Taking Care

Of

Grace

A Camden Falls Novel

Jean A. Smith

Copyright © 2020 Jean A. Smith
All rights reserved.

ISBN-13: 9798615844041

Cover design by Jean A. Smith

No part of this book may be reproduced in any form or by any electronic or mechanical means including information retrieval systems, without permission in writing from the author. The only exception is by a reviewer, who may quote short excerpts in a review.

This book is a work of fiction. Names, characters, places and incidents are either products of the author's imagination, or are used fictitiously. Any resemblance to persons, living or dead, events or locales is entirely coincidental.

Printed in the United States
First Edition: February 2020

Dedication:

This novel is dedicated to my aunt, Wilma Jean Powell. She has shared with me her love of reading and supported this writing journey.

To my dad, Fred Smith, who is and will always remain my hero.

To my mom, Betty Smith, who continues to cheer me on.

Thank you:
To family and friends, who without their love and support I would be lost.
To Jeffrey Williams, retired Marion City Police Officer and Educator, for answering my endless list of law enforcement questions.
To Ashley Wingert, for reading my work and offering comments and insights that helped shape this novel.

Missing College Students Now Total Five in Ohio:

The Columbus Dispatch; Columbus, Ohio:

Five college students have gone missing from three Ohio universities in the past 11 months: Cameron Shaw, 18, and a freshman at Capital University in Bexley, disappeared Tuesday, August 20. He was last seen leaving a fraternity party around 3 am. Shaw did not appear for chapel services later that morning. The Resident Assistant on his floor section in the dorm and two of his friends checked his room at approximately 11 am and Shaw was not there. His bed had not been slept in. Shaw is 6'1, 200 pounds, blonde hair, hazel eyes and a semi-colon tattoo on his left wrist. If anyone has any information regarding Shaw, please contact the Bexley Police Department or the Capital University Security Office.

Shaw is the fifth college student to go missing.

Previous Victims Still Under Investigation:

-Shonda Hayes, 21, a sophomore at Ohio Northern University, Ada, disappeared May 12th, 2018. Hayes is 5'5", curly brown hair and brown eyes. She was last seen wearing an ONU sweatshirt, shorts and sandals. A security camera shows Hayes leaving Heterick Memorial Library at around 10 pm and has not been seen since. The case is still open.

-Darren Green, 22, a junior at Ohio State University, Columbus, disappeared October 26, 2018. He was last seen leaving The Library Bar on High Street. His body was later found in an alley near the bar. There are no leads in his case.

-Pamela Grange, 21, a freshman at Case Western Reserve Cleveland, disappeared on January 15, 2019. Grange is 5'8" has red hair, hazel eyes. She was last seen wearing her uniform and leaving The Jolly Scholar restaurant around 9:30 pm, after her evening shift. She has not been seen or heard from and the case remains open.

-Lindsey Prater, 21, a sophomore at Ohio University, Athens, disappeared May 29, 2019. Prater is 5'9" with black hair styled in a pixie cut and brown eyes. She was last seen leaving the university Aquatic Center at around 3 pm. Prater was later found off-campus. She had suffered severe head trauma as well as several broken ribs and a punctured lung. She remains in a medically induced coma.

While university and law enforcement officials are not certain if these cases are related, they are sharing resources to find information regarding these disappearances. The public is urged to contact local law enforcement if they have any information regarding these missing persons.

Chapter One: September 20

Officer Hastings hated investigations that involved missing girls. They rarely turned out well. The young girl goes missing. Her family has no idea where she could be. No, she doesn't have any enemies. Her boyfriend is distraught and has an airtight alibi. Granted it's a frat house alibi, but more than likely, it had been early enough on the evening of the disappearance that any alcohol consumed hadn't taken effect yet. The girl is usually popular, active, smart, and pretty and possibly a little too naive for her own good. She is well liked in the community with a guardian or family who is beloved as well. No mother or father wants to hear that their daughter fits the stereotype of so many missing girls. And as is often the case, the weather never cooperates in these circumstances. Even if she went missing in perfect weather, the search would inevitably be conducted in violent snowstorms or in this case a torrential downpour.

Grace Winters had been missing for almost three days. So far, the Camden Falls Police Department, the sheriff's department and campus security had come up empty. Sheila hoped they found her soon. The longer she was gone, the slimmer the odds of a favorable outcome. She also wondered if this disappearance was linked to the other five college students that had gone missing over the last year. She had entered Grace's information into the state and national databases within 24 hours of the disappearance. She had also sent a text to her friend, Angie Rossi, a detective with the Columbus Police Department. Angie had been working on the missing college students' case from the beginning.

Sheila Hastings hated these nighttime searches. The rain was beating a noisy tattoo on her umbrella making it almost impossible to think, let alone hear anything such as someone calling out for help. The extremely hot August days had stirred up a series of severe thunderstorms with the threat of tornadoes in the surrounding counties. When her partner, Detective Evan Green returned with their coffee, she hoped his update would contain more promising information than the last two times he had questioned the patrons at the coffee house.

Evan was a good kid, but he had a lot to learn. Sheila had been an officer in Camden Falls for 20 years and the first African American female on the force. Ten years ago she had been promoted to detective. In Evan, she saw a lot of the same traits and inexperience she had when she first started out. Word around the department was that when Matt Brady, the first African American police chief in Camden Falls, Ohio, retired or moved on, she would be next in line for the job. She spent most of her time training the new detective recruits. She could tell within a few minutes of meeting a freshly minted rookie whether he or she would make it through the on-the-job training. She was rarely wrong. Evan needed practice questioning potential witnesses. That's why she had sent him to the coffeehouse and why she was out here searching the college campus for Grace Winters.

Sheila checked her text messages. No new information on Grace and no reply from Angie. She knew that as soon as she had a spare moment, she would be in contact. Her radio squawked with the usual drunk and disorderly, underage consumption and various traffic violations that came with the day-to-day operations of law enforcement. She had been searching the streets and alleyways of Camden Falls for three hours but didn't feel any closer to finding Grace's whereabouts. At least now they had brought in some of the community to help in the search. Peace Lutheran Church had been set up as headquarters and the congregation as well as the local fraternities, sororities and a wide variety of community members had been recruited as well to search for the missing teen. This church had been one of the first to volunteer due to the fact that the missing girl was related to the presiding minister, Melody Cline.

To be honest, if Grace had been abducted, they weren't going to find her within the city limits. Law enforcement and campus security had been keeping an eye out for sex trafficking rings that were offshoots of organized crime in the area. Gang activity could not be ruled out either. These heinous crimes had been plaguing the universities around the state. Luckily, Camden Falls had not fallen victim as of yet. Sheila and Matt both felt it was just a matter of time. She hoped Grace's disappearance was not an indicator that the crime had made its way into the sleepy college town.

Unfortunately, in either case, once the girls had outlived their usefulness, they were killed and abandoned along some country road. In some cases, the victims were stuffed in a dumpster behind one of the seedier bars on the outskirts of town. For the past two days, she and Evan had been canvassing Grace's haunts, talking with friends and acquaintances and were still coming up empty. It had been the same with Detective Carl Coleman and Tristan Bennett who had been trying to establish a cyber trail for Grace. They had come up empty so far as well.

Sheila decided to check out some of the more obscure areas of Camden Falls University. It was a beautiful campus during the day and night, as long as the weather cooperated. Tonight it was a smeared watercolor of lights, clouds and puddles making walking and searching a challenge and dangerous. She radioed dispatch and texted Evan to let them know she was headed towards the older part of campus that was less traveled and a little sketchy.

She wasn't sure why this particular area hadn't been searched. According to Arden, Grace's guardian, as well as Grace's friends, she would have no reason to be in the area. It couldn't hurt to take a look. She would feel better being able to say to the family, her superiors, and the media that no stone had been left unturned.

As she checked out the walkway between the dance studio and education building she replaced her smaller flashlight with a more powerful Maglite. The two looming three-story buildings cast shadows on the walkway and blocked the streetlights. No one, male or female, should be walking here at night. It was an area where a lot of drug deals and assaults played out. She was glad she had worn her waterproof boots as she sloshed through the pooling water on the sidewalk.

Earlier in the day, Grace's 2015 Toyota Camry had been found two blocks over with four soaking-wet parking tickets tucked under the windshield wipers. But a thorough search of the car, houses, yards and alleys had resulted in nothing but false leads. She was glad that Jack Phillips had gotten involved. Ever since he left the force in Chicago and came back to Camden Falls he had been a real asset to the police department as an occasional consultant. She hoped that Matt or someone on the force would talk him into joining their ranks.

Her Maglite illuminated the way and she was dismayed to smell the unmistakable odor of death and decay. Despite the stench, she was relieved to realize that the pungent smell was that of a dead animal and not rotting human remains. Her beam hit the source and she saw a dead raccoon partially hidden under a bush near the dance studio.

As she neared the grate that gave access to the heating tunnels that ran a twisty, curvy network under the town and campus, she noticed that it wasn't fastened properly. It was probably nothing but anything out of place was worth checking into. There wasn't any yellow caution tape or sawhorses blocking off the area that would indicate the city or university crews were working there. Rather than navigate the bureaucratic red tape that would delay investigating this lead, she took the direct route. Shouting over the continuous drumbeat of rain, Sheila said into her radio microphone, "Hey Betty Jo, Sheila Hastings, badge number 246. Can you get Clyde on the phone and patch it through? I have a question about a heating tunnel grate and I know he'll be able to help me."

Betty Jo Sherman and Sheila had started out on the force together. Betty Jo enjoyed being a dispatcher because of the quick thinking it required. Her very recognizable voice was born of a two-pack-a-day Marlboro habit that made the officers and detectives feel reassured that Betty Jo would get them what they needed. "Sure thing, Sheila. It doesn't sound like the rain has let up. Any luck out there?" Betty Jo asked knowing the answer would be no.

"Not yet, but I've got a heating tunnel grate that doesn't look right. It needs to be checked out" Sheila was silent, trying not to get her hopes up. She continued, "although it's probably a dead end."

"Okay, doll, I got him on the line. Stay warm and dry," Betty Jo's smoky voice signed off to answer another call from an officer in the field.

"Sheila, honey, are you there? Is everything okay?" Clyde said out of breath. He must have had to run from another room to pick up his phone.

"Yes, but that's Detective Honey to you. I am calling on official business." She paused, looking around. The rain and wind were gusting making it almost impossible for her to catch her breath. "Have your crews been working in the area between the Carver Dance Studio and the Galloway Education Building on campus?"

Clyde let out a long slow breath; both picturing the area and thinking through the list of places his maintenance crews had been working on. Clyde worked for the university and had worked his way up to the coordinator and supervisor of the tunnel crews. He grabbed his iPad and looked at the schematic of the campus that highlighted current repair and inspections.

Clyde shook his head and said, "No, we have been working mainly on the south end of campus. The area you're talking about isn't due for maintenance inspections for a couple of months. Why? Did you find something? That area is notorious for drug deals and God knows what else."

Sheila directed the Maglite beam at the lock on the grate. She snapped a couple of pictures with her phone and said into the microphone, "I'm sending you a couple of pictures. Is there something off about this grate and the lock?"

The line was silent while Clyde downloaded and looked at the pictures. If this lead panned out they could subpoena the transcript of this call. "You're right," Clyde said, "It looks like the lock had been jimmied and the grate has been moved. Whoever put it back didn't know what they were doing."

Sheila said "It could be nothing, but could you send one of your crews over here to take a look at this? I'll let dispatch know I put in the request."

"I'll get Jed Holmes on it. He is working the night shift and lives for any little bit of excitement."

"Ok," Sheila said somewhat distractedly, "gotta go." As she steadied the beam through the crosshatch holes of the grate, she realized that the maintenance lights in the tunnel seemed irregular. Several lights were off and a couple were flickering making it extremely difficult to see what lurked beneath. The only thing giving off a steady glow were the emergency lights that had back up generators and battery back up. She gasped when the beam landed on a bloody backpack confirming her worst fears. She moved closer to the grate, enabling the light to further illuminate the tunnel and she could see a foot in a red Keds tennis shoe twisted at an unnatural angle. Both items had been detailed in the subject's description. Even though she had hoped that Grace would be found alive and healthy she knew the odds were not in her favor. Sheila rarely got rattled on the job, but the shock of finding Grace and the wet conditions made her fumble the radio as she called in the information. "Possible subject found, Dispatch. I've got a city crew on the way to look at this heating tunnel grate." She gave her coordinates. "I repeat, possible subject found." As Officer Hastings continued to follow the light beam on the subject she detected the slightest bit of movement from the twisted leg. She grabbed the radio frantically, practically shouting, "Get an EMT here ASAP. I think the victim could still be alive." Now, this was not only an active crime scene but time was running out for Grace.

Chapter 2: Later that Same Night

Detective Evan Green arrived just in time to see his partner, Detective Sheila Hastings descend into the heating tunnel through an adjacent grate. Other officers had come to the scene and had placed yellow caution tape around the grate and a tent over the grate where Sheila had discovered Grace. A couple of officers were standing guard to preserve the crime scene as much as possible. The elements and the human factor could wreak havoc on a crime scene. No matter what precautions were taken to preserve the evidence, a crowd formed, each with his or her assigned tasks. .

Several Camden Falls police officers were standing around the perimeter to secure what was becoming a rapidly deteriorating crime scene. Unfortunately, the rain had not let up, in fact, it seemed to be increasing in speed and intensity. Without waiting for Clyde's crew to arrive, Sheila and Evan used a bolt cutter on the latch adjacent to the grate where Grace was found and carefully and quickly made their way down the ladder and to the victim. She could tell from the clothing and dark brown hair that this was the missing teen, Grace Winters. Evan had followed Sheila down the ladder as she quickly moved toward Grace to check her pulse. It was thready. Close behind Sheila and Evan, the EMTs carefully rolled Grace onto her back to assess her injuries. Grace groaned at the movement and Sheila took that as a good sign. Her breathing was slow as well.

"Hang in there, Grace," Sheila whispered, "Help is here." She didn't know if Grace could hear her, but she hoped that the young woman could feel her presence and the reassurances she was sending her way. She always sent up a silent prayer when she came across the victims. Sometimes it was the only way to process the horrific situations she faced on the job. The EMTs carefully loaded Grace onto a backboard, attached an oxygen mask, and inserted an IV. Grace had not responded to any questions that were asked of her or reacted to the sharp pain of the pinprick from the IV.

"Hey, Hudson, could you be sure to swab Grace's hands? We will want to check for DNA under her nails. Judging from the bruising and lacerations on her hands and arms, I think it's safe to say she put up a fight." There were noticeable scratches and bruising on Grace's face as well. Until a more complete examination could be made, they wouldn't know if Grace sustained the injuries while fighting off an attacker or from the fall.

Sheila hoped the young girl would make it to the hospital. She would check on her later. But for now, she and Evan had their work cut out for them. Between the inclement weather and the extraction of Grace from the tunnel, the crime scene would need their immediate attention.

Evan said, "This the girl that has been missing for almost three days."

Sheila nodded, "She fits the description. And I recognize her from seeing her around The BrewHouse."

"Wonder how she got down here?"

"Hard to say," Sheila said, "It's going to be our job to find out. And the city won't sleep until we do."

Taking Care of Grace

*****

Hastings and Green had been down in the tunnel for two hours. With Camden Falls being a small college town, there was no high tech CSI unit to bag and tag the evidence as seen on television. In real life, the detectives and officers involved had to do their own investigation. To Sheila, it felt as if they had barely made a dent in figuring out what happened to Grace and how she ended up in a heating tunnel.

Evan asked, "What are the tunnels for? All I've ever heard about them is that it's a great place for drug deals to go down."

Sheila answered, "That is partly true, unfortunately, but it's also a great way to keep the utility wires and heat circulating on campus. It used to be underneath the whole city. Kids could sneak through and come up through trap doors in bars all over town. That was a long time ago and most of those trap doors have been removed and replaced by more permanent flooring."

Officer Alex Brooks shouted down into the tunnel, "Hastings! Green! The chief wants to see you."

"Be right up!" Sheila shouted, and to Evan she said, "We will have to come back and take some measurements. I think we have enough photos for the time being. Sheila climbed up the ladder first with Evan following close behind. When she reached the top she saw the officer she was looking for and said, "Hey, Hudson, we'll be back after we talk to the chief and check-in at the hospital."

"Okay, let's do this," Evan said, following Sheila into the driving rain.

*****

Police Chief Matt Brady stood under the police-issued, large umbrella that really wasn't keeping the rain off of him. With his towering size and stature, the umbrella looked more like a child's toy rather than one used by an adult. It was actually just redirecting the rain, soaking his shoes and the bottoms of his pant legs. When he saw Hastings and Green approach, he said loudly over the rain, "The campus student center is across the commons. Let's go there where we can get out of the weather and you can fill me in on what you've found."

Sheila radioed Brooks and his partner, Susan Smith, to let them know where they were going and would be back to continue the investigation. She also told them to notify Bennett and Coleman to get over to the BrewHouse and transport Arden, Grace's guardian, to the hospital. The area around the tunnel would have to be blocked off for a while so that every detail could be logged in and studied. Hudson, Smith and several other cops had been called in to keep watch over the crime scene so that it would remain as intact as possible. The public couldn't be trusted. Thrill-seekers and amateur detectives would show up to see if they could outwit law enforcement. All they really succeeded in doing was compromising the crime scene and slowing down the investigation.

The trio headed across the commons to the welcoming lights of the Babb Student Center.

*****

After removing soaking wet, hats and overcoats, the chief and the detectives settled into overstuffed chairs in a quiet corner of the common room. It was a brightly lit lobby that took some getting used to after being stuck outside in the dark, persistent rain. There were sitting areas arranged around the room for chatting, studying or just relaxing after a day of classes.

Once they were situated, Matt said, "Sheila, could you get us some coffee from the vending machine? Evan. What have you got for me?"

Sheila got up and headed to the vending machine area, *"Get your own damn coffee,"* she thought. There was no love lost between Sheila Hastings and Matt Brady. They had both grown up in Camden Falls. She had come from the wrong side of the tracks while Matt's family had been able to break through barriers that Sheila's family had stumbled over. Besides, she was used to the other male police officers denigrating the females in subtle little ways unless it was their partner. Then strict trust codes were put into place.

It really irked Sheila that everyone seemed to see Matt as the chosen one. Granted, on paper, he looked like the perfect police chief. He had a stellar arrest record. He had a beautiful wife, Julia, and the two adorable kids that they had adopted through the foster care system. They had lent their support to a series of charities that benefitted the citizens of Camden Falls, making them the picture-perfect family. Julia was seen as a hero for her work as a trauma nurse and being a cancer survivor. While Sheila respected Julia and what she had been through, it made it difficult to show any kind of negative thoughts regarding the Bradys. To the community, negativity towards the Bradys was the equivalent of kicking a puppy.

When she got back, Evan had relayed the events leading up to finding Grace, calling the EMTs and removing Grace from the crime scene. He added, "Sheila was the one who discovered the victim. She has details about what she initially discovered at the scene."

Matt held up a hand to stop the account so that he could ask a question. "Hold on, what makes you think this is a crime scene? Is it possible that there was an accident?"

Sheila spoke up, "Possible, but not likely, sir. There are several factors that lead us to believe this was more than just an accident."

"Such as?"

"The most solid factor I observed was the fact that the heating grate had been moved, and put back in place and was latched, albeit somewhat haphazardly. When I approached the grate that was the first thing I noticed. Those grates are inspected routinely so that unfortunate accidents are avoided."

"Okay," Matt said, "But there has to be more that makes you think that it's a crime rather than an accident."

"Near the grate and around it, there appears to have been a struggle. There were muddy footprints in the tunnel in the area surrounding her body. The angle from which she fell and the partial footprint on her head leads me to believe that someone at the top pushed her, causing her to lose her balance. The perp told her to go down into the tunnel, possibly armed, threatened her and as she started down, they pushed her. The weight from her book bag as well as her slippery shoes, etc. made her balance on the ladder precarious. She fell at an awkward angle adding to her injuries."

Matt nodded his head, thinking over what the officers had told him, "What do we know about this situation? I have personally known Grace for most of her life, I can't imagine why she would be in a heating tunnel on campus."

"That's what has us puzzled, sir," Evan said. "We have been canvassing friends and classmates even before finding the victim. We haven't made much headway. We recovered her backpack and her cellphone was in the outside pocket. There has been some damage to the cellphone but hopefully, the tech guys will be able to salvage some info from it. It's the strongest lead we have right now."

Matt sat forward in his chair, forearms resting on his thighs, hands clasped together, "How soon before Grace wakes up?"

Sheila shook her head, "It's hard to say. She was not in good shape when the EMTs took her."

"Who notified Arden?"

"Coleman and Bennett went to the coffee shop and were then escorting her to Camden Falls Memorial. I plan on stopping by to check on Grace's progress and see if Arden can give us any insight."

"Sounds good. Now that we have found her we need to start filling in the blanks in the timeline. We need to find out what happened between the time she was last seen and when she ended up in the tunnel."

"We're on it," Evan said.

"Go to the hospital, check in with Arden and the doctor. The sooner Grace wakes up, the sooner we will have some answers.

"Will do, sir," said Sheila.

"I want whoever did this to be found. Grace means a lot to my family and this community. Whoever is responsible will pay."

The officers nodded, they and the chief cleaned up their coffee cups and headed out the door. Finally, the rain was starting to let up.

Chapter 3: September 20, Hospital

The EMTs, Carol and Jim, barreled through the emergency room doors shouting Grace's vital readings to the trauma nurses on duty, one of them being Lenore Gantry. Lenore had been an ER nurse for longer than she or anyone else, for that matter, could remember. She had seen nurses come and go. To be able to think on your feet and ignore the gore was too much to ask of some. One of the finest nurses she had seen in years was Julia Brady. With her short blonde hair and kind, blue eyes, she had an uncanny knack for putting patients and their loved ones at ease while still getting the job done. When treating patients, she seemed to know what the doctors needed even before they did.

She was covering for Julia tonight, who was headed out of town, to consult with another treatment center. This one had a stellar reputation for helping those fighting cancer obtain and sustain remission. She hoped Julia would be back in fine form soon. The hospital, as well as the community, needed her. Before she left, she had been visibly shaken by Grace's disappearance. Grace had been the house/baby and pet sitter for the Brady family for a number of years. Julia hated leaving town during this crisis, but the community was becoming aware of Julia's setback. She almost canceled her appointment in Utah, but Lenore promised to keep her updated and insisted that she make her health the top priority.

Lenore ran along with the gurney and the EMTs directing them into ER Bay 12. It had been a busy night. The first few weeks of the semester always were. Freshmen who were away from home, partying and drinking for the first time or were caught up in pledge week hazing kept the ER hopping.

It will break my heart if we lose this little girl, Lenore thought. She, as well as many of the hospital personnel, and the whole town had watched Grace grow up before their eyes. Lenore had been a regular at the BrewHouse long before Arden took it over.

Now as she watched the young woman fighting for her life, she knew the odds were not good despite the efforts of the EMTs as well as the quick thinking of the officers that found her and were investigating the case. Carol and Jim briefed Lenore and Dr. Millicent McGregor on Grace's condition. Grace had serious injuries and possibly massive internal bleeding. She had coded twice in the ambulance. Officers were on their way to notify Arden and transport her to the hospital to be with Grace.

Lenore was confident that if anyone could pull off a miracle it was Millicent McGregor. Lenore wanted to make sure she was available for Arden to answer any questions she knew were coming her way.

Chapter 4: Late August 2001

The sounds of the diner were familiar and comforting. Ever since the siblings had found their way to grown-up jobs in New York City, Arden and Ben Winters had been meeting at the Empire Diner for breakfast once every two weeks to catch up. It was the one time they both threw caution to the wind and ordered a real midwestern breakfast of eggs, sausage, hash browns and toast with a side order of biscuits and sausage gravy for Ben and a fruit cup for Arden. Orange juice and coffee rounded out the feast. Ruby, the waitress that had been there since the early 80s had started leaving the coffee pot on the table so that Ben and Arden could help themselves.

After the usual conversation about their respective jobs, Ben a tax accountant and Arden an advertising executive, they moved on to more personal matters.

With a twinkle in his eye, Ben said, "So, how did that blind date go that Jess arranged for you?"

"So how is my adorable niece?" Arden countered.

"That good, huh?

"Let's just say that as soon as I found out that he lived with his widowed mother and cared for her three cats, Winkin, Blinkin and Nod it was 'Check, please!'"

Ben shook his head, grinning, "I knew it would be a bust, but Jess is determined to trap you a man."

"Trap being the operative word, " Arden laughed. After a brief marriage that lasted about five minutes shortly after graduating from college, Arden had decided to focus on her career, rather than searching for more marriage material. "I know Jess means well, but I'm not ready to settle down."

Ben nodded, realizing that what she said was true. Arden had been saying it for the last ten years. She did seem very happy in her career and life. He and Jess just wanted to see her settled and happy.

Arden was so proud of her brother. They were a little over a year apart with Arden being his senior. He was successful at his job and so was his freelance photographer wife, Jess. And since Gracie had entered their lives last January, their little family was finding their stride. "Sounds like you and Jess have turned a corner."

Ben nodded in agreement. He was the spitting image of their dad, blond hair and hazel eyes that lit up at the mention of Jess, little Grace or the Columbus Blue Jackets. You could take the boy out of Ohio, but... "Absolutely. Those first few weeks after Gracie was born, we were both really struggling. Neither of us could believe that the hospital was letting us take this squirmy, sleepy bundle home with us. But, we have come a long way. It's hard to believe she'll be two in January."

"Don't I know it? It's amazing how quickly they grow up and yet we stay the same," Arden said in her self-deprecating way. She had grown from an awkward teenager with glasses and braces into a blond-haired, blue-eyed beauty with arresting good looks and a sense of style that was understated yet professional. "Pretty soon, she'll be sneaking out to meet boys," she teased.

The shock of her statement had Ben ready to spit out his coffee in her general direction. "Don't even," he said with a dark and equally teasing look. "No daughter of mine will be taking after her wayward aunt."

"Wow, Dad, I think she might have to master walking and potty training before you have anything to worry about. And let the record show that your kid is incredibly lucky to have a fabulous aunt like me. Who else will be able to show her the exciting world of advertising and the best clubs in New York City?"

Now they were both laughing. This conversation had become an oft-repeated bit between them. "So," Arden continued. "I am going to Chicago in a couple of weeks and my client is looking for a new freelance photographer. Should I mention Jess, or is her plate pretty full right now?"

Ben didn't hesitate, "Yeah, of course. She has been staying close to home because of the baby, but I can tell she is getting antsy. She always says that some of her best jobs come from your recommendations."

"Always happy to help. She is a very talented photographer, your wife."

Ben nodded, obviously pleased and proud, "I'll send you some of the pictures she's taken of Gracie. They are spectacular." A smile wreathed his face and he paused wistfully, "I love Jess and that will never change, but I never realized how much I could love another human being as much as I love Gracie."

"I'm so happy for you," Arden said, tears of nostalgia threatening to spill from her eyes, "I think that little one has brought our family closer together. It's hard to believe that last year at this time we were in Camden Falls celebrating Gracie's baptism. I'm so glad that Melody agreed to officiate. And mom got a chance to be there…," Arden's voice trailed off.

"I know. It kills me that she will never really know Grace and Grace won't really know her."

"Me, too. But I feel that on some level, she knows what's going on. When we took Grace to meet her, she recognized you and me, at least for a little while." Amanda Winters had been in the memory unit at Sunrise Assisted Living Facility in Camden Falls for three years. Their cousin Melody went to see her twice a week and either had lunch or dinner with her. Being a Lutheran minister, it gave Melody a chance to check on her aunt as well as her other parishioners who were living there. Twice a month, she held a Sunday afternoon service in the sunroom.

Arden nodded in agreement, "I know, thank God for Melody. She keeps us posted on Mom's condition. Whenever I travel West, I try to swing back through Ohio and spend a couple of days with mom. This insidious disease really takes its toll on the victims. At least mom still has moments of clarity. I don't know how much longer that will last." Arden smiled. "And thanks again for getting her the walker and the new nightgown set. They are wonderful."

"It's the least we could do. I don't get out there to see her as you do, but she's never out of my thoughts."

"I know that Bennie, and I think on some level mom feels it too." Trying to get the conversation back on a more positive note, Arden said, "You mentioned that Jess has been staying close to home. Is it the first time uncertainties of motherhood, or is something else going on?"

Ben didn't meet her eyes. He seemed suddenly very interested in the last piece of toast on his plate. "Sure, everything's fine. You know, with Grace and all she doesn't want to be too far away." Ben continued to butter his toast like it was his job.

"Alright, Bennie, what's up? You can't keep anything from me. What is it? Work? Jess's work? The baby?"

"Baby? What baby?" Ben's face grew pale then red then pale again.

"I mean Grace, of course," Arden paused and then it dawned on her, "Is there another little Winters in the works?" She couldn't keep the delight out of her voice.

"Shhhhhhh," Ben looked around the practically empty diner hoping no one had heard. "Jess would kill me if she knew I told anyone." Ben searched the diner again to ensure no one had heard. "She's only a couple of months along. It's still that scary time."

Tears of joy welled up in Arden's eyes. "Ah Bennie, that's wonderful news! I won't tell a soul until you're ready. Now there will be two of them to corrupt!"

Ben shook his head in mock irritation, "You have not heard anything about this. If Jess says anything you play dumb.

"Your secret is safe with me, Bennie."

"I know and stop calling me Bennie." He could never stay mad at his big sister.

Arden looked at her watch. "Uh-oh, I've gotta go. I'm supposed to be pitching a new campaign to one of our biggest clients in an hour. I hate to cut this short but we'll do it again once I get back into the city from my Chicago trip."

"Sounds good," Ben said, reaching for his wallet to settle the bill, "When are you due back?"

Rummaging in the bottom of her purse, "Let me see," Arden said consulting her Blackberry, "I fly out the 8th and I'm due back September 11. I've got an afternoon flight. I'm stopping in Camden Falls on the way back and flying into and out of Columbus."

"September 12, it is."

"Works for me. If I get any info on the job for Jess I'll call. I can also update you on mom when we meet. And as for keeping state secrets if it's a girl, I expect her name to be Arden."

Ben laughed, "I think there is only room in the world for one Arden."

Arden was laughing, too. They paid the bill, hugged outside the diner and went their separate ways to their offices. It was the last time Arden saw her brother alive.

Chapter 5: September 11, 2001, Camden Falls

Arden was glad that her business meeting in Chicago had finished up early. She had been able to get the clients to agree to not only print and a media campaign but also put some of their products on a website so that consumers could research and hopefully purchase them. Several of their competitors were giving it a try so it wasn't as hard to sell the idea as she thought it was going to be. They were also open to meeting with Jess about photos for the ads. She had been able to get to Camden Falls a couple of days early.

She was glad for the extra time to spend with her cousin Melody and Melody's husband Victor Cline. They had been college sweethearts. They had married right after Melody graduated from seminary. Victor had finished his masters in international relations and the two thought they would embark on a missionary trip. When the plans for that fell through, a call to a church in Victor's hometown became available. Victor and Melody were pleased and Victor found a teaching position at Camden Falls University.

Melody and Arden were more like siblings than cousins while growing up in north-central Ohio. The cousins were still very close even when the Winters had both ended up in New York City. When their mother Amanda started to have memory issues, Melody had helped them secure her a place in an assisted living facility in Camden Falls.

The church offered spiritual guidance for the community as well as many outreach programs that helped those locally and internationally. The Clines were expecting twins and Melody had felt increasingly uncomfortable to the point that she was short with Victor and tried to downplay her mood swings in front of the church members. Arden had been a huge help for the last few days and had eased the tension that was steadily building. She cleaned the house from top to bottom. The grocery shopping was done along with a few frozen casseroles that could easily go in the oven after a long day of working and twins. Arden had a way of sensing Melody's needs and knew when to back off when it was necessary. The sisterly connection never seemed to waver.

The sun was beginning to stream in the windows of the cozy house. Arden had been up for a couple of hours, drinking coffee, looking over the paperwork from her Chicago meetings and consulting her Blackberry to double-check her schedule for the upcoming week. She smiled when she saw the notation for her breakfast date with Ben. She always looked forward to seeing her baby brother. She had picked up an American Girl Doll for Grace at the store in Chicago. She knew that Grace was still too little to enjoy it, but she couldn't resist. Besides, Little Gracie would soon have a baby brother or sister to love. The doll could help her prepare for that.

Arden rinsed out her coffee mug and put it in the dishwasher. She decided to walk into town and enjoy the beautiful morning. She wanted to stop by the book store and pick up some reading material for the flight home. She had been wanting to read the latest Sue Grafton alphabet murder *P is for Peril,* and the flight back to the city would give her an opportunity to relax. Her hectic life rarely allowed her to sit, drink a cup of coffee and read a book. Ben has always been an athlete and she and Melody the bookworms.

Arden checked her watch. It was 8:45 am. Her plane didn't leave until 3 pm; that gave her plenty of time for a walk. She was already packed and would leave Camden Falls around noon so that she could make it to the Columbus Airport in plenty of time to make her flight. Arden grabbed her Louis Vuitton Canvas Speedy handbag and her keys. She carefully closed the back door so that she wouldn't wake up Melody. She was about a block away when Melody's landline began to ring.

*****

It had been a long night at the bedside of a pillar of the church. Mrs. Adelaide Griffith, Melody's oldest parishioner, had succumbed to cancer that had been slowly draining the life from her. At 99, she had outlived most of her family and Melody had spent as much time with her as she possibly could. Adelaide had always been an active member of the church, long before Melody began to serve there. Miss Adelaide, as she had been called, had worked in the church nursery during the church services, when they needed volunteers. She had taught Sunday School from preschool through adult for over 35 years. She had been the honorary grandmother to many of the children who attended Peace Lutheran Church.

Adelaide had been a widow for a number of years. Her husband started out as an attorney and eventually was elected to the municipal court bench. He was a judge for 30 years until he died suddenly at the age of 60 from a heart attack. She had outlived most of her family save for a few great-nieces and nephews. She had sold the family home and had lived in a condo until this third bout of cancer started to take its toll. Melody had sat holding her hand, offering prayers and communion when asked. She occasionally sang softly with Adelaide the old hymns she loved so well, "Amazing Grace" and "I Love to Tell the Story." At times, she was a silent comfort to the elderly woman.

When Melody returned home, it was around 6 am. She allowed the exhaustion to overtake her once she walked in the door. Victor was already at the university fitness center for his workout. Melody had stayed with Adelaide until the funeral home attendants arrived and took her to the funeral home and the Hospice volunteers had prepared their equipment for removal later that day. She walked into the house and relaxed into the welcomed silence. She had been completely drained by the experience. Adelaide hadn't just been a member of the church. She had been a friend, confidant and shining example that Melody looked up to. She would miss her stories of growing up in small-town America during World War II and her many travel experiences.

Melody glanced at the answering machine and sent up a small prayer of thanks that there were no new messages. As she made her way, more like waddled her way to the bedroom, she shed the clothes she had been wearing for over 24 hours and headed into the master bath and straight for the shower. She had no worries about waking Arden. The guest room was on the opposite side of the house and Arden slept with earplugs. One of the habits she retained even when she wasn't in the big city.

Melody's shoes felt incredibly tight and when she looked in the full-length mirror attached to the closet, she realized her ankles were swollen. *I'm quite the sex kitten now, Victor,* she thought ruefully; *will I ever feel normal again?* She padded to the shower where the steam and hot water washed the weariness and sorrow from her bones. Still, in her fluffy, pink bathrobe, she tumbled into bed. Her last thought before falling asleep was that she had a couple of hours before she had to get ready to take Arden to the airport.

*****

Is that my alarm going off?...No,...I think it's the phone. Why is it ringing? Isn't it the middle of the night? Who could be calling? Is Victor okay? I hope none of our parishioners are in trouble. Melody climbed out of her fog of sleep slowly trying to remember what day it was and what time it was. The light, pastel yellows and greens of the bedspread and curtains made the room that much brighter. She had forgotten to close the blinds before falling asleep. It had been a cool but beautiful day for September giving everyone the false hope that summer wasn't quite finished yet. She lay in bed willing herself to get up, but not wanting to leave the comfort of the bed.

The phone ringing again made her realize that something important must be going on. She sat up slowly, slipped on her slippers and shuffled her way to the kitchen. The answering machine was blinking an angry 5 at her. The first call came in at 9:02 am. It was Sue, the church secretary, "Melody, hey it's Sue. Can you call me when you get this? I don't know where you are but you might want to turn on the TV. Something is going on in New York."

The second call was from Sue as well, three minutes later, "Sorry to bother you but I really need to speak with you and Arden. Call me. I'm at the church office. We are kind of concerned."

The third call was from Ben at 9:07 am, "Hey Mel, it's Ben. I know Arden was going to stay with you a couple of days on her way back to the city. We've got a situation here. A plane just flew into the North Tower. It looks kinda bad. I tried to get a hold of Jess but-" a loud crash and screams could be heard, then, "Mel? Arden? Listen I think we've been hit, too. They are telling us to go to the stairs. Call Jess. Love you." And the line went dead.

The last two calls were from Sue again. Melody searched for the remote and turned on the TV. At this point, the South Tower where Ben worked was folding into itself and collapsing into a pile of dust, smoke and heat. Fear and shock paralyzed Melody momentarily. She made herself calm down and focus on what she was seeing on the television screen. Melody said a prayer for help and guidance. Melody found the note that Arden had written before she left to run errands. She had to find Arden.

Chapter 6: Columbus Police Department, Vice Division, Columbus, Ohio: September 21

Detective Angie Rossi had been staring at the computer, reading through the report on the latest missing college student, Cameron Shaw. Hector Esposito, of the Capital University Security Division, had asked her to take a look. He wondered if this latest case had any similarities to the others.

Angie rubbed her eyes and tried to focus as the words on the computer screen started running together. She could feel a potential migraine developing at the base of her neck. *Time to get out of this building and breathe some fresh air,* she thought. She had drunk too many cups of coffee and had nothing to eat since a bagel from the food cart for breakfast. These poor eating habits were taking their toll on Angie's 37-year-old body.

She got up from her desk chair feeling her 5'7 frame tense and release. She grabbed her black, tailored jacket that matched her black pants and boots. They were in stark contrast to the white blouse that had become part of her standard detective uniform. She opened the right-hand drawer of her desk and felt around until she found the spiral hair coil and tamed her unruly black curly hair into a manageable ponytail. *Air and some water will do me some good.*

Angie had been twelve years on the job and in vice for four of those years. Currently, the vice division was pretty quiet. A lot of the detectives were either out in the field or off duty. The only reason Angie was still there, two hours after her shift ended, was to prepare for the feds coming in tomorrow. By this time tomorrow, the case would no longer be under her control. Now that there were multiple missing persons, the feds would be taking over the PD's investigation as well. *We'll never gain back the trust of our informants once the feds get involved. Those contacts will slither back into hiding.*

She passed through the vice division and stopped in the hallway near the reception desk to get a bottle of water from one of several vending machines. The cuisine ranged from stale snacks and sandwiches past the expiration date to something pretending to be coffee.

She signed out and told Granger Holbrook who was working the reception desk that she was going out for a while and would be back in a few. Granger gave her a nod and knew, based on past experience that Detective Rossi would be back in the station half an hour from now.

*****

The walk and water had done the trick. Angie felt she could review the files again with a fresh perspective. As she made her way back to her desk, her phone buzzed with a text. It was from Sheila Hastings. *Good,* thought Angie, *I was hoping she would get back to me before tomorrow.* In response, Angie texted: Any word on your missing teen?

After a few blinking dots, Sheila replied: Yes, we found her a few hours ago. She's in bad shape. Might not make it.

Angie shook her head in disgust. These cases never got any easier. She started texting. Have you got a few minutes? Feds are coming tomorrow and I have a couple of questions for you.

The blinking dots started and then: Sure. Call me at this number. On a break.

Angie hit the call button and got an immediate answer. "Hey, Ang, what's new in C-Bus? Catching all the bad guys?"

Sheila, Matt Angie, and Jack had all been at the academy together. Angie had been a new recruit as Jack and Sheila were getting ready to graduate. Angie had proven helpful in a couple of crime scenarios during field experiences and Sheila had written her a letter of recommendation to get hired in Columbus. Their friendship had seen them through a number of happy and tragic family events. They also consulted one another from time to time regarding cases.

Angie said in her distinctive husky voice, "Sorry to hear about the girl in your area. Hope she makes it."

Sheila sighed, "Me, too. She's a great kid. Her mom runs the BrewHouse. You've met her, I think, Arden Winters."

"Oh, sure, I remember. Best coffee in the area. Her daughter, Grace, is the one you found?"

"Yes, she had been missing for three days. We found her in a heating tunnel, barely alive."

Angie shuffled through the papers on her desk, jotted down some notes, and then started typing on her computer. "So...what can you tell me about Grace? Was she prone to running away? Hanging out with a sketchy crowd?"

Sheila smiled, "No, not at all. Grace is one of the most straight-laced kids you'll meet. Arden keeps a pretty tight rein, very overprotective. You remember the story about her parents and 9/11."

"Mmhmm. Arden is actually her aunt, correct?"

"Yes," Sheila said, "so what's this all about?"

Angie went on to explain the other missing students and the fact that the feds were coming to take over the case the next day. "We have reason to believe that three of the five missing students could have been victims of sex trafficking."

"God, I was afraid you were going to say that, "Sheila and the rest of Camden Falls had been afraid that it was going to make its way to them. This town was the perfect set up for it. A small college town, with a lot of young people who felt reasonably secure in their surroundings. All of these factors added up to a prime spot for trafficking. "I have been keeping up with the cases online. What haven't you told the press?"

Angie looked at the list of similarities she had jotted down on the legal tablet when she was looking through the files. She tapped her pen on the pad as she spoke. "As you know, most of the victims have been found near college campuses. Two of the attacks were carried out in broad daylight because we had witnesses that came forward. They were both taken away in nondescript white vans. What we haven't told the press is that two of the victims had a brand on the back of their left thigh. The other one had a gang sign tattooed in the same spot. We think we've got two different rings operating in the state. Either that or they are using two different signs to throw us off."

"I can tell you that Grace doesn't have either one of those markings on her. They have had Grace in surgery from the moment they got her stabilized. None of those markings were reported. To be honest, Evan and I are treating this as an attack. Grace put up a fight. But I don't think anyone was trying to abduct her. I think she was trying to defend herself based on the bruising and lacerations."

"Got it," Angie said, "Just trying to get all the information ahead of the feds so they will keep us in the loop."

Sheila laughed, "Good luck with that. I'll keep you posted if anything matching your information turns up."

"Thanks," Angie hesitated then said, "So how's Jack Phillips? Still chasing the college co-eds?"

"You know he's not like that. Still single…"

"Thanks again for the info," ignoring the implications. "We'll do lunch when I'm in the area."

"Sounds good," Sheila said knowing that it wouldn't do any good to push her friend. Clearly, her past with Jack was still a part of Angie's present.

Chapter 7: September 11, 2001, New York City

Jess Winters and freelance writer Andy Christie had gotten an early start that morning. Andy had been writing an article on spec about the architecture of Old Manhattan. After a breakfast meeting finalizing the areas Andy wanted her to photograph, they hit the streets. The two had met in college when Jess had answered an ad for a freelance writer looking for someone to take photographs for a travel piece he was working on. They had been instant friends from the beginning. They had seen each other through many ups and downs and failed relationships until Jess met Ben and Andy met Trevor. Now whenever Andy needed photos for his writing gigs, he called on Jess. Both of them had been looking up because that was where the old city structures revealed their stories.

They had just gotten to Fulton Street near St. Paul's Chapel. Jess was adjusting the light filter on her vintage Nikon when she heard what sounded like a plane flying too close to the city. Then came an enormous explosion, lifting both of them off their feet. Once they ascertained that neither of them was hurt, they scrambled to their feet and ran into the chapel for shelter along with several other people who were on the street with them. Confusion and fear were written across their faces.

She and Andy ventured out to see what was happening. Jess began snapping photos. Smoke, dust, sirens and screaming met them as they walked cautiously out of the chapel. Men and women were running, covered in dust, racing past them. "A plane hit one of the Towers!" Another shouted, "What is going on?" Still, another shouted, "It must be an accident!" From then on, an otherwise peaceful, sunny Tuesday morning turned tragic. Fear gripped Jess and she instinctively placed a hand on her abdomen. Trying to focus, she frantically searched her camera bag for the cellphone Ben had surprised her with on her birthday. Jess stepped around to the side of the chapel cautiously to try to get a better signal to call Ben. When she called Ben's office she kept getting and an "all circuits are busy, please try your call again later," message.

"I have to see if Ben is alright," Jess called to Andy above the confusion and she started running towards the Towers. Andy tried to grab her to stop her, "No, Jess, we don't know what's happening. I'm sure he's fine. We need to find somewhere safe for the time being."

Jess pulled away, tears streaming down her cheeks, "No, I have to find Ben!"

Andy tried to reason with her but she was already running towards the Towers and into danger. She bobbed through the crowds of people covered in blood, dust and shock. Most had dazed and confused expressions etched on their faces. Jess kept trying to call Ben as well as the babysitter to check on Grace until her cellphone died. She had received the same recorded message for both.

"Ben!" Jess shouted, "BEN WINTERS! Have you seen my husband Ben Winters?" Jess asked the people fleeing the wreckage as she worked her way towards the chaos rather than away from it. Soon the dust and smoke made it difficult to breathe let alone scream for her husband.

The crowds and quickly arriving first responders had shoved Jess toward the South Tower. As Jess looked at the useless cellphone, the roar of a second jet engine too close to be safe, drowned out the cacophony of the panicked crowd. As she and others looked up to locate the sound, they watched in helpless horror as the second plane crashed into the second Tower sending a ball of fire and flying debris into the crowd below.

    Andy caught up and spotted Jess in the crowd and also witnessed her getting hit with the fiery rain of debris. By the time he reached her, and he scooped her into his arms, her eyes filled with tears. She whispered, "My baby" and died in Andy's arms. A firefighter shouted to an EMT to tend to Jess while he pulled a sobbing Andy away so that his burned hands and face could be treated before he went into shock.

Chapter 8: October 2001

The first days after the terrorist attacks gripped the nation in grief, disbelief and resilience. It was an excruciating two days before the telephone lines calmed down enough to allow Arden to get through to the authorities and hotlines and get any information regarding Ben and Jess. Melody's congregation at Peace Lutheran had been wonderful. In a matter of days a team of 12 firefighters, EMTs and Red Cross volunteers loaded up four vans of people, water, food, first aid supplies, clothes and hope. There had been no question that Arden would join them. Her main concern was getting to Gracie. Thankfully, Grace's babysitter, Jeanette Pearson had been caring for the toddler who was blissfully unaware of the chaos surrounding the city and her own life. She had cried for her mother and dad a couple of times but Jeanette and been able to distract her with toys, games and videos.

Arden had tracked down Andy at one of the local hospitals. Physically, he was recovering more quickly than expected. Mentally, however, was another story. Trevor, Andy's partner, had been out of town in upstate New York appraising artwork at a gallery and drove all night to be by Andy's side. Worry and exhaustion etched Trevor's face. He was glad to see Arden and hoped her visit would ease Andy. Arden and Andy cried together over the loss of Jess and Ben. Arden, with a broken heart, explained Jess's last words. They made a vow to keep in touch.

She was relieved to find her apartment intact. Her home was far enough away from Ground Zero that it didn't sustain any damage. However, dust and debris still filled the air, shrouding the streets. There was no escaping it.

*****

The day was warm and sunny for late October. Melody and Arden along with Jess's parents, the Whitakers, had scheduled a joint memorial service for their loved ones in Jess's hometown of Erie, Pennsylvania.

As Arden drove them to the graveside service, Melody kept her eyes on the scenery out the passenger side window, letting the tears fall down her cheeks unchecked. She was still recovering from Nick and Billy, the twins' delivery. They had been born a few days after the 9/11 tragedies and this was the first time she had been allowed to ride in a car for more than doctors' appointments. In the days following the attacks and the birth of the twins, she wondered what kind of world they were coming into. At this point, her faith was the only thing getting her through.

Arden, breaking the silence, said, "For as long as I can remember, you and Ben and I have all been weirdly linked. Now it's as if we have lost a part of our foundation and things feel wobbly beneath my feet."

Melody put her hand on Arden's arm, "We will find our balance again. It's going to take a while, but with God's help and being there for each other and that little angel in the backseat, we will find our way." Arden gripped Melody's hand to seal the deal.

Arden paused then said, "I want you to know how much I appreciate what you and your church have done for me. Everyone has been absolutely wonderful."

Melody nodded, "You are more than welcome. And I have some thank yous to give as well. Losing Ben and the twins being born in the midst of all of this, they have provided a great deal of love and support.

"You have a legion of guardian angels in your congregation. I couldn't have cut through the red tape without their help. A couple of them were able to contact law enforcement and expedite the process for us." Arden still had a hard time saying the words.

Melody agreed and tried to lighten the mood, "You know, you and Grace aren't going to be able to go back to New York until you eat up some more of the casseroles in my freezer. I think we'd survive at least ten years after Armageddon based on the stacks of freezer-to-oven containers stacked in the garage freezer alone. Victor took fifteen more over to the church to store in the walk-in freezer until we can bring them back here. Plus we haven't even touched the ones you made before the twins arrived."

Arden smiled, "You make a good point." She paused. "I've been giving this a lot of thought." Arden pulled into the cemetery and the gravel of the driveway crunched under her tires. She parked the car near the gravesite and turned off the ignition as Victor pulled up behind her. She turned and looked into Melody's eyes. Arden's were filled with fear and haunted by grief, "As much as I hate to admit it, I'm afraid to be in the city right now. It would be different if I only had myself to think of," she paused and looked into the rearview mirror into the back seat at the peacefully sleeping baby Grace. "But I've got this little one to consider."

Melody nodded. She understood her cousin's fears. Since the twins had been born and the terrorist attack happened, every action was measured against a different filter, more cautious and careful than ever before.

Arden continued, "If 9/11 has taught us anything, it's that we're all vulnerable, no matter where we are, whether it's the office you work in every day or the flight you've made hundreds of times. Things have changed." She paused, "I think I want to be closer to family."

Melody, secretly pleased but cautious, said, "Are you sure this is what you want to do? We've suffered a huge loss. This is a pretty big step to take."

Arden nodded and said, "I know what you're saying. I've read and reread all the books and articles that say you shouldn't make any big decisions after a tragic event. But playing by the rules feels alien to me. It always has. But now," choking back tears, "I've never felt so alone." Arden took a deep breath and said, "What would you think if Grace and I came to Camden Falls?"

Melody paused; she didn't want to scare Arden by putting too much pressure on her. But she had secretly been hoping and praying that Arden would come to this conclusion. "I think it would be wonderful. But I want you to be sure. Do you have any idea what you will do?" Melody knew Arden's thought processes almost as well as she knew her own. This wasn't a spontaneous decision. She was sure Arden had done her research.

"I've been doing a little research while I've been going back and forth to the city."

Melody smiled to herself.

Jean A. Smith

Chapter 9: September 17

The rain had started to pick up just as the weatherman said it would. Jack Phillips shook out the umbrella as well as his raincoat and took a seat in the dimly lit booth. This cozy pub had become a regular hangout for Jack. It was off Main Street, away from campus, and it reminded him of a place he used to frequent back in Chicago.

Maggie, the waitress, with short red hair and wisdom-beyond-her-years green eyes brought him a scotch neat. The amber liquid shot warmth into his body alleviating the dampness of the rain. He liked the fact that this pub had not turned into a college hangout with drunken frat boys and desperate sorority sisters. An undercurrent of jazz played in the background, loud enough to be noticed, but not overbearing. The rain was coming down hard enough to beat a comforting rhythm on the roof.

The first few weeks of the semester were always a bear with schedule changes, meetings and new regulations to follow. He had just wrapped up a pile of paperwork at his university office and couldn't face going home to his empty house.

It had been two years since Edie's murder and today would have been her fortieth birthday. Edie had loved birthdays, especially those marking a milestone. When Jack had turned forty, she had gotten him box seats at a Cubs game. It had been perfect, even if they had lost to the Cincinnati Reds by one run. For her, they had planned to- his thought was cut short by his smartphone buzzing in his pocket. He had been so caught up in university paperwork and red tape that he hadn't checked his phone in hours. This was quite a departure from his days working as a cop, protecting the streets of Chicago.

According to the notifications lighting up his phone, he had 12 new emails and 5 new text messages. The emails could wait. They usually consisted of the cyber variety of junk mail and university announcements and reminders. Texts were the main venue he used to communicate with his friends, siblings, and his mother, Rachel, as she updated all of them on their father's progress.

Jack scrolled through the texts. Four of the five were indeed from his mother, Rachel. Texts one through four were details about when his siblings would be in town and was it possible for Jack to pick up his brother and sister at the John Glenn Columbus International Airport? A quick reply of "yes" and he "could work it in" was sent to Rachel.

The last text was an alert from the university. The red, bold letters kicked Jack's law enforcement training into high gear. The alert had gone out around four this afternoon. The name of the missing girl was Grace Winters, which sent a wave of panic through him. Grace had been dating his youngest sibling, Grant, for several months. She also was a house/pet/babysitter for his best friend, police chief, Matt Brady. As he read through the text noting description, clothing, and place last seen, he realized the alert had been sent five hours ago. *Why hadn't Grant or someone let him know?* He hadn't heard any of the students or faculty members talking about it. His focus had been on schedules and upcoming lectures. He hoped she had found her way back by now, but he couldn't shake the uneasy feeling. He had seen too many cases like this and they rarely ended well.

Jack slid from the booth and put on his black trench coat all in one swift movement. He tossed a bill on the table, nodded to Sam the bartender who always seemed to be drying the same whiskey glass, and strode out in the torrential rain and headed to the frat house to check on his brother.

Chapter 10: Later That Same Day

Since Jack had walked from campus to the pub, his car was still in faculty parking. He didn't want to waste time getting to his little brother so he called an Uber and gave the driver the address to the frat house.

"Man, is this rain ever gonna stop?" The driver asked.

Jack wasn't interested in making small talk, but was not one to be impolite, "I sure hope so. Makes getting around campus difficult."

"Sure does. But it's good for business." he said as he looked around the area making sure the road was safe and clear of debris. "This weather makes it hard to look for that missing girl."

Jack tried not to let the shock of his statement show on his face, "Yes, it does. Have there been any updates on the situation?"

"Nah, must be killing her family not knowing where she is."

"Yes," Jack said, a little preoccupied with his own questions about the disappearance. He was also wondering how long it was going to take to get to the frat house. His patience was wearing thin. He needed to see Grant now.

*****

When Jack got to Grant's room, Grant had been waiting for him.

"Jack! Am I glad to see you! Any news?"

"Afraid not. How ya holdin' up? I just saw the text alert and came right over. Why didn't you get in touch with me?"

"I did! I sent you like 5 texts!"

Jack checked his phone and sure enough, he had not scrolled down far enough after reading the text from the university. "Sorry, kid. No excuse. I'm here now. Do you have any idea where she could be? When did you last talk to Grace?"

Grant grew so pale, Jack thought the kid was going to pass out. "Why are you asking all these questions? Am I a suspect?"

Jack sat on the end of Grant's bed and motioned for his brother to have a seat in his recliner. "Sorry, my law enforcement background is a knee jerk reaction. Look, you have watched me in action and you've watched enough of those true crime documentaries with Grace to know that in missing persons' cases, the first suspects are the people closest to the victim, the parents and a significant other, if there is one in the picture."

Grant sighed and sank into the recliner near his desk, tears welling in his eyes, "I guess that makes sense."

"So, back to my original question. When was the last time you saw Grace?"

Grant hesitated, "Here at the frat house before the party." Grant avoided looking his brother in the eye.

Jack sensed there was more to this story than what he thought. "Spill, Grant. This is no time for holding back. A girl's life could be in danger." Jack paused, "Did you say here at the frat house? I didn't think Arden wanted Grace to come here."

Grant looked sheepish, "She doesn't and it doesn't happen very often, but yeah she was here." Jack looked annoyed and was about to say something when Grant held up a hand and said, "I got her out before the party got started so we wouldn't be caught with someone under the drinking age in the house."

Jack nodded, relieved. "Okay, so why was she here?"

Grant hesitated and said, "We were making plans for after the party. We were going to meet up later."

Jack took on the parental role, "Would this have been after her curfew and after the legal curfew? Was Arden going to be made aware of this plan?"

Grant shook his head, "Of course not. It's not like it was the first time we've done it."

"Why? Why all the sneaking around? Mom and Dad love Grace and I thought Arden was supporting this relationship. Whenever I'm at the BrewHouse and you two come up in conversation, she has nothing but positive things to say about you."

"I don't know. It just seemed fun. You're right, everyone supports us, but Arden keeps a pretty tight leash on Grace and sometimes she likes to sneak out and meet when we both know Arden would freak."

"Well, of course, she would. You realize that Arden has good reason to keep a close eye on Grace."

"I do and I know Grace knows it, too. But sometimes she wants to shake things up and rebel a little."

"I just hope that her rebellion hasn't gotten her into trouble."

"When Grace comes back, if she gets back-"

"She will come back and then I think both of you will be grounded until you are ready for the nursing home."

"Way to make me feel better. Actually, if it meant Grace walking through that door right now, I would be willing to be grounded for life."

"Grant, listen, most of the police force, as well as friends and family, will be looking for Grace. We will find her. You can't give up hope. Unless-"

Grant let what Jack had just said to him sink in and then when the realization hit, he practically jumped out of the recliner, "What do you mean, unless? What are you implying? Do you think I had something to do with Grace's disappearance?"

Jack sighed and rubbed his neck, "Look, you have already admitted to sneaking around. The next leap to make is that something happened and-"

"No, stop right there. Nothing happened."

"Okay, so was hooking up later all you talked about?" Jack asked quietly,

"No."

"No?"

"No."

"What else did you talk about?"

"It's private."

"Look, Grant, nothing is private in a missing person's case, especially if you are a prime suspect. Now level with me. Are you two in some kind of trouble? Did you two argue and things went south? Tell me! I have to know so that I can help you."

Grant shook his head. "That's it. Nothing to tell."

Jean A. Smith

Chapter 11: Las Vegas- One Year Ago

The redhead sat at the bar lazily stirring her drink. She was wearing a short black skirt and a cerulean blue spaghetti strap top that flowed around her curves in all the right places. She had been doing quite well at the blackjack table, but tonight, it felt a little too routine. The slots had lost their appeal within the first few hours on the Strip. She had come back to Vegas to recapture the excitement that had been missing in her life for so long. So far, the trip had been a bust. She had given the blackjack tables a try and at first, had a hard time getting the rhythm of the game.

One thing the redhead was good at was reading people. She could identify their tells almost immediately. Once she had gotten a feel for the players, she was able to adjust accordingly using their tells against them. She had a short attention span and Blackjack had fallen into the boring category file in her mind. In the past few months, poker had captured her attention. That game intrigued her. She had been spending some of her free time watching how-to videos on YouTube and had also watched some of the championships on TV. The tension, the hushed play-by-play of the announcers, and stacks and stacks of beautiful chips made her a little dizzy at first trying to take it all in.

She had finally gathered the courage and confidence to get in on a couple of games with friends. It had been fun, however, she took it a lot more seriously than they did. So she started searching for out-of-town games and began to gain more confidence and experience. Now she was hoping to either find a mark that would buy her a few drinks and show her a good time or get her a buy-in at one of the high stakes poker games. Those games were usually by invitation only. That was why choosing a mark had to be done with care. They were the hardest to wrangle. If they were any good, they were looking for tells just as she was.

She was getting ready to order a second drink when a smoky voice said, "I'll have what the lady is having and put it on my tab."

"Sure thing, Trey," the bartender said.

The redhead turned towards the smoky voice and found herself looking into the eyes of an extremely attractive man. He was wearing a black suit and tie. His red shirt set off his dark skin. His stunning good looks almost took her breath away. All she could say was, "Thank you."

Trey kept his arm around the back of the bar chair trapping her, but she didn't mind. "So, Red, I'm looking for a good luck charm. Think you are up to the task?"

Red appraised Trey with a long look up and down his body that made him feel a little exposed. "I don't believe in luck."

Their drinks arrived and each took a sip not breaking eye contact with each other.

"Aww, Red, don't toy with me."

Red smiled, "If I toy with you, I guarantee you'll enjoy it."

Trey laughed a deep, throaty laugh, "Ah, Red, I like you. You are spunky." He started drawing a lazy circle on her bare shoulder, "What do you say, we get out of here and find our own kind of fun."

Red leaned in and whispered looking directly at his mouth, "What did you have in mind?"

"Well," Trey said, "what turns you on?"

"Let me think," she said, "I came to Vegas to gamble. So I guess gambling turns me on."

"What a coincidence," he said, "me, too. Are you into poker? I happen to know there is a poker game upstairs in this very hotel."

"Lucky for us," she said.

"I thought you didn't believe in luck."

"I do when it suits me."

"Does it suit you now?"

"I believe it does."

"Let's go, I didn't get your name."

"Lola. Just call me Lola."

The slightly swaying couple made their way to the elevator and took it to the penthouse suite.
*****

"Oh, my God! That was amazing!"

"You were amazing. You've been holding out on me, Lola. I think we've worked out quite a system here."

"It has possibilities," the redhead said this as casually as possible but inside the excitement was ready to burst. This was exactly what she had wanted to accomplish.

"I have never played that well in my life. This is the biggest pot I've won in a long time. Like it or not, you are my good luck charm."

Lola used the money to fan herself, "Don't sell yourself short, Trey. You were very skillful, even masterful in that game."

Trey walked toward her taking the money from her hands and throwing it on the bed. "That's not the only place I'm skilled and masterful."

"I have no doubt," she whispered, as she sank down on the bed and grabbing his tie pulling him towards her finishing what they started in the elevator.

Chapter 12: Present-September 13

    Grace unlocked the side door and punched in the security code for the Brady house. At the last minute, Julia had been approved for new immunotherapy treatment and she and Matt had to make a quick trip to the airport to catch a flight in order to see if she was a candidate. Matt and Julia both had texted her, asking if she could meet the kids at the bus, get them to karate class and spend the weekend taking care of them and their mini-pinscher dogs, Trixie and Nancy. Matt had named the pets after two fictional detectives from children's mysteries when they rescued the sisters from the Camden Falls Humane Society. When she opened the dogs' crate, they sprang out practically knocking her over and headed to the glass-sliding door so they could run around the back yard.
    Grace was secretly happy that this opportunity presented itself. Not only was it good news for Julia, but Grace needed the money to add to her college fund and she would be able to get a lot of her school work done. She knew the Bradys' Wi-Fi password, so she could access her College Credit Plus classes, too. Arden never gave

her a hard time when the Bradys called and needed her. Everyone was now aware of their situation and lending a helping hand was never questioned. She had an hour before the kids got home. She made her way to the kitchen and tossed her backpack on the center island and headed for the fridge. The Bradys always had the best selection of food and snacks. She was not disappointed. She grabbed a Coke Zero, a container of cheese chunks and a bowl of grapes. As she turned to shut the refrigerator door, Trixie and Nancy were jumping around and panting at the glass-sliding door. She let them in and they immediately started jumping for the cheese in her hand.

"Hey, no human food for you. I'll grab you guys some treats." Grace put her snacks on the island and went to the canister by the microwave and grabbed a handful of treats the Bradys bought at the local gourmet pet bakery.

"Now sit," both dogs obeyed. "Good job!" she gave them the treats and scratched their ears. She put a few of the treats in their dishes just for good measure. She also made sure that their huge metal water bowl was filled. Since the weather was still a little warm and humid, she added some ice cubes to the water bowl to cool it off.

Grace made her way back into the kitchen island and seated herself in one of the comfortable chairs that surrounded it. She loved this kitchen with its white walls and fixtures with the gray and yellow accents. She could imagine herself as a successful veterinarian coming home from work and the live-in housekeeper would have started dinner. Her successful husband, who looked a lot like Grant, would get home from the office and they would walk the dogs while their children, a boy and a girl, rode their bikes ahead of them. They would make their way back home, get the kids ready for bed and share a glass of wine and talk about their respective days at work. A notification ring from her phone brought her back to reality. Grace sighed, her best friend, Lyndsay texted again. This was the third time today.

Lyndsay: Where r u?

Grace paused then texted: Brady gig. Waiting for the kiddos. Here all weekend. What's up? She thought she might regret asking that. Grace had really been looking forward to getting a chunk of

Advanced Government done and she was behind in her reading for AP English. She needed to post a question regarding *Pride and Prejudice* and her perceptions of Elizabeth Bennett's character and a couple of answers to other posts by Sunday.

Lyndsay: Out of town for the weekend. The 'rents want one last camping trip before cold weather sets in. Pray for me. (Praying hands emoji).

Grace: LOL. I'll get Pastor Mel on it. So you're on kid patrol, too. She was secretly relieved that Lindsay was going to be busy for the weekend as well. She loved spending time with her, but senior year and her course load was turning out to be more stressful than she originally thought.

Lyndsay had three little siblings, two boys and one girl, all stair steps. Madison was in kindergarten, Bryson was in first grade and Austin was in second grade. Lyndsay and they were half-siblings. When Lyndsay's mom left her and her dad to "go find herself," her dad "found" a younger woman. They married after 6 weeks of dating and started having kids almost immediately. Now the family fun time was taking camping trips. Lyndsay, though not a fan, was given no choice in the matter. Dad and stepmom had dubbed her live-in babysitter/nanny.

Lyndsay: Yes. Can't wait to see what trouble they get into this time.

Grace: LOL. Once the kids are asleep I'm going to see if Grant wants to come over for Netflix and chill.

Lyndsay: Or maybe just chill! LOL!

Grace: I'll take what I can get! Text if you get bored.

Lyndsay: No doubt!

Grace checked her other messages. They were school-related on Remind. Many of Grace's teachers used this system and it was much quicker to use than emailing. Sometimes, the teacher didn't check the inbox until it was too late. This way the response was usually a lot faster. Who didn't check their texts on a regular basis? It made it easy to get assignments and the teacher or anyone else she didn't want to have her number could still get messages to her. The first message was from Miss Bishop. She was reminding them to post their questions and responses to others to the *Pride and Prejudice* board. She also included book emojis and nerd faces. *Miss Bishop needs to get out more,* Grace thought.

Another message was from her Advanced Government teacher. Their paper on Game Theory had been changed to a later date. *There is a God,* Grace breathed a sigh of relief.

The siblings, Hazel and Neil would be home soon and not expecting her. She would fix them each a treat bag with trail mix and a juice box that they could eat while she drove them to their karate lesson. She would drop them off and park the Bradys' SUV in the nearby parking garage. The beauty of driving their SUV gave her free access to the parking garage rather than spending money on a pass. It was close enough to the karate class that she could walk across the street to the university library and get some of her AP reading done.

******

Hazel and Neil were as excited to see Grace as they were to go to karate class. Grace was able to get some of her homework done at the library and the siblings were chatty all the way home. Thank goodness they weren't arguing this time.

Once they got home and dumped their karate bags in the laundry room, Grace made a deal with them. If they were good, took their baths and got into their pajamas without fighting, she would order pizza for dinner and they would eat it in front of the TV. Food bribery always did the trick. The Bradys always left money for "treats and emergencies." In Grace's mind having pizza delivered covered both.

While Hazel and Neil got a bath and put on their pajamas, Grace checked on them twice and then went into the laundry room to empty their karate bags and start a load of laundry. She went back into the kitchen and opened their backpacks in search of important forms and half-eaten snacks. Grace could always count on finding one of three treasures. Today was no exception. She found a part of a granola bar in Neil's bag. She was thankful it wasn't the chocolate-covered variety. A split-open banana was lodged in Hazel's backpack. Thank goodness the banana smell funk had not permeated the rest of the bag.

Taking Care of Grace

Just as they tumbled into the kitchen the doorbell rang, signaling that dinner was ready. When Grace opened the door expecting the delivery boy, she found Grant instead, holding the pizza box.

"Grant!" the kids screamed, Grace grabbed the pizza and Hazel and Neil grabbed Grant's hands, dragging him to the den. Grace laughed. Grant was so good with them and they loved him as much as they loved Grace.

Grace called Grant, from the kitchen while she was plating the pizza, "Hey, how did you know I was here and that we'd ordered pizza?"

It was Grant's turn to laugh as he tried to extricate himself from the wiggly siblings. "I called the BrewHouse and Arden told me where you were. The pizza delivery was a happy coincidence. I paid the driver and tipped him well."

"I'll pay you back," Grace said, sensing him behind her, she turned and looked into Grant's blue eyes.

"We'll think of something," he murmured and leaned in to kiss her. From behind her, Hazel and Neil were melodramatically gagging and throwing themselves on the floor, collapsing into giggles, "NO KISSING! EWWW! GROSS!!"

Grant and Grace parted, laughing. They were used to this reaction by now. The gang made their way into the den where the family spent most of their time. It had that lived-in, cozy look. The gas fireplace that was on constantly throughout the winter, took up an entire wall. The brick was from the original police station in Camden Falls that had been torn down a few years ago when the new facility was built.

On the inside wall, a giant smart TV and various home theater accouterments were standing at the ready to entertain. The comfy leather sectional sofa held carelessly placed throw pillows and blankets to ward off a chill. Grant herded the kids back into the den with the pizza on paper plates while Grace grabbed the napkins and soft drinks. As she entered the den she paused watching Grant with Hazel and Neil. They were trying once again to get him to talk Grace into letting them watch *Stranger Things*. Grant was gentle but firm.

"You know your parents don't want you to watch that. *I* even get scared," he said with mock exaggeration. "And we don't want to get

Grace in trouble." The siblings nodded in agreement somewhat reluctantly. Drawing them in, Grant said in a conspiratorial tone, "Have you guys ever seen *Goonies*?" Neil and Hazel shook their heads in unison, hanging on Grant's every word. "Really, no One-Eyed Willie, buried treasure, Chunk?"

"No," Hazel spoke up. "Grace and our parents said the next time it was on TV we would watch it. Can we, Grace?" She asked as Grace entered the room.

"Sure, you guys are gonna love this movie." She turned to Grant, "Is it on Netflix?

"No, Hulu." Grant answered.

Grace gave a sigh of relief, "*Goonies* it is!"

******

The evening was a huge success. Hazel and Neil loved the movie and they also loved hanging out with Grace and Grant. Fairly soon after the movie, the kids started to nod off. Grant carried a sleeping Neil to his room to tuck him in and Hazel walked sleepily to her room holding Grace's hand. Once Grace had her tucked in and kissed her on the forehead, Hazel reached out a hand and took Grace's.

"Grace?" Hazel whispered. "What's it like to kiss a boy?"

Grace was taken aback, but didn't want to embarrass Hazel.

"When it's the right guy, it's pretty great. Why do you ask?"

Hazel blushed, giggled and pulled the covers over her head. Grace tickled her through the covers and Hazel came up for air.

"Seriously, Hazy" Grace asked, calling Hazel by her nickname, "Why do you ask?"

Hazel sat up and whispered, "Trent Anderson tried to kiss me during recess today."

Grace asked, "Really. So what happened?"

"I slugged him in the arm and ran away."

Grace stifled a laugh, "I guess that's one way to handle it. You might want to talk to your mom about this when she gets home."

Hazel flopped back in the bed, sighing heavily, "Okay. But Mom only kissed Daddy and that doesn't count."

"Why not?"

"Cause he's our dad, not a boyfriend."

Grace was not going to argue with that logic. Changing the subject she said, "If the weather is nice in the morning, do you think you and Neil would want to play a little driveway hockey?"

"Yes!" Hazel whispered excitedly.

"Okay, time for bed. And no spying on Grant and I, deal?"

"Deal," Hazel agreed, "Or no hockey."

"Or no hockey." Grace repeated. They had made this deal many, many times before. She tucked her in and kissed her on the forehead again. Grace left the door cracked so the hall light spilled in and joined Grant in the den.

Jean A. Smith

Chapter 13: September 14

"That goal was good and you know it!" Neil shouted at the top of his lungs.

"It was OUT! You, Butthead!" Hazel screamed.

"No, it wasn't, Dogface!"

"Enough!" Grace yelled. "Now, if you two can't play nice, we will go back inside and no Netflix or video games!"

"Aw, Grace come on, you always side with her," Neil whined.

Before Grace could answer, Hazel yelled, "Oh, yeah? That's 'cause she knows I'm right."

"That's it, we are done for the afternoon. Pick up your hockey sticks and goals from the driveway, take off your skates and put everything where it belongs in the garage. I think it's going to rain soon anyway."

"See? Now you got us in trouble! You always do, Neil!" Hazel skated up the driveway to the house. Blinded by her anger, she didn't see the stone that locked in her skates and threw her to the ground scraping both of her palms.

"Ow, ow, ow, ow, ow!" Hazel howled. Anger forgotten, Neil rushed to her side along with Grace. Grace knelt by the crying child and looked at her hands.

"You're going to be okay, sweetie. It's just a little blood and a few scrapes. Some cleaning up with soap and water and a little antiseptic will do the trick." Grace surmised that Hazel's outburst was more about the game. Her injury appeared to be linked to the shock of falling and her anger at Neil.

"Come on, Hazy" Grace said, "let's go inside and get you fixed up. Neil, would you put away the skates and the rest of the equipment?"

"Sure, Grace," then Neil directed his comments to his sister with a wicked grin trying to cheer her up, "I'll get you next time, Butthead!" Neil skated away quickly before Grace had a chance to reprimand him. Besides, Grace couldn't help but smile. The insult seemed to do the trick. Hazel rolled her eyes and said disdainfully to Grace, "Boys." As they walked towards the house Grace thought about the Brady kids' relationship. Being an only child, Grace sometimes wished she had a sibling to share the good and bad times with. Arden had told her that her mother had been pregnant when she was killed during 9/11. Grace often wondered what her sibling would have been like. Would they have gotten along? How different would her life be if her parents had lived and she had been raised in New York? She never gave this line of thinking too much time. It was pointless. She loved the life she had with Arden in Camden Falls. It was hard to imagine an alternative.

******

"Yow," Hazel said. She and Grace were in the bathroom the kids shared. Grace had helped Hazel get up on the vanity so that Grace had a better vantage point in which to treat Hazel's wounds.

"Blow on it," Grace said, "It will help take the sting away." Hazel obeyed and Grace racked her brain to find a topic to engage Hazel in that would take her mind off of her medical treatment. Hazel did that for her.

"Grace?" Hazel hesitated.

"Yeah," Grace said off-handedly, concentrating on the work at hand.

"Grace, are things okay with our mom and dad?" Hazel started to swing her legs with nervous tension; Grace stilled them and looked into the little girl's fear-filled eyes.

"What makes you ask that Hazy?" concerned etched Grace's face.

Holding back tears, Hazel continued, "I overheard mommy and daddy talking and daddy was crying!" Hazel's eyes widened as she shared this information.

"Hmm," Grace said trying not to alarm the child, "you know, Hazy, sometimes grownups talk and when you hear only part of the conversation, you can really get the wrong idea. Why don't you tell me what happened and maybe we can figure it out together."

Hazel sighed, "Okay. But I don't want to get in trouble for this."

"Why would you get into trouble?"

"Because I was doing something I wasn't supposed to be doing."

Ugh, this is a tough one, Grace thought. *This is tricky because I might need to ask Julia and Matt about it.* Grace put her hands on either side of Hazel, leaned and looked her in the eyes. "Look, Hazel, I won't say anything to your parents unless I have to and if I do, we'll do it together, deal?"

Hazel hesitated, "Deal," and she reluctantly nodded. "Okay, so I was sitting up in my room reading *Escape from Mr. Lemoncello's Library.*"

"Okay, so far, so good."

"But I hadn't finished my science homework and it was past my bedtime."

"These are minor crimes at this point, except for the not finishing the homework thing."

"I know, but I didn't understand it and I was going to ask the teacher during homeroom tomorrow."

"Fair enough, continue."

"So I was reading and I thought I heard someone yell in the other part of the house."

"You mean yell out in pain, or what?"

"I couldn't be sure and I wasn't even sure I heard anything."

"Got it. Go on."

"So I continued reading and I heard it again, louder this time and I could hear some of the words."

"What did you hear?

"The only thing that was really clear was 'Why are you doing this?'"

"Who said it, your mom or your dad?"

"I wasn't sure until..." Hazel trailed off.

"Until what?" Grace had no idea where this was going. She knew from her friends that parents fight, argue, disagree, whatever. But Julia and Matt were solid. From her standpoint and pretty much all of Camden Falls saw Matt and Julia as the perfect couple. Both were gorgeous, had great jobs, gave to charity, adopted two of the sweetest kids out of foster care and were always ready to lend a hand. She also knew that the kids didn't know the whole story of Julia's relapse. They had told the kids that Julia was going out of town to make sure her treatments were working. They didn't want the kids blindsided if someone brought it up to them at school.

Grace didn't think about marriage a lot, but she knew her parents had been solid from what Arden and Melody had told her. She hoped that whomever she married, if she got married, she and her husband would have a relationship like that.

"This is the I-could-get-in-big trouble part."

"Remember our deal."

Hazel blew out a breath. "Okay, so I snuck out of bed crept down the stairs."

"How did you make it down those squeaky stairs?"

Hazel said with knowledge only a ten-year-old could have, "Years of practice, Neil and I figured out how to go down the stairs silently so that we could peek at what Santa brought us. We spent a whole afternoon figuring it out while mom and dad were cleaning the garage."

Impressive, Grace thought, *these two have a future in government intelligence.* "We'll talk about that aspect of things later. So you went down the stairs and..." Grace encouraged the young girl to continue.

"And I could tell that the voices were coming from the den, so I tiptoed through the kitchen and listened at the door. It was then that I figured out that it was Daddy that had been asking the question I had overheard in the beginning."

"How did you know that?"

"Because he was asking it again and what were they going to do about me and Neil."

"Neil and me,"

"That's what I said." It went over Hazel's head that Grace was correcting her grammar.

"Hmmm." Grace was at a loss. She went back to cleaning and bandaging Hazel's cuts and scrapes. *This is something I am going to have to think about and talk to Arden about. Or maybe Melody would be a good choice. Melody counsels people all the time, right? Maybe she would know what to do?*

"Grace, what do you think? Do you think it has something to do with Mommy being sick?" Hazel's questions brought Grace back to the present.

"Listen, I don't think we should jump to conclusions. Who knows, maybe your mom wants to go skydiving and your dad doesn't want her to." Grace tried to lighten the mood, feeling that what the little girl was saying was at the heart of a much more serious problem.

"You're not going to tell on me, are you?"

"Hey, we have a deal. Besides, if I say anything to them, you will be with me," Grace paused, "Listen, I know this sounds serious. Let's just see how the rest of the weekend goes."

"Okay," Hazel seemed somewhat relieved.

"Okay, so you're all set. Your cost for these services is... a hug," Grace smiled.

Hazel's face broke into a smile and threw herself into Grace's arms.

"That's my girl. So let's see what that crazy brother of yours is up to, I think some ice cream is in order."

Hazel and Grace left the upstairs bathroom that the siblings shared. They were downstairs and out of earshot when a chirping sound came from the master bedroom.

Chapter 14: Columbus Police Department, September 19

"Knock it off, Ramey! You're having a bad dream! Hedren called from the intake area. It was a monthly occurrence to have Joseph Ramey in holding to sleep off a bender. He could only behave himself for so long before Faith Mission kicked him out. Then once on the street he would drink whatever booze he could beg, borrow or steal and pick a fight with the first vagrant he encountered. He must have gotten a hold of some cheap whiskey. That's what usually brought on his nightmares.

Angie shook her head as she walked back to her desk. *Sometimes I think he goes off the rails just so he can surround himself with familiar faces.*

Taking Care of Grace

As she sat down at her desk to check messages and update her other pending cases, she ran a hand through her hair trying to release the tension of the day. Angie was exhausted. The Feds had insisted on retracing all the steps she and the CPD had already covered and had come up with the same results. They were no closer to solving the case than the locals were. The only positive elements to surface were that no other college students had gone missing within the last 36 hours and it appeared that the case Sheila was working on was not related to the sex trafficking cases. *Thank God,* she thought *we don't need another innocent kid added to the list.*

Since she had spoken to Sheila, Angie had been fighting to erase the images of Jack Phillips that kept sneaking into her mind as soon as she let her guard down and tried to relax. She, Jack, Sheila and Matt Brady had all been at the police academy around the same time. Even though the three of them were in the class ahead of her, they had adopted Angie into their close-knit group and had treated her as an equal. While Sheila had been very aware of Angie's feelings for Jack, he didn't have a clue. While he admired Angie, his priorities were in a different place. Once he left for Chicago, the next thing she knew, he was married to the love of his life, Edie.

Angie threw herself into her work after that announcement and quickly made her way up the ranks and was one of the top detectives in the division. The FBI had come sniffing around twice, trying to recruit her, but Angie was happy in Columbus. She had family here and she knew the streets. Now she was having a hard time doing that job with the likes of Jack Phillips in the vicinity. Sheila had casually dropped information into their monthly phone calls regarding Jack. Angie adopted a cool and casual demeanor during the conversation but found herself thinking about it later when time permitted.

Hedren interrupted Angie's train of thought, "Hey, Rossi, Ramey is asking to talk to you. Says he knows somethin' about those missing kids."

Angie sighed, "Do you believe him? Or is this another cry for attention?"

Hedren rubbed his chin thoughtfully, "Hard to say. When he's off the booze, he's a pretty credible source."

Angie nodded, "I never want to be accused of leaving a stone unturned." She got up from her desk and headed toward the interrogation room with a bottle of water and a legal pad and pen.

Hedren nodded, "I'll bring him down in a few. Thanks for hearing him out. You never know, I guess."

Angie smiled, "All part of the job."

*****

Angie paced the interrogation room while she waited for Hedren to bring Ramey up from holding. *Just consider this your good deed of the day.* Taking Joe seriously and questioning him as an informant usually fell to her. Joe had been a friend to the Rossi family before the death of his wife and the loss of his pizza carryout to fire. Those two tragedies had sent him into the depths of alcoholism and homelessness. Angie and Hedren were the only two at the station that treated Joe with any real respect. He had ticked off more than one officer with his ranting. Angie knew that under all the street filth and demons was a caring man who had lost more than he could manage.

Joe's stench of vomit, urine and cheap alcohol arrived in the interrogation room before he did. Angie willed her eyes not to water, but years of experience didn't curb a person's natural instincts. Hedren had Joe cuffed in front, pulled the chair facing Angie away from the metal table and planted Joe firmly in it. He landed with an "Oof" and belched out toxic air into the already cold, confined space. "Hey," Hedren said loudly, "Manners in front of the lady."

Joe nodded as tears started to flood his eyes. *Here we go,* thought Angie, *angry to a puddle of tears in 5 seconds flat.* Angie sat, folded her hands on the table and said, "Hi, Joe. Hedren said you might have some information for me. Feel like talking?"

Joe looked up bleary-eyed trying to focus on who was talking to him, then said, "Yeah, I got somethin' to say."

Angie waited. Joe seemed to be clearing the cobwebs swirling in his brain and grasping at thoughts and images just out of reach. Angie sat there patiently hoping that this wasn't just a waste of time. Finally, Joe cleared his throat and began.

"Word on the street is that you guys are trying to track down some missing kids that might have been caught up in sex trafficking."

Angie exhaled trying to keep the impatience out of her voice, "Joe, that's old news. Hedren said you might have information about it?"

Joe leaned back in his chair and said very confidently, "As a matter of fact I do."

Angie asked, "Care to share?"

Joe looked at her thoughtfully, "Maybe, if the price is right."

Angie sighed, "Come on, Joe, you know it doesn't work that way."

Joe waved a grimy hand, "I don't want money, I want a favor."

"I can't let you out until we see if the guy you fought with is going to press charges."

"Aw, Come on, Angie, can't you let me out on my own recog-, recogna-

"Not until you can say it clearly and even then it's not up to me." She paused. "I tell you what, if you actually have some usable information, I will treat you to a burger at the Inn Towne Diner and talk to the people at the shelter to see if they will let you back in. Deal?"

"I knew you'd come through for me."

"Joe, the deal is null and void unless you give me something I can use."

"Okay, so I was minding my own business, sitting on a bench near the campus entrance and this food truck pulls up and sets up shop."

Angie began taking notes. She remembered from some of the reports she had read that they had reason to suspect that a food truck called The Paddy Wagon was one of the covers in the operation. "Where was this bench and which campus were you near?"

Joe scratched at his patchy beard that shadowed his neck, "I'm not sure."

This is getting us nowhere, Angie thought and then said, " And you hang out at both OSU and Cap. Can you remember if it was one of those campuses?"

Joe continued to scratch which made Angie slightly queasy. He then stopped rather abruptly and said, "Cap. Definitely Cap. People walkin' around in clothes that look like rags a bum would wear, but cost more than a week's wage."

On the nose, Angie thought. *You are more observant than anyone gives you credit for. They don't call it Bucksley for nothing.* Focusing on the job at hand, Angie continued to write and ask questions. Through her interview with Ramey she concluded that based on the activity Ramey had observed and the odd hours of operation, this might be the lead they had been looking for. She wanted to do some digging before she turned this new info over to the feds. If it turned out to be a dead end, they would be none the wiser. Just as Angie stood up, Hedren knocked and opened the interrogation room door, "Hey, Rossi, can I see you a minute?"

"Sure," Angie said trying to figure out why Hedren would interrupt now. She said to Joe, "Listen, Joe, I'll be right back." She followed Hedren out of the room closing the door behind her so that Joe couldn't hear their conversation. "What's up, Hedren?"

Hedren nodded toward the interrogation room, "Your boy in there lucked out. No charges are being filed. He is free to go as soon as you are done with him." Angie breathed a sigh of relief. Hedren continued, "However, I think getting him back into Faith Mission is going to take a little arm twisting."

Angie nodded and said, "Good news for Joe. Let me take care of the Mission. Hopefully, I can put a little fear in Joe." She turned to go back into the interrogation room and then turned back to Hedren. Laying a hand on his arm and giving it a squeeze, she said, "I owe ya one, Hedren. Thanks."

Hedren blushed a little and said, "Don't thank me, I had nothing to do with it. As soon as the higher-ups heard you were questioning him, they backed off."

Angie smiled, "Whatever works. I'm going to let him sweat a little more. I don't want this victory to come easy. He has to work his way into the Mission's good graces again. Leave him in there while I give the Mission a call."

"I like the way you think, Rossi." Hedren smiled and turned to head back to the reception desk. Angie took out her cell phone and called the Mission.

Chapter 15: Present: September 16

Arden sat drinking coffee on her enclosed deck making her daily list of things that needed to be done. It has been sixteen years since she and Grace settled into Camden Falls. She smiled to herself, *the best decision I ever made.*

Becoming Grace's guardian had come as a surprise. The Whitakers, Jess's parents had not objected to Ben and Jess's wishes regarding Grace's guardianship. But that wasn't the only major change that Arden had to adjust to.

When she settled in the quaint college town, she was not a coffee expert, at least not in the business sense. Did she like coffee? Yes. Did she drink coffee? Absolutely. It was part of her morning routine as it was for millions of other people. Her decision to go into business for herself hadn't been easy. With the love and support of Melody and Victor, the congregation and the Whitakers, she had been able to secure this new life for herself and Grace.

She had loved being an advertising executive in the Big Apple. She was energized when trying to zero in on what was going to grab the public's attention and she didn't rest until they bought the product she was promoting. She had worked her way up the corporate ladder and had broken through her share of glass ceilings. She had a substantial list of clients who were achieving their own success due to her advertising expertise.

Arden had captured the attention of the top brass in the agency. She had been offered a position to head up the company's new office in London on the heels of landing her tenth national campaign when the attacks came. Even before that life-altering event, her success was beginning to feel stale. She felt as if she was fighting and succeeding in the same battle over and over again. The job had lost its challenge. She started to know what to expect. She knew she needed to look for something new. The fear and added responsibility of Grace made those fleeting thoughts a necessity.

She still missed Ben every day. He, Jess and Grace had been the perfect little family. She had loved Jess as well, thinking of her like the sister she had always wanted. They had been sensible people with 401ks, insurance policies and college funds set up for Grace and the little one who had been on the way. They vacationed in the Hamptons and hosted clever dinner parties for associates and friends. They always included Arden and arranged for a potential love interest or two to be in attendance in the hopes that Arden would find the love of her life and finally settle down.

While all the men had been handsome and wildly successful, none of them had made her feel the connection she was looking for. She wasn't getting any younger and while she loved her job, she was beginning to realize that she needed more in her life. It might have been watching Ben and his family that had started her thinking. She also knew that as soon as she was offered the London office, she was going to turn them down. She loved traveling and visiting different places, but the thought of being so far away from family had her declining the offer. She felt secure in the fact that New York was just a short plane ride away from family.

Now, since Grace had gotten older and was getting ready to start college, Arden was open to dating although she wasn't sure if there were any prospects on the horizon. She had been married for about five minutes right out of college. Her focus had always been education first and then her career. If she had one regret in life, it was that she had put Simon and herself through the pain of a failed marriage. She was glad they had parted amicably and pursued the lives they had envisioned for themselves. She had gone on to pursue her dreams in the advertising world. He had settled in upstate New York and opened a furniture refinishing business and antique store. He had been happily married for a number of years and they had three children, two boys and a girl. The divorce, while incredibly painful, had been the best decision for both of them.

So while the city and the rest of the country as a whole were trying to put itself back together, Arden's life was a rebuilding project as well. Once the legal matters were sifted through and finalized, Arden had been named the legal guardian of Grace and took custody of her. It became grudgingly apparent within the first few weeks of bringing Grace permanently in her life, that living arrangements needed to change drastically. New York, with its fast pace and loaded schedule no longer appealed to her. This new responsibility brought with it a sense of fear and a need to protect. While she had the financial means and resources to hire nannies and other staff, she did not want Grace to be raised by strangers. Her parents had been hands-on and present in Ben and her life. That was what she wanted for Grace. Her life, BG, Before Grace, didn't allow for diaper changes, snuggle time and naps.

With Melody's support, Arden and Grace embarked on a new lifestyle. What better place to raise a child than the Midwest? County fairs, farmland for miles, football games, walking trails and small-town living gave Arden a feeling of security and not of confinement as it did when she was young. It sounded perfect and more importantly safe for both of them.

While the ad agency was supportive of her decision, they hated to lose her. Her clients, though understanding, were even unhappier. Being the planner and list-maker she had always been since childhood, she created piles of lists and goals as well as research about Camden Falls. She sought out a profession that would allow her to make a living as well as create her own hours and have Grace close by.

Melody put her in touch with the owners of the BrewHouse, a local coffee shop. Tom and Gladys Gleeson had been a mainstay in Camden Falls, but Tom had passed away suddenly from a heart attack and Gladys didn't want the pressure of running the coffeehouse by herself. It was filled with too many memories. She had decided to sell and move into a retirement community near her daughter and son-in-law in Savannah, Georgia. Gladys and Arden had several lengthy phone conversations and both parties agreed that Arden and Grace would be a good fit for the business and the town.

Becoming a single parent had been a huge adjustment for Arden. She had been so used to looking out for only herself that adding a new, little, needy person into the mix had been both terrifying and amazing. There were so many things to get used to and learn. Arden worried that she didn't have the mom instinct one needed to be a successful parent. She remembered a time, after they had recently moved to Camden Falls when Grace was three and they were on play date at one of the neighbor's homes. Grace and her little friend Olivia were eating lunch and both of them held out their banana sections to Arden. Arden said to the girls, "Yes, those are yours to eat." It wasn't until Olivia's mom, Randi took the sections from the girls and peeled them for them that Arden realized the girls needed help peeling their banana sections. Arden slipped into the bathroom and cried. When Randi found her later, she hugged her and said, "You'll get the hang of it. Unfortunately, there is no handbook to follow but you have nothing to worry about. Your love for that little girl will show you the way." And as Arden reflected on those early days, she realized that was true.

The beauty of running the coffee shop allowed her to set up a pack and play in her office and not run up enormous daycare fees. Besides, Arden was very protective of Grace. Both of them had lost so much and images from that fateful day and the days that followed still haunted her. Melody was a godsend when it came to offering parental advice or a sounding board when Arden needed it. The twins, Nicholas and Billy, were a little younger than Grace but as the trio grew the boys were very protective of their older cousin. Grace fascinated the twins with her dark brown, wavy hair and startling green eyes. It didn't take long for her to figure that out and she soon became the leader of the trio.

Arden and Grace learned from each other. Arden became an expert at figuring out which cries were for hunger, a scraped knee, a fever or just wanting to snuggle. Along with Melody, the local pediatrician and other parents she met along the way, helped Arden to ease into her new role by providing calm, patient answers whenever Arden called, day or night. The toddling threes gave way to the preschool fours and Arden marveled at the developing personality of this amazing little person.

When the first anniversary of the attacks came, Arden started the tradition of she and Grace making a pilgrimage back to New York and Ground Zero to pay tribute to Ben and Jess. Every year, Jess's parents made the trip as well. It was bittersweet for them, mourning the loss of their daughter and watching the astonishing growth of their granddaughter, Gracie. Sometimes Melody would go with them, offering comfort and prayers to the grieving survivors. After the visit, they would spend a few days in Erie, Pennsylvania and visit the family memorial there.

As Grace grew older, she became the unofficial mascot of the coffee shop. The college kids loved her as well as the current and retired professors from the university. Grace would entertain them by drawing pictures or telling endless stories about her adventures with her imaginary friend, Petey. In turn, they would include her in their conversation or read one of her storybooks to her. Eventually, she was able to read her favorite stories to them.

Once the tween and teen years hit, her friends from school would come to the shop and hang out and get a snack. And as the twins got older, she was sure to include them in her after school activities. Arden fixed up the back room that had a huge picture window that looked out over the Camden Falls University campus. She furnished it with overstuffed chairs and a sofa as well as offset areas for studying. She let the kids decorate it, call it their own and amuse themselves under her watchful eye. As they grew older, she extended the Wi-Fi from the shop so they could get a jumpstart on their homework. It had seen its share of birthday parties featuring a certain boy wizard. Eventually, heated discussions and raucous laughter accompanied the debates as to which "team' they were on-Team Vampire or Team Werewolf. Recently, she had added a flat-screen TV and Roku stick so that they could watch Netflix or Hulu or whatever streaming network they were currently into.

Now the room wasn't seeing as much action. Grace and her friends were on the fast track both during school hours and after. Between high school classes, extracurricular activities and jobs, the only time they could get together were Friday nights after a home football game. The kids piled in, pizzas were delivered and music and laughter and riotous games of Cards Against Humanity could be heard late into the night. It wasn't unusual for Arden to come in early to open and find kids asleep on the comfy couches, lights still burning bright from the fun the night before.

As she looked back on her life in the city, it seems as if it belonged to someone else or like a movie she had caught in the middle of the night. Motherhood had not been easy but it was the most rewarding and satisfying job she had ever had. She felt she had learned a lot about herself and Grace in the process. Despite the annoyances of being a small business owner and a single parent, Arden was happy with the way their lives had turned out so far. She missed Ben and Jess every day but she made sure that Grace was fully aware of her parents through old scrapbooks, yearbooks and home movies. Grace had so much potential. Tears filled Arden's eyes, thinking how proud Ben and Jess would be. She hoped they were looking down and watching the marvel they had created.

Arden shook her head trying to set aside the sentimental memories that she rarely indulged in. Time to get back to business. She looked over the coffee inventory next to her to-do list and realized the chocolate cocoanut blend and Havana Delight would have to be pushed, hopefully creating new favorites while she waited for the back-ordered favorites to come in. She would ask Stacy, one of the many college students she employed to give her some feedback as to the customers' reactions to the new blends and any other comments they were making about the shop in general.

She looked at the time on her phone and realized she needed to open in an hour. A shipment of Camden Falls University memorabilia was coming in just in time for the new semester crowd. While she wasn't crazy about stocking these items, the travel mugs were good advertising with the university logo on the front and the BrewHouse logo on the back. The incoming freshmen sometimes bought them but it was the parents and alumni who were the best customers. She was considering establishing a reward system with the mugs or giving customers a discount if they brought them in to fill them up.

    She picked up her own mug of coffee, savoring the last quiet moments before driving into the organized chaos of the university town. She had a 15-minute drive from the Cape Cod-style house that she and Grace lived into the heart of Camden Falls and bustle of the BrewHouse. She left a sticky note on Grace's backpack that was sitting on one of the chairs near the kitchen island. She needed Grace to come and meet her at the Golden Palace Chinese Restaurant for dinner this evening. Arden wanted to talk to her about her class load and the fact that she was spending a lot of time on campus. She knew that teenage years could be problematic and so far she and Grace had been lucky. There had been a few bumps in the road but for the most part, their disagreements had been minor. She hoped that discussing Grace's course load and future wouldn't bring about the battle that other parents talked about regarding their teenagers. That's one reason why she had opted for a public place that also happened to be one of their favorite hangouts. Arden hoped that all of the elements combined would create a calm atmosphere in which to discuss a serious issue. She grabbed her purse, tote and a bottle of water and headed out the door.

Chapter 16: The Same Morning

    Natasha Bedingfield belting out "Pocketful of Sunshine" brought Grace to the surface of the much-to-early morning alarm. She peeled her chemistry worksheet from her face where she had fallen asleep studying the periodic table. Grace slid the alarm to "dismiss" on her phone. No time for the snooze button today. She had to get to school early for a student council meeting. Plans were underway for Homecoming Weekend and Grace, like several of her friends, had been making predictions for weeks as to who would be voted in as royalty.
    Lindsay thought Grace was a shoo-in. Grace blew it off but secretly hoped she would at least be on the court. According to Arden, her mom, Jess had been Homecoming Queen her senior year. Grace wanted to carry on the family tradition. Normally, Grace wouldn't

have to be at school until the second period because her schedule included both high school and college classes. She was only at Washington High School for four periods. Then she left, grabbed lunch at home or popped by the BrewHouse on her way to her college classes at Camden Falls University.

Luckily, today was a pretty easy day. After the student council meeting, she would go to the student lounge, hang out with her best friend Lindsay and Lindsay's sister Ellie until second-period chemistry. It was the only class she had with Lindsay. After chemistry, Grace would head to AP English and then to Art, where she was a photographer for the yearbook. And her last class at the high school was Advanced Government. Then, in the afternoon, she took Abnormal Psychology and Advanced Composition classes through the university. Parts of those classes were held in a classroom, but the papers and discussion topics and responses were submitted online. At the rate she was going, she would be able to enter her first year of college as a sophomore, getting her that much closer to the classes in her major.

She was looking forward to her free day. After her high school classes, which met daily, her college classes met on Monday, Wednesday and Thursday. Today was Tuesday, so Grace was going to go home and eat the veggie pizza leftover from last night's supper and get started on her Advanced Comp paper. It was due to the professor's inbox by midnight Friday. Most of the time, Grace was on top of her assignments and wasn't one to put them off until the very last minute. She just wanted to get it over with. The only thing she really procrastinated about was running errands. She hated running to the store to pick up random items. She usually waited until the list was so long and the needs were urgent that she didn't have a choice. Then she hated the fact that she had to spend so much time at the store. Vicious circle. And then there was her college composition class. It wasn't that she didn't enjoy the class, she did. But writing wasn't as easy as it looked. Seeing the blinking cursor almost mocking her because she didn't know where to start gave her an unsettling panicked feeling. She needed to stay focused. If she kept her eye on the prize, she would be that much further ahead when she got to college full time.

Grace gathered up her books and papers before shedding her pj's and jumping in the shower. That and a steaming cup of tea, ironically she hated coffee, would get her ready to face the day.

After her shower, she pulled her damp, dark unruly hair into a ponytail, put on a little makeup and lip-gloss. She slipped the white t-shirt on and a pair of skinny jeans. She grabbed her black, *Hamilton!* Hoodie. Wearing layers was a trick all the students knew. You could never be sure if the classroom was going to feel like a sauna or a meat locker. Her classes at the high school had fairly consistent temperatures since the new building opened five years ago. But her college classes were another story. Even though she wouldn't be on campus today, the weather was so unpredictable that it wouldn't hurt to have an extra layer of clothing along just in case.

Grace used the arms of the hoodie to tie around her waist; she collected her books and phone and headed downstairs to the kitchen. Her Vera Bradley backpack was right where she had left it. There was a note taped to it from Arden. *Aw, Mom. What now?* Grace thought. Grace had called her Aunt Arden Mom from the beginning. She had been the only Mom she had ever really known. She had vague, shadowy, out-of-focus memories of Jess and Ben. Through photo albums and home movies, Grace sometimes wondered which of her memories were real and which did the pictures and movies she had seen fuel her imagination.

The yearly trip to New York City was always scheduled for a couple of days around September 11. They visited the memorial at Ground Zero, placed flowers on her parents' names and attended the memorial service. Then they would spend the remainder of the trip in Erie with her grandparents. The yearly trip this year took place over the Labor Day weekend. Arden and Grace had taken Nickolas and Billy with them. It was their first visit to the City. Grace loved spending time with her grandparents and looked forward to the visits. She Face Timed them weekly and they had attended some of her tennis matches and other programs that she had participated in over the years.

Taking Care of Grace

Grace sighed, Arden did her best to be a mom and Grace loved her for it. It hadn't been easy for independent Arden to take on the custody of a toddler. They had grown up together and even though Grace called her Mom she felt more like a sister than a parent. Rarely, did Arden play the mom card and demand to know where she was and whom she was with. Grace normally volunteered that information anyway. But she noticed that overprotection mode kicked in around the end of August and lasted until the end of September. She learned to ride it out realizing it had more to do with Arden losing a brother and sister-in-law in one day than pressuring Grace. She plucked the note from her backpack and stuffed it in her pocket. She would head over to the campus library to work on her composition and get some studying in before heading to the Golden Palace. While she was at the library she could research some of the colleges she was thinking about. Maybe tonight would be the night to talk to Arden about going to college somewhere different than Camden Falls.

*****

Grace should be here any minute, thought Arden. She put on a pot of lemon tea for Grace. *I will never understand how the coffee gene missed that kid,* Arden chuckled to herself. She grabbed a couple of discarded newspapers off of vacant tables and stopped to talk to Tabitha. "Hey, Tabby, will you let me know when Grace gets here? I'm going in the back to check on a couple of orders and update our schedule. The Java Book Club is going to meet on Saturday morning instead of Wednesday evening this month."

"Sure thing, Arden. Do you want me to put on some tea for Grace?"

Arden shook her head and smiled. "Got it covered." She threw the newspapers into the recycle bin and headed to her back office.

*****

"You summoned?" Grace asked in a joking manner, as she stood in the doorway of Arden's office. Arden had been so absorbed in checking orders and updating the schedule that she didn't hear Grace walk in.

"Ah, daughter, good of you to stop by," Arden continued the running joke that they often adopted with one another. *We really need to stop binge-watching* The Crown, Arden thought.

"So what's up?" Grace asked.

"I just wanted to check in with you. With the beginning of school and the influx of students new and old to the campus, we haven't had a chance to chat."

"Everything's fine," Grace said.

"Are you sure? This is your senior year and you are only spending half a day at the high school. I don't want you missing out on quintessential experiences."

"Mom, high school isn't like what it used to be for you."

"I realize that, but I also know that some things never change. Plus dating Grant, a college guy. I know there is only a couple of years' difference in your ages, but there is a world of difference in your experiences. I doubt he will want to hang out at high school dances or go to high school football games."

Grace was silent for a moment. Then she said, "I know you're worried, but you don't need to be. Grant and I have already worked this out. If I'm on the court, he'll be my date for the game and the dance. If I'm not on the court, Lindsay, Ellie and I will go to the dance together and have a sleepover here? If that's okay."

"Of course it's okay," Arden said, "It sounds like you have it all figured out." Broaching a subject that always feels uncomfortable, Arden said, "So how are things with Grant?"

"Good," Grace answered.

Great, thought Arden, *I love those one-word teen answers. How was school? Fine. Did you learn anything? No. Where are you going? Out. With whom? Friends. Ugh. What happened to the chatty little Grace, who used to tell a story about finding a seat on the bus that took what seemed like hours to tell?* Arden decided to change the subject and double back to Grant later. "I left you the note because I was concerned about you missing out on your senior year. I just don't want you to look back years from now and think, I wish I would have done this or that." Arden paused. *The last thing I want to do is start a fight. Time to take a different tact.*

Arden said, "Look, let's talk about this later. Feel like Chinese tonight? We could meet at the Golden Palace. We haven't actually had dinner there in a long time.

Grace sighed, "Okay. I can be there by 7:30."

Arden let out a breath she didn't realize she had been holding. "Good. Sounds like you have a busy day if 7:30 is the time you can meet."

Grace nodded, "After school and college classes, I have to go back to school to shoot the girls' tennis match and the boys' soccer game for yearbook. Then I am meeting up with the chemistry study group at the BrewHouse from 6 to 7."

Arden smiled, "Your dad and especially your mom would be so proud of you. I'm glad you got the photo gene, someone has to record our lives."

Grace blushed, she hoped that somewhere her parents were aware of how her life was turning out. Pleasing them and Arden was important to Grace. "My mom had a good eye for capturing everyday people in interesting ways. I hope my photos do the same for the yearbook."

Arden offered, "No doubt they will. You and your friends can use the back room if you like. I'll make sure that Tabby has drinks and snacks ready for you."

Grace smiled, "Thanks. That will help; we have a quiz and notebooks due tomorrow. Plus, the Wi-Fi is stronger back there."

"Good. Since you are already at the shop we could go to the restaurant together but I'm going to be over at the church meeting with Melody about the Fall Festival/Halloween Trick or Trunk activities." Arden paused, "Listen, kid, I need you to do me a favor. In fact, it is more like you need to do your Aunt Mel a favor."

Grace laughed, "Let me guess, the twins need help with something."

"A mind reader, too. Is there no end to your talent? They are setting up for the fall festival/trick or trunk event at the end of next month and they wondered if you could help out? You know, dress up, pass out candy, and help decorate ahead of time?"

"Yeah, no problem but it's a little early to be thinking about this, It's not even October yet?"

"Agreed, but you know your aunt, she likes to plan, make lists and schedule her spontaneity."

"Sounds like someone else I know."

"Hey," Arden said, mock offended, "if that's a crack about my managerial skills, well, guilty as charged."

Grace laughed, "It's fine. I see the twins sometimes in the lounge. I'll text them and maybe we can meet some morning before school."

"Sounds like organization is a family trait. Not a bad one to have."

"Okay, okay. Maybe we can work out another costume theme that we can wear. The Harry Potter costumes went over big last year. Maybe if I can talk Lindsay into it, we could be the Scooby Gang. She's always liked Nicholas. She'd probably be up for it."

"I like the way you think. I'll let Mel know you're on board."

"Cool," Grace looked at her phone. "Gotta run, the Bradys asked me to walk Hazel and Neil to the bus stop and let the dogs out."

"Okay," Arden said, looking at her own phone to check the time. "See you at the Golden Palace?"

"See you there." Grace grabbed her things, gave Arden a quick kiss on the top of her head and bustled out the door calling, "Bye!"

"Bye, see you later," Arden called, marveling at the young woman that Grace had become.

Chapter 17: September 18

Jack was finally catching his stride with his class schedule. His timetable and the college timetable were not always in sync with the first few weeks of school. Jack was and always had been organized and methodical. It was these qualities that made him an excellent cop. His colleagues knew that if Jack was on the case, every detail would be addressed.

As a kid, he had confounded his parents and siblings by reading and rereading Sherlock Holmes and Hardy Boys mysteries. He would then stage his own investigations and recruit his siblings to help solve the case. Jack, being the oldest, had his younger siblings willing to follow his lead.

Lauren, the only girl in the Phillips band of siblings, would join in, but only if the case "involved lost or stolen items that needed to be dug up or dirt sifted through." She loved poking around in attics and basements. No matter what the circumstances whether it was actual dirt or figuratively sifting through clues to questioning suspects, that girl loved to dig. She was more ruthless during interrogations than all the boys put together.

The suspects usually included younger brother Cory and Jack's best friend, Matt Brady. Lauren flatly refused to play the femme fatale. As they got older, Jack and Matt were the only two interested in pursuing these investigations, which led them to become part of the sheriff department's young explorers club that segued into law enforcement careers.

As Lauren grew older, she started volunteering at the local historical society which led to a double major in archeology and history. She had been a professor at Camden Falls University for 12 years. When she wasn't teaching, she was leading a group of students and colleagues on digs all over the world. Her brothers were extremely proud of her, but loved to tease her as well. One Christmas, they pooled their resources. They presented her with a hat and a whip in homage to Indiana Jones. These items were lovingly displayed in her campus office.

As Cory got older, the fun of going on these elaborate investigations lost its charm. His interest was sports and he became an all around athlete practically from the time he could walk. There was not a sport he wouldn't try and he appeared to excel at most. He had set and broken numerous records in high school and in college, mostly in track and tennis and to this day, most had not been exceeded. His real love, however, was rugby. He was fueled by the sheer aggression of the sport, much to his mother's dismay. The injuries were the only downside to rugby in Cory's mind. However, it was through his love of this sport and the numerous injuries suffered by both himself and his teammates that drew him to sports medicine. Now he traveled with the state's pro hockey team as one of the trainers and team doctor.

As Jack mused about his siblings and how far they had all come, he settled on baby brother Grant. Grant had been a surprise. Jack had just left for the police academy, Lauren was in high school and Cory was in middle school when Grant made his appearance. Throughout the pregnancy, Cory and Lauren were horrified and completely embarrassed by the fact that their parents had let themselves get into this situation. But as soon as they saw that sleeping angel face at the hospital, the three siblings fell in love with the newest Phillips family member.

Oliver, their father, felt like he was given a second chance with the birth of Grant. Grant was the hope to take over the family business. None of his other children showed any interest in carrying on the family business, Phillips Candy and Confections. Oliver could see that there would be no one to pass down the business to and that had been a source of frustration for years. They had all worked at the factory during school breaks and loved the chance to make some extra money, but none of them were interested in carrying on the tradition. Oliver was a proud man and very proud of his children, but now he saw Grant as a possible CEO to the business and the heir he had been looking for.

From day one, Oliver paraded Grant around the candy factory as his junior assistant. Grant's devilish smile and dimples won over the employees and they loved answering his questions and showing him how certain aspects of the factory worked. Eventually, Grant became the official youth guide when people visited the factory.

Oliver was determined that his children would not have the same struggles he did when he was just starting out. He had built the Phillips Candy and Confections business from the ground up. He knew he had made it big when local and national amusement parks picked up his products to sell to their visitors. Even though the Phillips family did not want for anything, Oliver insisted that his children earn money, keep a savings account, get good grades and attend college. Grant was the last one in college and he worked in the factory during breaks and while classes were in session, he worked under an internship program that his father set up a long time ago in partnership with the university.

Now as Jack thought about it, it appeared that Grant was going to slide right into his father's plan. He would see Grant around campus and they met once a week for lunch. On one occasion, Grant brought his new girlfriend, Grace, and she and Jack had hit it off almost instantly. When Lauren was in town, she would join her siblings. Cory, who lived in Columbus, was usually on the run with the team, he would show up unexpectedly to reconnect with his siblings.

Jack was concerned about his baby brother, however. He was a sophomore with a dual major in business and pre-law. He worked at the factory and squired Grace around town and was working his way up in his fraternity. He had hoped Grant and Grace were being careful. After they had been dating for about a month, Jack had asked Grant if he and Grace were using protection. Jack had been relieved to find out that Grace was on the pill and she and Grant had decided to wait until they had been together a little longer before they took their relationship to the next level.

Jack had never liked the idea of Grant pledging a fraternity, but Grant insisted that it was a great way to make contacts and eventually be good for business in the future. While in theory that sounded good, Jack had seen too many hazing incidents go wrong when he was in Chicago. Grant living at the frat house was something else Jack had reservations about. Now that Grace was missing and it had thrown Grant into a tailspin. He never got rattled and now the terror was evident in his whole demeanor. Even though Grace was a high school senior taking some college classes, he hoped that she would continue to be a stabilizing force in Grant's life. She seemed to keep him grounded. He hoped they found her soon. If they put together any search parties, he and Grant would volunteer. He hoped that wouldn't be necessary.

Jack's phone buzzed with a notification bringing him back to the present. There was a cocktail party for faculty at the Dean of Students house in ten minutes. It was an unwritten rule that attendance was mandatory. Jack sighed. One drink that he could nurse for awhile through polite conversation and a few stale hors d'oeuvres and maybe he could sneak out and make it home by 8:30. Wishful thinking.

*****

When Jack had left Chicago to come home to start over, he welcomed the suggestion from his parents that he stay in the guesthouse on the property. It was a one-floor cottage style house with two bedrooms, two baths, a kitchen and a deck out back. The living room was cozy with an overstuffed couch and chairs and a gas fireplace. There was a large flat screen TV and a laundry room off the kitchen.

Jack had made one of the bedrooms into his office. He had built floor to ceiling cherry wood bookcases that framed the huge picture window and added a Royal Stewart Tartan cushion and various throw pillows making it a comfortable alternative to his desk. He reviewed his lectures, graded exams and studied the latest in criminology techniques. He also caught up with former colleagues in Chicago as well as law enforcement contacts around the country. After reading the papers and pouring himself a second cup of coffee he headed to his office to do a little research. It felt like home, but it wasn't a situation of the kid who comes home to invade the privacy of the empty nesters. As always, Rachel and Oliver insisted that he stay there rent-free but Jack was an adult and too proud to take that kind of generosity that he suspected was laced with a good dose of pity. Instead, he found other ways to "pay the rent." First of all, the last person to live there was Rachel's mother, Darla. A true southern belle who, even in her 90's, insisted on dressing every day in case friends "came calling." She and her live-in nurse, Jodi had stayed there until pneumonia had claimed Darla at 98. For quite a while, the guesthouse had a nursing home feel to it. Jack felt that for him to live there, or anyone else for that matter, some updates were needed.

Jack came in and painted the walls of the kitchen and the two bedrooms. A soft, eggshell neutral seemed to be the safest choice and add color via the furnishings. He stripped the pink wallpaper with the frolicking kittens in the master bath and had replaced it with light blue and white subway tiles. *That is definitely a big improvement,* he thought.

This part of the guesthouse looked out over the private pond that was situated between the main house and the guesthouse. In the morning and all throughout the day and night various forms of wildlife could be seen from his windows. No matter what time of year it was, deer could be seen on the property as well Canadian geese and occasionally a family of red foxes.

The only thing missing was a dog and Edie he couldn't help thinking. While he didn't completely buy into the idea that time heals all wounds, he had begun to realize that thoughts and reminders of Edie were getting easier to deal with. Tears didn't flood his eyes at her memory. He didn't look for her in every crowd. The memories were finding their place in his life and were a source of comfort rather than a source of sorrow.

Before leaving for the faculty cocktail party, Jack checked the media and campus websites to see if there were any updates on Grace. Unfortunately, it was the same news cycle with no new updates. If there wasn't information from Grace soon, they would start forming search parties. If it came to that, he and Grant could be counted on to help. He closed up his laptop, breathed a heavy sigh and headed out to his car to drive to campus. He would be glad when this evening was over.

Chapter 18: The Same Evening

Jack arrived at the cocktail party feeling that slight twinge of unease he had whenever he arrived at a social gathering. When Edie had been alive, she had been able to escort him to the obligatory functions with the law enforcement top brass and almost made him look forward to it. Not because he enjoyed these parties but because Edie made it a game. Before arriving, they would place bets with salacious rewards as to which colleagues would get drunk first, who would hit on whom and just how dreadful the food would be. They would make their way through the party obeying their unwritten rules.

Edie would take her place with the police detectives' wives as well as a few of the female detectives and Jack would be left to network with the other officers and administrators of the department. Throughout the evening, Edie and Jack would play out their own mutually agreed upon game of signals. An index finger tapping on a drinking glass meant, "I'm bored." A hand near the throat meant, "Rescue Me." And then at some point in the evening, and Jack was never sure when, Edie would find him across the room, and give him a wink that meant "I Have Plans For You." Once that signal was given, Jack made the routine good-byes and whisked Edie out the door. Sometimes they barely made it home before they were tearing each other's clothes off. Sometimes they didn't. After "collecting on their bets," they lay in each other's arms laughing about the evening, taking turns relaying scandalous tidbits and formulating gossipy theories about the other partygoers.

Now Jack navigated these types of gatherings solo and his attitude was quite different. After grabbing a glass of cheap white wine that seemed to be a staple at these functions and a fig stuffed with goat cheese and prosciutto, he made his way over to a cluster of professors standing near the fireplace and collection of captain's chairs and a sofa all in varying shades of wine and navy. His colleagues were debating the national government's antics and the up-to-the-minute university gossip. The elephant in the room was the missing teenager girl. No one seemed to know what happened to her. They offered the usual murmurs of sympathy for the family. Luckily, none of the partygoers had realized Jack's connection to the boyfriend and he had been spared the litany of uncomfortable questions.

"Hello, Old Chap! Glad you could join us!" Dennis Crabtree had been a pretty interesting conversationalist until he took his sabbatical in the UK. Post UK, he had become an insufferable bore. His affected British accent and careless insertions of "Old Chap" and "Bloody Hell" into conversations made him sound like a recycled Dickens character. He had been back a couple of months and everyone had been hoping the new Dennis would wear off soon. For Jack, it wasn't soon enough.

Even worse than Dennis's silliness was the ongoing game of avoidance he would soon be playing with Liza Duncan, wife of Diplomatic Policies Professor, Dr. Joel Duncan.

Liza was the stereotypical professor's wife who strolled into any gathering in a wave of Chanel No. 5, hairspray and desperation. She was older than she looked thanks to Botox, perfectly chiseled features that could cut ice, a personal trainer and a string of lovers that kept her busy when she wasn't parading around the tennis court in her short, short skirts. Liza had been unhappy for years but was of an age that in her universe, divorce was not an option. It was a well-known secret that she had been carrying on this way for years. The majority of the faculty felt bad for Dennis for putting up with his wife's odious behavior. Liza was that rare creature who was popular because of her husband's position at the university, but feared because of her aggressive approach to life. She had no true friends; only people who wanted to stay on her good side. But Jack knew that Joel had a life of his own. Joel had been involved in an affair of his own for the past several years.

 Three years ago, Jack had flown back to Chicago to meet with some colleagues from the precinct to celebrate the retirement of their former boss. They had made their way to various haunts and had ended up at The Redhead Piano Bar. Jack had decided to call it a night and came out of the bar to flag down a taxi to take him back to the hotel. As the taxi pulled up, he noticed Joel across the street talking to someone in the shadows. He almost called out to him, until Joel started laughing and grabbed the hand of the other person pulling him out of the shadows. Joel then kissed Quantum Physics professor Steve Graham.

Jack watched the couple, obviously happy to be together and oblivious to their surroundings as they faded into the shadows once more. Jack never told anyone about his discovery. The only person he would have told was Edie and that was no longer a possibility. So he tucked the information away and vowed to be a little kinder to Liza but not get caught up in her web. He didn't know if Liza was aware of her husband's situation, but he wasn't about to tell her.

Word around the water cooler was that Liza's latest conquest, a young fitness pro had left for a job in another state. When Liza was at loose ends, that was when she became her most dangerous. Jack always seemed to be her target at these functions. As soon as she entered a room, heads turned out of curiosity and jealousy to see what stylish and wildly overpriced cocktail dress she would be wearing. Tonight it was an emerald green, strapless fitted dress with a slit up the left thigh and green kitten heels to match. Her compact body made the emerald material shimmer in all the right places. Her stylishly cut, short blonde hair, large blue eyes and understated makeup made her look glamorous, not cheap. Jack couldn't help but wish that Liza had decided to go to one of the numerous spa retreats that she went on several times a year.

As soon as she spied Jack, she strode with casual purpose across the room and gently took his arm. She leaned in close and almost touching his ear with her lips whispered, "What does a girl have to do to get a drink around here?"

Not missing a beat and ignoring the flirtatious overtones, Jack deftly extricated himself from her grasp and at the same time grabbed a glass of white wine from the tray of a passing waiter.

"Here you go, Liza. You're looking well as always."

"And you look delicious," she said, under hooded eyes. She then looked around at the others in attendance and said just a little too loudly, "I hate these parties, why don't you and I go somewhere and get a proper drunk, I mean drink," she giggled. With glassy eyes and teetering heels, it was obvious that Liza had started her party before arriving.

This took Jack by surprise somewhat. He was used to Liza flirting but she had never been this forward. At least not to him. Something must be up and his cop instincts told him that nothing good could come from this.

"I've got a better idea, Liza. Let's get you something to eat. The hors d'oeuvres are really good."

Liza drew herself closer to Jack and whispered in his ear, "You're the only thing I want to nibble on."

"Okay," Jack laughed embarrassed, "I hate to break this up, but I see one of the law professors I need to speak with." He peeled Liza's hand from his arm and gracefully navigated her to a cluster of wives he knew to be made up of acquaintances and a couple of frenemies. As he backed away, he said, "Hello, ladies. Enjoy your evening."

As he walked away, all eyes were on Jack Phillips. With his jet black hair and piercing blue eyes, he had no idea the effect he had on the women in the room, or any room for that matter. Only Liza saw him slip into the dean's study. After a brief chat with a couple of other partygoers, Liza weaved her way through the crowd and slipped into the study.

*****

Jack looked at the books in the study-library and walked over to the glass wall that looked out into the dean's garden. After speaking with Jeb Brown, a transplant from Texas who had rather unorthodox ways of teaching his business law classes and was well liked by the students, Jack slipped into the dean's study to get away from the crowd. If worse came to worst, he could sneak out through the French doors that secured part of the window wall and jog through the garden. The rain was finally letting up. Maybe he could get home before it started again. He was heading towards the door to go and make his goodbyes when the door opened and in walked Liza.

"Ahhh, so this is where you've been hiding."

Feeling trapped, Jack tried to get around her and out the still-open door. In one quick move, she had the door closed and Jack pinned against it, her trim, toned body against his.

"Liza, look, I-"

"Jack, please," she said with an air of disdain, "I don't know why you're fighting this. We are two consenting adults..." Her voice trailed off while her hand trailed down his arm and reached around to grab his backside.

Jack grabbed her wandering hand and brought it between them. "Liza, stop this before you embarrass both of us. You're married to a man I have to see every day. And I still feel married to Edie," Jack pulled out his cell phone, "I'm calling you a cab."

Liza would not back down, "Good idea. Let's go to your place."

Jack shook his head, "Liza, listen. You are very attractive and if circumstances were different...who knows? But whatever you have in mind, it's not happening tonight with me."

Liza's eyes flashed anger, "Really, Jack. What's this bullshit about being married? Dennis and I haven't had a marriage for years and you claim to still be in love with a ghost."

Jack was shaken by her harsh words. "I think you'll regret your words in the morning or when you sober up, whichever comes first."

As if she didn't hear Jack's comment, Liza said, "Besides, we all know you have a thing for the coffeehouse matron, what's her name, Alice, Annie?"

Jack chose to ignore her. Luckily, his cell phone buzzed with an incoming text. He saw it was from Matt, the perfect excuse to leave. "I'm leaving. Something has come up. I suggest you start drinking some coffee and lay off the wine."

Jack gently but firmly removed himself from Liza's clutches, walked out of the study door and pulled it closed behind him, just as Liza's wine glass crashed and broke against it. Shaking his head, he read the text from Matt. Come to the Pub. Urgent. God, he hoped it wasn't bad news about Grace.

Chapter 19: September 18

The rain was back with a vengeance as Jack shook out his umbrella just outside the door of the pub. As he entered he immediately started scanning the dimly lit bar for his friend. Sam, the bartender, cocked his head towards the back booth and Jack nodded in acknowledgment. Jack and Matt had been friends from the first time they met on the playground in kindergarten. They had seen each other through scraped knees, chickenpox and poison ivy, first dates, Edie's murder, Julia's cancer and Matt and Julia's adoption of their foster kids. They were there for each other at a moment's notice. Even though both had siblings to count on, they were honorary members of one another's families. Jack slid into the booth across from Matt and could tell that his friend was in pretty bad shape. Matt's big paw hands were shaking and tears were threatening to course down his cheeks.

Alarmed, Jack said gently, "Hey, Buddy, it can't be that bad, what gives?" Jack could tell this was something more personal to Matt. This was not something he could tease Matt out of, but was instantly obvious that something horrible had happened, but his instincts told him that it didn't have anything to do with Grace.

"Julia is leaving me," Matt whispered, trying to hold back his tears.

"What do you mean Julia's leaving you?" Jack asked, practically holding his breath.

"Julia's cancer," Matt said, "It's worse than what they thought. They warned us the experimental treatment could be risky but there was also a chance it would put her into remission. Then there was also the possibility that it would be worthless. Unfortunately, it has done nothing and the cancer continues to grow."

Jack hung his head, not wanting his friend to see the defeat on his face. "Matt, I'm so sorry. She has been looking healthy for over a year. I don't get how leaving you, and I assume the kids, helps this situation. Is she leaving the kids, too?"

Matt nodded, "Julia thinks that if we divorce, it will be less of a financial burden. Plus," Matt found it hard to continue, "She doesn't want me and the kids to see her as she goes through this. From what she says, it's going to get ugly."

"God, that's awful. Certainly, there is something they can do. Doctors and researchers are making breakthroughs all the time."

"Chemotherapy and radiation are out. She won't put herself through that again. The doctors don't think it's a good idea either. There are some drug trials she could be eligible for. The doctor referred her to a couple of specialists. However, it means more traveling out of state."

Grabbing on to any hope he could, Jack said, "Good. That's good." He tried to focus on what Matt was saying. He knew the pain of losing the love of your life. He was trying to keep that from filtering in.

Matt was trying to keep his composure, but the larger than life police chief seemed to shrink before Jack's eyes. "I just don't think splitting up is the answer, I know she is trying to protect me and the kids, but we are here for her. The one drug trial they mentioned seemed tailor-made for her type of cancer, however, it's not FDA approved so insurance won't pay for it." Matt couldn't hold back any longer and started sobbing silently in his hands, "I can't live without her."

Jack put a hand on Matt's arm, "Listen, we will get through this. I know the department is behind you. We will find a way to get Julia what she needs without breaking up your family. You said these are experimental trials, don't they usually pay the patients to participate, or offer deep discounts? Can't the hospital help since Julia is an employee there?"

Matt grimly shook his head, "They are both out of state and you're right the treatments themselves are free, but the expense of the hospital room and other expenses aren't covered. We've maxed out our insurance, our health savings accounts and our credit cards." Matt looked ashamed. The last thing he wanted was word to get around that the chief of police was on the verge of bankruptcy and bawling like a baby in the local bar. He pulled himself together long enough to say, "Look, I'm sorry I bothered you with this. You've got enough going on with your dad's recovery and a new semester starting. Julia and I will figure it out." He paused, "I'm checking into liquidating our pension funds."

Jack didn't want to argue, but said, "Wait, isn't there another way? What about your parents? Can't they help? Or some of your siblings? I know that Julia doesn't have any relatives since she was raised in the foster care system."

Matt shook his head as tears threatened again, "No, my parents are tapped out from the last time. Jen and her husband Peter are putting all their money into repairs and renovations since Hurricane Harvey practically leveled their house. And Trey..." Matt trailed off. Trey had been the bad seed in the family. He had been in and out of jail so many times for petty crimes that it was hard to keep up with where he was. Matt continued, "Plus, Julia doesn't want to worry them. She wants to see if the latest treatment works before she tells them."

"How are you going to explain the trips out of town and your separation?"

"We are telling them these are follow-up consultations not that the cancer is back. I don't think my mom could take it. She has always had a soft spot for Julia since she was brought up as a foster kid, too. As for the separation, they think I will be going with her or I might have to stay in town for work reasons."

Jack agreed to a point, "Olivia did take it hard and rightly so. But I don't think lying, even if it is to protect them, is the best course to take. It will only hurt them in the end."

"No!" Matt was adamant. "I have to do this Julia's way."

Jack backed off, "Okay, I'm sorry. I can only imagine the pain you are in." Jack shook his head and then continued, "How much do the twins know?"

"I'm sorry," Matt said, " you're not *like* a brother, you are my brother and I know you are only trying to help. The kids think we are going to consultations. At 8 and 10 years old, we want them to worry only about school. No need to tell them anything until absolutely necessary. The divorce, we are going to keep under wraps for as long as we can. I am hoping I can talk her out of that part of the plan by finding a more lucrative financial plan. Besides, I don't care what she looks like as long as we get this cancer beaten. She is always beautiful to me." Matt stopped as the tears were threatening again.

Jack tried to lighten the mood, "Since we're 'related' I know who to contact to fix a speeding ticket." Matt was able to laugh a little and Jack continued, "Listen, before you two raid your pension plans, let me check out some alternatives."

Matt started to interrupt and Jack stopped him, "Look, you are a hometown hero. Let's explore some other avenues before you put your future on the line."

Matt nodded and found it hard to look Jack in the eye.

Jack put his hand on Matt's arm again. "We'll beat it. I'll see what I can find out. Let me drive you home." He paused, "I know this has nothing to do with your situation, but are there any updates on Grace?"

Matt shook his head, "No, I've got patrols out looking all over campus and beyond. Thanks for the offer but I need to clear my head. I'm gonna walk home. Julia doesn't need to see me like this."

Jack nodded, "Call me anytime." Jack gave Matt's arm a reassuring pat. Matt gave him an appreciative smile. He slowly got up from the table and lumbered out of the bar. Jack had never seen Matt so down. Even when Julia went through the first bout of cancer, he had been more positive. It didn't seem possible that Matt and Julia's marriage could be on such shaky ground. Jack slid from the booth, settled the bill and left the pub, determined to see his friend through this crisis.

Chapter 20-September 17

Arden sat shivering in the police interrogation room. Everything about it seemed austere and unforgiving. The gunmetal grey chairs and tables added to the clinical coldness of the room. Tristen Bennett and Carl Coleman, partners on the Camden Falls police force and regulars at the coffee shop, had asked her to come in and give her official statement regarding Grace's disappearance. While she knew she wasn't a suspect, the official metallic atmosphere of the police station and her guilt at having argued with Grace the day before her disappearance sent a renewed set of shivers through her body. The observation made her feel like she was on display and those observing were judging her and her parenting skills or lack thereof.

She couldn't help thinking about the countless hours that stretched into agonizing days waiting at the New York City police precinct hoping for news regarding her brother and sister-in-law after 9/11. Even though the atmosphere was the same, the temperature was not. Those endless hours spent in the police station had been hot and sweaty, crammed with people and desperation. She and her cousin Melody along with 2-year-old Grace had waited with shell-shocked faces and reserved hope that Ben and Jess would be located at some hospital or urgent care center and then the only reason they hadn't been in touch was because of overloaded phone lines.

Eventually, the only items found were Ben's wallet and Jess's battered camera bag. Inside, the camera was so badly damaged that none of the pictures could be saved. This had been hard to accept and the devastation took its toll physically on her and Ben's mother. Amanda Winters had been dealing with dementia issues and even though Arden had kept as much information about the attacks as she could from her mother, Amanda had found out and became very agitated when Arden tried to evade her questions. Maybe it was a blessing that Amanda had passed away several years ago. She wouldn't understand this latest crisis. Arden started to recognize the same feelings of panic and fear in herself resurfacing with Grace's disappearance.

Bennett and Coleman came into the icy interrogation room and had brought Officer Sheila Hastings with them. Sheila took a chair next to Arden and the other two officers sat across from her. Even in her frightened state of mind, she could tell that these officers felt bad about dragging her to the station on official business. Arden fought to keep her tears under control. She was afraid that if she gave into them, they may never stop. Sheila took Arden's hand and said, "How ya holding up?"

Arden tried to keep her hysteria in check, "Hanging in there," she said with a forced smile. "Is there any news? I have to know, did you bring me down here to tell me the bad news?"

"No," Tristen said, "we called you down here to update you on the search and to see if you remember anything that could give us insight into where to look."

As if reading each other's minds, Coleman and Bennett each reached into a coat pocket and took out a pocket tablet and pen.

Arden looked at each officer in turn, "I'm not sure what else I can tell you…" her voice trailed off.

Sheila got up and took Arden's hands firmly into her own. "I am going to check with the search teams. We will talk after you get done here."

"Thank you for everything, Sheila. Just bring my girl home."

Sheila gave Arden's hands a reassuring squeeze. She left the interrogation room and went to the main desk to check for updates. Then she would wind back around to the other side of the observation mirror.

This time Carl Coleman said with sympathy in his voice, "Look, I know you have been asked this a thousand times before, but could you tell us again what happened the days before Grace's disappearance. Was everything okay at home? Were her grades okay? Fight with a boyfriend?"

Arden was starting to feel frustrated, "You're right. I have been through this a thousand times before. As far as I know, everything was fine at home, her grades were on track although she had been worried about her chemistry class. She dates Grant Phillips and they are the picture-perfect couple. No problems." Arden paused to take a breath, "Now, I thought you were going to update me on the search. Where do things stand, where have you looked? Have you talked to her friends?"

Tristan said reassuringly, "I know you're scared and frustrated. As you know, the search party headquarters has been set up at Peace Lutheran. Folks will be searching around the clock in groups of two or three. They are working in tandem with the Camden Falls police department, the sheriff's department and campus security."

Arden nodded, "I'm sorry. I don't mean to make your job harder or act like I'm not grateful. I am." Arden paused, then whispered, "I'm just so scared."

Carl nodded thinking how he would feel if anything happened to one of his two daughters or his son, "I know and we are working as hard as we can to bring your daughter back to you. All of Gracie's friends are out looking for her and Grant has his fraternity looking for her as well."

"I know. Everyone has been wonderful. Anything to help. What do you need from me?" Arden said, trying to regain her composure and not fly into hysterics, which seemed to be inevitable.

Coleman and Bennett gave a slight nod to one another and Bennett said, "Arden, do you need a minute? Can I get you some water?"

Arden nodded her thanks and Coleman said, "Arden, while Tristan gets you some water, do you want me to see if Sheila is still around? Maybe talking to her would help."

"Thank you," Arden said, "I hate feeling so helpless."

"It is understandable. I will see if I can find her." Carl left the interrogation room and was met by Sheila coming from the observation room.

"I'll see if I can calm her down and get her to focus. Just so you know, no news, good or bad. Green and I will be going out again soon." Sheila said.

She entered the interrogation room as Arden looked up, fear, anticipation and panic etched her face. Sheila took a seat beside Arden and said, "You and I have been friends for a long time. You have seen me through Clyde's layoffs and the kids' shenanigans and we will get through this."

Arden held back the tears as best she could and then voiced her real fears to Sheila, "What the officers said about bringing my daughter back to me really got me. Grace is not my daughter. My brother and Jess entrusted that little life to me and I have let them down."

"Whoa, whoa, whoa, let me stop you right there. You have been the best mom Grace could ever have, biological mom or otherwise. You haven't let anyone down. Grace is out there and we are going to find her. You have to keep believing that."

"But what if…"

"No borrowing trouble. Look, I don't know how many times I have worried about Clyde going on a trip or what the kids are going to get into next, but I always knew in my gut that they were okay. I believe that about Grace, too. Now, what is your gut telling you?"

Arden took in what Shelia was saying to her and replied, "My gut is telling me that she is still alive but can't get in touch with me. I know it sounds crazy, but I had the same strange connection to her dad. I knew as soon as we arrived in New York after 9/11 that Ben and Jess were both gone. I could feel it. Thankfully, I don't have that same feeling about Grace. I feel that if she were…" Arden couldn't bring herself to say the words.

Sheila turned Arden to face her and grabbed both of her hands in hers, "You have to hold on to that."

"Thank you, Sheila. I guess we better call the boys back in. Maybe together we will discover something that we overlooked before."

Sheila patted her arm and nodded, "That's the spirit." As if on cue, Carl and Tristen came back into the interrogation room.

After they had seated themselves across from Arden and Sheila had left, Carl took the lead, "First of all, we searched Grace's room and didn't find a whole lot that could help us. As you know, we took her laptop and the tech guys are going through it right now. So far, there's nothing out of the ordinary. I'm sure Grace has a cell phone and it's probably with her. Do you have any way of tracking her through it?"

Arden shook her head, "I know other parents have activated that app, Life360, but I never felt the need to with Grace. She and I always check in with one another. That's why I panicked when she didn't answer calls or texts. It's not like her."

"Okay," Carl said, "Is it possible she's lost her phone or the battery died and that's why you haven't heard from her?"

"No, she lost her phone once and called me from Lindsay's phone to let me know."

"Okay, what about other devices? Does she have a smart watch? Fitness tracker?"

Arden shook her head, "No smart watch, but she does have a Fitbit."

"Good," Carl said, "we can track her through the app"

"No, you can't. Grace left it at the BrewHouse a couple of days ago. It's in my desk and dead as a doornail. The charger is at home."

"Why did she leave it at the BrewHouse?" Tristen asked.

"Grace is only serious about counting her steps when she is in training. She, Lindsay and some of the other girls from school were going to go shopping at the outlet malls. She took it off because it didn't go with her outfit."

"That sounds about right." Carl said, thinking of his own daughters and hiding his disappointment that the fitness tracker was a dead end. "Her maternal grandparents, any help there?"

Arden shook her head, "When I spoke to them yesterday to let them know what was going on, they had not heard from Grace and they were getting ready to contact me as to why Grace hadn't been in touch."

It was becoming clear to the three officers that the information they had was all they were going to get. Carl made the move to end the meeting, "Listen, Arden, we appreciate you coming in and talking with us today. I know you're anxious to get back to the search headquarters. We will keep the lines of communication open."

"Thank you so much," Arden said. "Yes, we will keep the lines of communication open." Arden left the police station and headed to Peace Lutheran.

Chapter 21: September 18

Matt walked blindly through the rain-soaked streets of Camden Falls, trying to put his life into perspective. *How did it ever get to this point? Where do we go from here? What do we tell the kids? I can't lose Julia. Not now.*

Memories of their life before the cancer invaded their family flooded his mind. His parents Matt, Sr., and Olivia had been movers and shakers in the community just as long as Jack's had been. Matt Sr. had been a financial advisor who had an almost supernatural sense about knowing which stocks to invest in and when it was time to sell.

He was also, along with the help of Olivia, able to secure substantial amounts of money through donations to local, national and international charities. They kept the family grounded. Matt Sr.and Olivia agreed early on that their children would have a healthy work ethic instilled in them at an early age. Most of the Brady children subscribed to this mindset. Lorrie, the next in line after Matt, had loved traveling early on. It came as no surprise when she established a thriving bed and breakfast in Camden Falls 15 years ago. Five years into the operation a national hospitality group bought her establishment and brought her on as a consultant. Now she travels around the country putting her expert touch on the new B and Bs that follow her original model. The family has accepted the fact that she will never settle down in one area. Her home base is still Camden Fall but she is never there for long.

Jen, the third sibling and her husband Peter had moved to Texas to be close to Peter's ailing parents. Peter made a good living as an architect, which allowed Jen to stay home with their three kids. Now that they were school age, Jen was volunteering more and working part-time at the local library.

If there was a disappointment in the family, it had been Terence or just Trey for short. He had been trouble from the time he was born in the hospital parking lot to the present. A cranky and stubborn baby from the start, he couldn't wait to see what kind of trouble he could get into.

Trey was angry and no one was able to figure out exactly why. Plenty of speculation had taken place both within the family and out in the community. The baby of the family, too smart for his own good, exceptionally good looking, highly successful siblings to live up to, fearing success because then it would be expected of him were theories offered and perhaps it was too much for Trey to live up to.

He started causing trouble as soon as he started preschool. The other children were afraid of him. He would steal their toys, chase them around the playground and "accidentally" spill his fruit punch on them. In elementary school, he was suspended in first grade twice for fighting on the playground and on the school bus. When they tested Trey for possible learning disabilities his skill set was off the charts. Once he was placed in the gifted program his grades continued to plummet and the acting out escalated. Trey hated being away from what few friends he had and he hated being singled out.

Once he entered high school, the out of control behavior continued. The Bradys were constantly shuttling between meetings at the school and pickups at the police station. Trey was either fighting, shoplifting, or running an illegal gambling operation having students place bets on the high school as well as college games. Trey finally pissed off the wrong gambler, got into a fight and Trey was the only one that ended up doing some jail time. It had been a knife fight in an alley next to a bar that led to Trey's opponent losing an eye. Trey was behind bars for five years. That's where he spent his twenty-first birthday.

Since then, Trey had been in and out of jail on various charges, mainly from gambling debts gone wrong. He refused visits from his family except Matt. For whatever reason, Matt was the one who was able to get through to Trey. Matt wondered where Trey was now. His name had not come across the local or national police blotter in almost a year. Their parents had asked Matt to contact his friends in other precincts to see if there was any information on Trey's whereabouts. He told his parents he would, even though he had already done that months ago.

*****

Matt's parents and siblings couldn't have been prouder or happier when Matt decided to go into law enforcement. It had been the basis for friendship when he and Jack met in first grade, both of them grabbed for the toy police cruiser. They almost got into a fistfight as to which was the better cop show. Matt was obsessed with *21 Jump Street.* Jack liked *CHiPs.* When they discovered that they both liked *The A-Team,* their friendship was formed.

They had both taken college classes together and had entered the police academy together. Matt had been content to stay in the area and had worked his way up in the Camden Falls Police Department. Now he was the chief of police. He should feel happy with all he had accomplished, but this cloud of fear was pushing him in a more negative direction.

Matt thought back to the times he had spent with Jack and his family. How secure they had always made him feel. Jack had been one of the few kids in the public school system that came from a wealthy family like his, but kept their kids in public school rather than ship them off to boarding school. Both sets of parents emphasized a lifestyle of giving back to the community.

As he rounded the corner into his neighborhood, his thoughts turned to his marriage. Meeting Julia and falling in love had taken both of them by surprise. He had been on the force for about a year when he and his partner, Louis, had found a ten-year-old boy huddled in an alley on the sketchier side of Camden Falls. He had been beaten and bloodied for his lunch money and Starter® jacket. Matt had ridden in the ambulance with the boy while Louis went to track down the parents and investigate any leads.

The ambulance screeched to a halt at the emergency entrance. The doors flew open and Matt came face to face with the most beautiful and fierce woman he had ever seen. She barely noticed Matt or so it would seem and focused totally on the bruised and battered ten-year-old.

She had gone with the child so quickly; he wondered if he had imagined her. The next evening after his shift, he went back to the hospital to check on the young victim and bring him a couple of comic books. He checked in at the front desk to get the boy's room number and was relieved that he was in a regular room in the pediatric ward and not in intensive care.

He stopped short before entering the boy's room and listened to the conversation. He heard a woman say that the police could take care of whoever had hurt him. The boy became tearful and said he didn't want to get his brother's friends in trouble. It would be bad for both him and his brother. By now, Matt was able to peek through the crack between the door and the door jam. He saw the beautiful nurse from yesterday in the ER gingerly hugging the fragile little boy. She had been able to get more out of him than Matt and his colleagues had. She told the little boy to lie back and get some rest and she would be back to check on him later. He nodded and slid down between the covers trying to get comfortable.

Julia almost hit Matt in the face when she exited the room. She whirled around to Matt and in an angry whisper asked, "Did you get everything you needed, Officer?" Her voice dripped with sarcasm.

For the first time in a very long time, Matt was speechless. When he recovered he said in the same angry whisper, "As a matter of fact, yes. You just gave me a lead. I only came to check on the kid. I didn't realize I would be listening to your heart-to-heart with him."

Julia's blue eyes flashed in angry shock. "I was just trying to make Ryan, if you care to know his name, comfortable and a little less scared. His parents are here as much as they can be, both of them work and their employers aren't as understanding as some regarding time off. And besides, Ryan has been through enough. He doesn't need the cops breathing down his neck." Her vicious tone made it clear how she felt about law enforcement.

"Look, I-" Matt said, getting annoyed with the nurse's attitude. Usually, his uniform garnered him a little respect.

Almost as if she had read his mind she interrupted him and said, "And don't think that uniform means you can throw your weight around in here, think again. That little boy is terrified and does not need you interrogating him!" Her voice rose ever so slightly making her look around to ensure that no one had heard their heated exchange.

Now it was Matt's turn to get a little heated. He was starting to lose his cool and professionalism. "Listen, lady. I don't know what your problem is, but I am not the enemy. I just came here to check on Ryan and bring him a couple of comic books about his favorite superhero according to this mom and brother."

Julia immediately relaxed and looked up at Matt somewhat sheepishly. It became obvious that she was trying to give Matt the benefit of the doubt and regain her composure. "I'm sorry," she paused, "It's just that there are so many times I see kids get manipulated by adults, even cops and Ryan reminds me of my brother. I shouldn't get personally attached but sometimes it can't be helped."

Matt nodded. He was beginning to get his emotions under control, "We both work in high-pressure jobs."

Julia nodded and said, "Which is why you should take me out for a drink."

Coming back to the present, Matt laughed to himself, despite the threat of tears. After that first date, they had become almost inseparable. He told her about Trey and his other siblings. She told him about her life in foster care. It was a sad story of separation from siblings, abuse and neglect. When she aged out of the system, she worked two jobs and put herself through nursing school. During her first year at her job, Julia was diagnosed with ovarian cancer. They were able to catch it early, not early enough to save her ovaries. She had a full hysterectomy at age twenty-five, giving up the dream of having children of her own.

Their whirlwind romance led to a wedding six months later. Three years into their marriage, they decided to adopt. They became foster parents to Hazel and Neil. They were brother and sister, Hazel was three and Neil just a year old when their parents were killed in a plane crash. There were no relatives to take the children in so they were placed in the foster system. Matt heard about them at work. Once they were placed with the Bradys, they wasted no time adopting them. The kids had made their life and family complete.

As he came up the walk he could see Hazel in her room reading as she always did right before bed. She was the Brady sibling that the teachers loved. Polite, funny and prompt with homework, she was a teacher's dream. She read the entire Harry Potter series over the summer and was now soaking up the wisdom of Judy Blume. He could see Trixie curled up on her bed keeping a sleepy but watchful eye on the youngster.

Neil on the other hand, was obsessed with video games. Matt could see through the window that intermittent flicker of the television screen as he defeated zombies, or worked his way up through the ranks of *Fortnite: Battle Royale*. He had even taught Hazel some of the dance moves featured in the game. Neil, however, was a worry for Matt because there seemed to be traces of Terence in him. Neil hated doing his homework, yet could ace tests and pull speeches out of thin air for class projects. He also ran with a pretty fast crowd, but Julia assured Matt that Neil was a normal boy. Nancy was probably curled up at his feet hoping that a corn chip or cookie crumb would fall her way.

Taking Care of Grace

As Matt entered the house, he feared they would never be normal again.

Jean A. Smith

Chapter 22: Vegas-September 13

    The games had been exhausting but worth it. His bank account would soon swell with the $1.2 million he just won two hours ago. It should be deposited within the next few hours. Antonio Cervantes sat down on the plush couch in his comped Vegas suite, leaned back, closed his eyes and let the victory wash over him.

    The slinky redhead snaked her arms around his neck and whispered in his ear, "You were fantastic tonight." He reached up and rubbed her silky bare arms and released a sigh of contentment, "You've become quite the good luck charm for me, uh… What was your name again?"

    "Lola," she whispered in the same seductive way she had reserved for the last three days that they had been together. They had met at a blackjack table where he noticed that every time she stood near him, he beat the house. Antonio was a practical man, but why tempt fate when she was putting a good luck talisman in your lap? She kissed his ear and whispered, "What would you like to do?"

He took a deep breath and said, "The usual, baby, gotta keep my winning streak going." He kept his eyes closed because he knew as soon as he opened them the magic of the winning streak and the evening would fade. He smiled; *who would have thought a lowlife kid from the streets of Pittsburgh would end up being one of the world's richest high stakes poker players? Those chumps from East High could suck it. They were still in the Burgh killing themselves at the plant and he was living the high life.*

Lola slipped around the edge of the couch and sat down on Antonio's lap, straddling him. Her short black skirt rode up revealing the top of her black, thigh-high hose and garters. One of the spaghetti straps of her purple tank slid down her arm, she left it. She slowly began to unbutton his Tom Ford black shirt kissing her way down his chest. He reached out and slid the other strap from her shoulder. She wondered how many more evenings would end this way before he started taking her with him to the exotic locals he frequented, if she was really the good luck charm he claimed she was. She had done her homework. She knew Antonio Cervantes lived the kind of life she wanted to become accustomed to. As she undid the belt, she thought, *As many nights as it takes.*

Chapter 23: September 15

Arden loved and hated the bustle of the new school year. Each semester and summer break provided its own unique set of schedules and patrons. The one thing she enjoyed was seeing familiar as well as new faces that entered the BrewHouse. The excitement of embarking on a new chapter in the lives of not only the students but their parents as well hung in the air. Just when she and her crew had the semester rhythm down to a science, routines would change and she and the shop would settle into a new normal.

Arden could spot first-time college parents a mile away. When she and Grace first settled in Camden Falls, the parents were enveloped in a flurry of forms, paper maps of campus, orientation schedules and book lists for their incoming college student. Now the pile of papers was almost obsolete. Both parents and students accessed the information through their phones or other devices. One thing that did not change over the years was the kaleidoscope of emotions that played out over the faces of the parents no matter what their experience level. The universal looks of fear, pride, joy, and sadness were a steady parade. She could tell which parents had been through it all before and which ones were rookies. The rookies were usually a little less organized and looked more panicked than the more experienced parents.

Luckily for Arden, they all wanted coffee and/or some sort of treat. She wasn't one to stay in her office and crunch numbers. She made her presence felt, chatting with customers, topping off coffees and answering questions about locations in and around the university. Over the years she had built on the clientele that the Gleesons had established. Catching up with returning families and faculty helped Arden stay up to date on university policy and gossip. Most of the faculty lived in town but took the summer break for relaxation and travel. Arden had her favorites who made the BrewHouse part of their daily routines.

Sebastian French had taught Shakespeare courses for years at the university. He is a big man with a gentle face. During the winter, he would grow out a snowy, white beard and for years, Grace was convinced that he was either Santa in disguise or one of Santa's elves sent from the North Pole to check on the naughty and nice of Camden Falls. He regaled Arden and Grace with stories about his time spent with the Royal Shakespeare Theater Company as a dresser. He shamelessly name-dropped a few celebrities that he had the pleasure to encounter. His British accent added character to the already colorful stories. Sebastian had been hinting for the past five years that he was going to retire and return to his native London. Arden hoped that if he actually went through with the retirement he wouldn't return to England. The BrewHouse wouldn't be the same without him.

Another favorite customer was Roxie Kincaid. Roxie taught Calculus at Camden Falls University but looked like anything but a math teacher. Her bohemian wardrobe and rings on practically every finger gave her the look of a gypsy fortuneteller. Arden enjoyed seeing what color Roxie's hair would be each time she came into the coffee shop. Cut pixie short, it changed color on a regular basis from blue to gray and Arden's favorite, lavender. Roxie had been married three times. Twice widowed and once divorced. She was willow thin and towered over almost everyone. Next to Melanie, she was Arden's best friend.

When Arden moved to the college town and took over the coffee shop, Roxie was one of the first faculty members to welcome her. But Roxie had a secret. Calculus professor by day, romance novelist by night. She had been writing steamy romances with scantily clad natives and regal knights gracing the book covers for decades. No one at the university was aware of her writing success because she wrote under a penname and she never let her picture appear on the back of the novels or in any publicity material. However, Arden in her previous New York life, had attended one of her book signings at a little independent bookstore with some of her friends from the office. This had been just as Roxie's popularity was starting to emerge.

They were two years into their friendship when Roxie dropped by Arden's house with flyers that Arden was going to hang in the BrewHouse for a Math Club fundraiser. One of Roxie's older romance novels was lying on the coffee table. Arden invited Roxie to sit down and have a glass of iced tea. While Arden was in the kitchen, Roxie casually picked up the novel and was startled to see her personal message and autograph on the title page. Arden entered the living room with a tray of iced tea and cookies.

Roxie surrendered, "How long have you known?"

"Almost since the day you walked into my coffee shop."

Bewildered, Roxie continued, "Why didn't you say anything?"

Arden sat the tray down and took a seat across from Roxie, "In watching you and those around you it didn't seem like anyone was aware. Besides, it isn't my story to tell. I figured you had your reasons."

Roxie sighed and relaxed, "That is true. No one at the university, as far as I know, is aware of my alter ego." She paused then continued, "My teaching job is fulfilling, but I wanted something that was just mine. I didn't really care if they sold or not. My first husband, Carlos, had been the love of my life. When he died suddenly, I wanted to relive the joy and love I felt with him. So I wrote my first novel based on our love story. It's really a tribute to Carlos and our marriage."

Roxie's eyes filled with tears, and she recovered with a little laugh, "One night after one too many glasses of wine I composed a somewhat flippant cover letter and dropped it and a copy of my manuscript in the mail. Six weeks later I got a letter and a phone call that they loved the book and wanted to publish it. I didn't want my colleagues to know and the pen name C.R. Townsend was born. C for

Carlos, R for Roxie and Townsend came from a flyer that I received in the mail. Next thing I knew, it was a huge hit and the publisher wanted more. So I started writing them and submitting them with the condition that my identity would be revealed only by me when I deemed the time was right." Roxie stopped and waited for Arden's reply.

"I can respect that and I am willing to keep your secret as long as I get advanced copies of all your new books," Arden said with a laugh.

Roxie relaxed and laughed realizing that Arden could be trusted. "Oh, is that all? Done." The two women had been friends ever since.

Roxie had fascinated Grace and Roxie became the "crazy aunt" who took Grace shopping, for her first manicure and to the Rock and Roll Hall of Fame. After one of their outings, when Grace came home with green fingernails and a blue streak in her hair, Arden he said sternly, "I swear to God, Roxie Kincaid, if she comes home with a tattoo…"

"Relax," Roxie had said, "we'll be sure to get it somewhere that doesn't show." That had been a running joke ever since.

As Roxie settled into her usual booth to catch up on course plans and grading, Arden brought her a soy latte and warm snicker doodles and slid into the seat across from her.

"What's up? How are the new classes going?"

Roxie looked up and smiled, "Good. I can face the planning and grading now that I have caffeine and sugar to fuel me. How are things around here?"

"Good," Arden answered. "We've been busy with the students moving in. Do you have any book signing scheduled?"

Roxie sighed, "Yes, over fall break they are sending me out west for a five shop junket. I told them no photos on social media or television interviews."

"Wow, J. D. Salinger, who knew you were such a diva!" Arden joked.

Roxie laughed, "I know and I realize with camera phones and social media everywhere my identity won't stay a secret much longer."

"So true," Arden admitted, "but would it really be so bad if your secret did come out?"

"Probably not," Roxie said, "before I was scared of what the university honchos might think, but now that I'm established in my department, it really wouldn't be a big deal." Wanting to change the subject, Roxie said, "How's my favorite high school senior?"

"Also busy. I hardly see the kid. Between high school classes, college classes, extracurricular activities, Brady house sitting and boyfriend we are more like roommates than family."

"Senior year is always crazy. Grace will pull through. She's got a good head on her shoulders."

Arden sighed, "I know. I just worry about her. Is she doing too much? Is she having fun?"

"Will she be the homecoming queen?" Roxie finished for her.

Arden looked down at her hands and then at Roxie, "You know I've never been a fan of beauty pageants, but Jess was homecoming queen her senior year and I want that for Grace, too."

Roxie nodded, "Understandable and I think pretty likely. Grace is well liked and popular."

"That she is, I'm trying to downplay it in my own mind and not get my hopes up. But I overheard Grace and Lindsay talking in the back room the other day and Grace is secretly hoping for it, too."

Roxie took a sip of her latte, changing the subject, "So, Grace's boyfriend has a mighty cute brother. Doesn't he come here occasionally?"

Arden smiled, "Yes, Jack is a frequent customer, however, our relationship is strictly business."

"If you say so," Roxie grinned.

"I do say so. Just remember I'm not one of your romance heroines."

"We'll see about that," Roxie said.

"Besides, Grace would never forgive me."

"So you have given it some thought," Roxie said just as Arden's phone dinged with a notification. As she picked up the phone to look at it, Arden said, "I hope this isn't Grace postponing our dinner again. The Bradys have really been keeping her busy."

Roxie nodded, "It's a shame what that family is going through. I hope one of the treatments work soon. Those kids need their mother."

"Agreed," Arden replied. "So when is your next book signing?"

Roxie laughed quietly, "Well, as soon as mid-October. I'll be gone for most of the fall break. They fly me out on Sunday and Monday through Thursday I will be hitting Phoenix, Vegas, San Diego and Sacramento. Then I fly out of Vegas and make it back here Saturday and return to class on Monday.

"Wow, that is quite an itinerary. Are you ever afraid that you are going to run into someone from back home?"

"Sometimes, but I think that if anyone did see me, it's out of context and they would just dismiss it as someone who looks like Roxie."

Arden nodded, "Good point." She absently nodded as she looked at her phone, startled by the name she saw associated with the text. It was from Jack Phillips and it said I need your help.

*****

Jack looked forward to Fridays just as many people did. It was the beginning of the weekend, and for Jack he didn't have to go to campus because he did not have classes on Friday. So, instead of getting up at 6 am he slept in until 8. He made a pot of coffee and fried himself an egg white omelet topped with salsa. He turned on one of the national morning news programs to get the headlines. He loved easing into his day in this manner. He had to vacate by 11 am so that the housekeeper could come in and clean his house.

When Jack had decided to leave Chicago, he had been at loose ends and not sure what he wanted to do. He knew that staying in Chicago was not an option. There were too many painful memories. He wasn't even sure if he wanted to stay in law enforcement. Then about a year after Edie's funeral, Matt Brady had called to check on him. His best friend mentioned that Jack should consider coming back to Camden Falls, at least for a little while. When he mentioned it to his parents, his mother Rachel screamed so loud with excitement that Oliver thought she had received either really bad news or really good news. With Rachel, it was always all or nothing, no in-between.

So he packed his bags, sold the furniture, kept the things he wanted, gave away the things he didn't and hit the road back to Ohio.

Instead of finding an apartment or house in town, Rachel and Oliver insisted that he stay in the guesthouse on the property. Jack had had some second thoughts when he first moved in but after Oliver's stroke, he was glad that he was nearby to help out when things got overwhelming for his mother.

Matt was also the one who gave him a heads up that the university was adding law enforcement and criminology to their curriculum. He asked Jack if he wanted him to mention his best friend at the next planning meeting.

"Sure," Jack had said without giving it too much thought. He didn't want to get his hopes up or give the University a false sense of security. He wasn't even sure he wanted any part of law enforcement. However, it didn't hurt to see what the university was offering. Maybe it could be challenging to be in on the ground floor of this new program.

Now looking back, he was glad he had made the move and become part of the university. He felt closer to his siblings, parents and the Bradys. A win-win all the way around.

He spent a forty-five-minute workout on the elliptical he had set up in the heated garage attached to the guesthouse. His workout playlist included everything from classic Who, the more recent Fall Out Boy to Imagine Dragons. He credited his sister and baby brother Grant for the updated music selections, while he tried to interest them in more classic rock. After the workout, he grabbed a quick shower. Then he read the online news sites and poured himself a second cup of coffee and headed to his home office to do a little research. He settled in behind his desk and started looking up fundraisers that other communities had used to support one of its members through tough times. Plenty of business, small towns and big cities had used an online fundraising app through social media, but Jack didn't feel as it would fit the Camden Falls style. Since Jack was a kid, this community with the aid of the university at times, had rallied around those in need that were close by as well as far away. The victims of hurricanes, tornadoes, forest fires and military families had all benefited from the generosity of the town and the university. Within the community they had helped victims of house fires, flooding and health issues. Jack flagged a couple of ideas on his iPad and printed them out for good measure, so that he could refer to them during his meeting with Arden. He smiled as he thought of his upcoming meeting with her at 11.

They had agreed to meet at the BrewHouse and discuss ways that they could help the Bradys. He had been glad to discover, when he came back to town, that the BrewHouse was still in operation. He knew the Gleesons who had been the owners for as long as he could remember. They always made the clientele feel at home, as if they were sitting in their own living rooms sipping coffee and eating comfort food treats.

Arden had continued that tradition but it had evolved, too. She had given the shop that homey feel and had balanced it with an atmosphere that also appealed to the university crowd. Probably raising a teenage girl helped in that regard. He had heard some of his students say that she encourages them to come in and study and is in the process of instituting a reward system. If they show their student ID it's 10% off the order. And she punches your card. After 10 coffees, you get one free. Jeb, one of his older students, said he was helping Arden develop an app that everyone could download and it would be a lot easier for Arden to keep track of the rewards.

He figured with her background in advertising, she would be the obvious choice to help with this fundraiser. He was well aware of her story, as he was sure she was well aware of his. He couldn't imagine the kind of loss Arden had suffered, losing so much of her family and possibly friends in one insidious terrorist act. Losing Edie had been devastating and grief is grief, but he had experienced his loss on a private level. Arden had to relive a very public tragedy every time someone mentioned it, or the news outlets found a new angle.

He admired her strength and sense of humor. He was glad that there was someone around his age that he could talk to and not have to explain his past or why he had returned to Camden Falls. He also felt it was important to keep the lines of communication open now that his brother was dating Grace and the two seemed to become more and more exclusive. He was also pleased that she considered him a "consultant" when it came to new treats they were considering offering in the shop.

He gathered up the papers and stuffed them in a folder. He grabbed his iPad and keys and he was off to the BrewHouse for his meeting with Arden.

Chapter 24: September 15

Arden checked the time on her phone. Jack was scheduled to arrive in twenty minutes. She topped off a couple of customers' coffees and headed back to her office. She was kind of a mess this morning. Her chestnut hair was working its way out of her already messy bun. She closed the door to her office and critiqued her look in the full-length mirror attached to the back of the door. The apron had to go. It had smudges and smears of butter, cinnamon and nutmeg on the front. She had a collection of aprons with witty sayings that Grace had given her every year for Christmas. This one said "With Coffee, All Things Are Possible" her only clean one left was "Bakers Gonna Bake, Bake, Bake, Bake," that Grace got her when she and her tween friends were going through their Taylor Swift phase. *Thank goodness that was short-lived,* Arden thought, *I'm really glad the new musical obsession is Fall Out Boy and Hamilton.* She took off the apron and threw it in the hamper glad that the baking was over for today. She grabbed the make-up bag and brush that she kept in the top drawer of her desk. A little mascara to accent her blue eyes, a little blush to highlight her cheeks and lip gloss made her look a little more human and a little less like a crazed baker. She tucked in some of the stray hairs on her messy bun.

She smoothed down her red, knit t-shirt, a chunky silver necklace and black jeans. Thank goodness she had worn her black ankle boots rather than the ratty Skechers she wore to work most days. They were incredibly comfortable to work in but she had other plans to accomplish today. She had planned on sneaking out this afternoon to meet with the other senior moms who were helping in the planning of the high school Homecoming festivities. Since Grace was on student council, the moms helped out with the planning and decorating. She hoped that Grace at least made it on the court. Jess would be so proud, Even better if she were crowned Homecoming Queen. She tried not to get her hopes up. All she wanted for Grace was what made her happy and put her on the road to future success. After one last look to survey her appearance, she opened her office door so that she could head out to the shop when Jack arrived.

Time to get back to the present. Soon the weather will be getting cooler and she can start wearing her favorite sweaters. She was glancing at the inventory lists when someone gave a light tap on the door. It was Jake, who was one of her newer employees that had taken to the coffee house business immediately.

"Hey, Arden, Jack is here for his meeting."

"Thanks, Jake. Get him some coffee and snicker doodle cookies and tell him I'll be right there."

"Will do," Jake said with a nod and headed to the counter to grab the coffee and cookies on his way to the table where he had seated Jack.

Arden grabbed her phone and planner. There were many things in the high tech world that Arden loved and appreciated, but when it came to keeping track of important dates and appointments she still liked to go old school as Grace said and have a paper planner. It was her lifeline and she rarely went anywhere without it. As she headed to meet Jack she thought, *I wonder why he wants to meet with me?*

*****

Jack watched Arden as she made her way through the shop, stopping to greet patrons and checking to see if they needed refills. She waved to others and greeted Jack with a smile as she moved towards his table.

It had been a while since he had seriously appreciated female company. For so long after Edie's death, he had felt guilty about even looking at another woman let alone going out with someone on a real date. Man-eaters like Liza Duncan scared the hell out of him. He didn't want that kind of betrayal-riddled situation causing complications he wasn't ready to deal with. The sneaking around and keeping secrets were fun for some but not for Jack. When it came to relationships, Jack didn't play games.

In fact, Jack really had no idea just how attractive he was. The jet black hair was starting to gray at the temples and his haunting blue eyes set hearts fluttering both in his former job at the precinct and his current job in the classroom. As a detective, he had always dressed in a suit and tie. It was hard to break the habit now. Today being his day off, however, the suit and tie were traded in for a Kelly green polo shirt, blue jeans and boat shoes.

Jack automatically smiled as Arden approached and he gestured to the snicker doodles, "Another baking triumph."

"Something we're considering for the fall. Be our Guinea pig and then fill me in on the deets," Arden smiled. She had come to like these frequent chats with Jack.

"If I keep being your taste tester, I won't be able to fit in the chairs. But if it means helping your business..." Jack trailed off.

Arden laughed, they had had this same conversation every time she asked him to try something new.

Jack took a bite of the still-warm cookie and the taste of fall resonated through his mouth. "Oh, wow, that is amazing. The customers will love it."

"Good," Arden said, "Your reaction is exactly what I was hoping for. We are hoping to introduce them during the mid-October Homecoming weekend. As the weather gets colder, the customers want comfort food to usher in the Halloween and Thanksgiving holidays.

"You know, I think I might need to sample a few more, just to be sure." Jack said winking. "I wouldn't want to put your customers or business in jeopardy."

"Very slick, Jack," Arden smiled. "Tabby, could you get more cookies from the back? I think a batch just came out of the oven."

"Sure thing," Tabby answered. Tabitha "Tabby" Myers was a senior at Camden Falls University and one of Arden's best employees. She had started working at the BrewHouse in her sophomore year and had worked her way up to assistant manager. Her parents both worked in the fine arts department at the university. They had five children, three girls and two boys all named after 60s and 70s television shows. Tabitha from *Bewitched,* Marsha from *The Brady Bunch,* and David and Danny from *The Partridge Family.* Tabby had confided that she was glad her parents stuck to television shows when naming their kids. Her aunt and uncle had spent several years in a commune, so her cousins had names like Moonflower and Glowing Star. Arden agreed that Tabby and her siblings had indeed dodged a bullet in the name game. Arden hated to think of Tabby graduating and moving onto bigger and better things. It was bittersweet. She knew that Tabby had great potential and should experience the world beyond Camden Falls, but she hated to lose such a fantastic worker.

"These snicker doodles are amazing. Come on, what's your secret?" Jack asked with a twinkle in his eyes.

"A baker never reveals her secrets," Arden winked.

"I am an officer of the law. You have to answer the question," he said with a grin. He always felt relaxed around Arden. The playful banter was always a part of their exchanges.

"Listen, Officer, I'm not givin" up the goods," Arden said in her best 1920s gangster voice.

"Wait a second, " Jack said as he took another bite, "is that …nutmeg I taste?"

"Ya got me, Copper," Arden laughed, "Don't give away my secret. See, that is why you are the official taste tester for the BrewHouse, after Grace, of course."

"Of course," Jack agreed, "How is Grace? Is she settling into the new school year okay?"

"Yes," Arden smiled, "senior year, I can hardly believe it. I am trying to get her to savor every moment. It seems as if she is spending more time on campus than she is at the high school. That worries me a little and I am hoping to talk to her about it. Adulting comes soon enough."

"I agree, I'm trying to get Grant to see the same thing. For what it's worth, I think Grace is really good for Grant."

"Thanks, I really like Grant, too. If I had to choose a first boyfriend for Grace which I was hoping would be when she entered the retirement home, Grant is an excellent choice."

Jack laughed, "For being the baby of the family, Grant is a lot more responsible than some kids I've seen. I realize I'm a little biased, but it seems like Grant and I are from two different families."

"That makes sense. There is quite an age difference between you and your other siblings and Grant."

"Yes," Jack smiled, but don't let my sister hear you say that. She doesn't like being reminded of her age or ours for that matter."

Arden nodded and then asked, "So what was it you wanted to talk to me about?"

Jack hesitated thinking about how much he wanted to reveal to Arden about Matt and Julia's situation. He also knew that if there was one person outside of his family that he could trust to be discreet, it was Arden. She had proven herself over and over again as being a good listener and not gossip about the conversations that take place in her establishment. Besides, she was probably more aware of the situation than others in the community since Grace worked for the Bradys. Jack took the plunge, "The reason I am here involves the Brady family and I was hoping you and your cousin Melody could help out."

"I thought perhaps that might be it," Arden flipped to the notes section in her planner thinking that taking notes might be necessary. Arden had started doing this when she worked at the ad agency because you never know when inspiration could hit. Also, Arden was a list maker. It was very satisfying to cross chores off the list or the steps in a project as she completed them.

"So," Jack told Arden the necessary information about Julia and Matt, the possible separation, the fact that her cancer is back and that they are running out of options for treatment and financial support.

Arden sat back in her chair, stunned by the news Jack was telling her. She knew that Grace had been helping them out more in the past few months and that Julia was facing a health crisis again. But she didn't realize how serious the situation had become. She didn't think

Grace was fully aware either. Recovering herself she asked, "Okay, what do you need me to do?"

The relief was obvious on Jack's face, "Good, I was hoping that between the BrewHouse and the Peace Lutheran congregation, we could put together a fundraiser or two to help the Brady family out."

"Since Matt is chief of police, do you think the department would like to be involved?"

"I've already spoken to Sheila Hastings and a couple of other cops. They want in on this, too."

"Good, this is very good," Arden said transitioning into ad executive mode.

Jack marveled at the transition as he watched her begin to scribble notes and diagrams.

Jack nodded and watched Arden write as quickly as the ideas formulated themselves. Jack said, "I take it in your former life you organized a few fundraisers in the Big Apple."

Arden was a little taken aback. No one had asked about her life in New York in a very long time. She wasn't sure why that was. Perhaps it was because they didn't want to pry and were respecting her privacy. When Jack casually brought it up, it didn't feel like prying. It felt like two people wanting to learn more about each other. Arden smiled, "As a matter of fact, yes, I did organize a couple of fundraising dinners. It was really up to my colleague, Dana, to set those up, but I was the fallback when she was out on maternity leave for two of her children."

Jack nodded, "So what worked for those events?"

Arden thought, "Well, first of all, they were for national charities and we were trying to appeal to the rich and famous. Many times these events were more about being seen giving a huge donation to make headlines instead of the actual charity needs."

Now it was Jack's turn to be taken aback. "That sounds a little cynical."

"It's not meant to. Many of the people we invited and worked with were very nice and genuinely cared about the people we were trying to get help for. My point was that what might work in the big city may not work in a small Midwest college town." Arden paused looking over her notes, excitement lit up her eyes, "Okay, we need to appeal to the hometown hero angle of this. Luckily, the Bradys are the poster children for the perfect family. Matt and Julia have been married for a number of years, they both work in jobs that serve the community. Matt's family has a stable, well-liked reputation and Julia brings a special kind of success story from the foster care system and the fact that they adopted foster kids adds to their likability."

Jack was amazed at the breakdown that Arden had just relayed. "All true, now how is that going to help us raise money to help them?"

"I'm glad you asked. I think we should focus on the family aspect of things. People in this area love festivals. Think about it, a few counties over we have the Pumpkin Festival. Up north where Ben and I grew up we had the Bratwurst Festival and a little further south from us, The Popcorn Festival. Most small towns in Ohio respect and attend family events. I propose we have a Pancake Breakfast in the fall so that we don't step on the civic club's events, and a family festival in the spring when the weather breaks and people are ready to shake off their cabin fever."

Jack nodded and smiled, "I like it. I see your two events and raise you another. What about an indoor family night in the winter? February is one of the dreariest months and summer seems to be forever away. We could possibly use the multi-purpose room at Peace Lutheran and have board games, snacks, carnival games, etc. We could sell tickets to the event that would cover admission and any games/activities the citizens wanted to participate in. Food would be the only additional cost."

"I love it and we could move the spring festival to early summer as soon as school is out. Same premise, only the activities will be outdoors as well. I think the first thing we need to plan is the pancake breakfast. Let me text Melody and see if she can stop over and we can get these events on the books."

"Perfect, while you do that, I'm going to check in with my mom. Dad has had a rough couple of days and a little moral support can't hurt."

Arden looked concerned, "I'm sorry to hear that. It must be tough for a person who is used to being so active to be restricted all of a sudden."

Jack agreed, "That's the problem. Physically he is ahead of schedule, but not fast enough for Oliver."

Arden smiled, "I'm sure it's difficult for everyone involved. If you'll excuse me I'll text while you give your mom a call."

"Perfect." Jack got up and walked towards the doorway and Arden headed back towards the counter to check on coffee and cookie levels.

Arden: Hey Mel, u busy?

A few seconds later.

Melody: Looking for a distraction.

Arden: Good. Come to the BrewHouse. We have something to run by you. Bring the church schedule.

Melody: Who is we?

Arden: Come and find out. (Wink emoji)

Arden started back to the table as did Jack. Arden asked, "How is your dad?"

Jack shook his head, "Up to his old tricks, sneaking around when he's supposed to be resting. He has been canceling physical therapy appointments and driving my mom crazy. Just another day in the life of the Phillips family."

"At least you know everyone is doing their part."

Jack laughed. "There is that. Were you able to get a hold of Melody?"

"Yes, she is on her way."

"Good," Jack said. "Listen, I want you to know how much I appreciate this. I know the Bradys will, too."

"I'm glad to help out. The Bradys have been wonderful to Grace and we both think a lot of them. I know Melody and the church will be happy to help as well. I've never met a more caring group of people."

"I agree. Mom and Dad are more faithful in their attendance than I am."

Arden was reassuring, "We all could do better."

The door to the shop jangled and in walked Melody. She waved and said hi to other customers as she made her way to Arden and Jack. "Hello, people! What kind of trouble are the two of you cooking up?"

Jack and Arden filled in the blanks regarding Julia's medical situation, the Bradys' financial situation and their ideas for the fundraisers.

"Wow," Melody said, "You two should run for office, you'd have the government in tip top-shape by dinner with time to spare."

"That's how we roll," Jack said and he and Arden shared a high five.

Melody laughed, "I see no problem scheduling the pancake breakfast. We have a farmer in the congregation who we can ask to sell us sausage and bacon at cost. And there is a Pillsbury factory that will donate pancake flour. It's a huge tax write off for them. Let's set the date. I have a church council meeting tomorrow. I will run this by them and get back to the two of you tomorrow night. Sound good?"

"Better than we could have hoped for," Arden said. "Melody, thanks so much for helping us out with this."

"Happy to do it. That family is an inspiration to us all. So, I'll be in touch. Arden, can I get a coffee to go? I've got to drive to Columbus to check on a parishioner that's having surgery."

"Absolutely," Arden said.

"Talk her out of some of the snicker doodles, they are amazing."

"Ooo, do you have any left? You know those are my favorite," Melody said.

"I think I can arrange that."

"Excellent," Melody said as she started to get her billfold out of her purse.

"Don't even try it, Reverend Cline. Your money's no good here."

"Wow, you're still as bossy as when we were kids."

"Some things never change," Arden called as she made her way to get the coffee and cookies ready. Melody reached into her billfold and put a ten-dollar bill in the tip jar. She winked at Jack and put her fingers up to her lips making the Shhhh sign.

"I saw that," Arden called.

"She missed her calling as a cranky study hall monitor," Melody said quietly to Jack.

Jack stifled a laugh as Arden came around the counter to deliver the coffee and cookies. She looked from Melody to Jack and back again. "You two are up to no good."

Also trying not to laugh, Melody grabbed the goodies and headed to the door, "Talk to you two tomorrow!"

Jack said, "I should get going too. Thanks again for everything."

Arden smiled. "No problem. Happy to do it."

Arden watched carefully as Jack went out of the door.

Chapter 25: September 15

Grace was exhausted. Arden hadn't been very happy when she had to postpone their dinner plans so that Grace could help out the Bradys. Julia had received word that she had qualified for another study and Matt was already out of town at a law enforcement convention. He would be out of town longer than Julia planned to be. So Grace had texted Arden with the change in plans and then threw some clothes and toiletries into her overnight duffle, grabbed her book bag and headed to the Bradys so that she could greet the kids as they got home from school.

Hazel and Neil had been far less cooperative than they had been in the past. Grace chalked it up to them missing their parents. Also, she figured it wasn't easy on them never knowing if their parents were going to be waiting for them at home. But Grace had finally gotten them to bed after much coaxing, bargaining and promises made that would probably be forgotten in the morning. Time to get back to *Pride and Prejudice*. Grace liked the novel for the most part, but assigned reading was not her thing. She liked the fact that her AP English teacher, Ms. Bishop, allowed them the freedom to choose their own supplemental reading materials, but assigned reading by the teacher was another story altogether.

She checked her phone for messages. She and Lyndsey had been blowing up each others' phones with texts about Grant, Chemistry, the upcoming Homecoming Dance and who was going to take over for the chemistry teacher, Mrs. Robinson, while she was off having her baby.

No texts from Grant, but she knew it was going to be a busy day for him. After his study group, he had fraternity business to attend to. She probably wouldn't see him until tomorrow and maybe not even then. She had been trying to decide if she was going to ask him to Homecoming. He was a sophomore in college, and going with your high school girlfriend to her school dance seemed pretty lame. Her other alternative was to go in a group with her friends, cut out early and go to the frat house. Arden probably wouldn't approve, but what Arden didn't know wouldn't hurt Grace.

The bucolic setting and Austen's gentle, country gentry along with her Spotify studying soundtrack and the comfy overstuffed couch put Grace to sleep. Nancy and Trixie had snuggled in relishing the quiet house and a human willing to give tummy rubs. A noise startled Grace awake. Her phone had long died but she couldn't be sure if she actually heard a noise or if she had dreamed it. She peeled herself out from under the blanket she had thrown over herself and the dogs. She extricated herself from the dogs and plugged in her phone to charge. As she woke up, she realized all the lights were still on downstairs, so it was easy to see that the clock read 3:05 am. She padded through the downstairs hallway and to the staircase to go check on the kids. Hazel's room was the first room on the right at the top of the stairs. When she peeked in, Grace had fallen asleep with the nightstand light on and a book in her lap. Not a surprise. It would be surprising if Hazel didn't have a book near her. Grace carefully bookmarked Hazel's page. She laid the book on her nightstand and carefully turned out the light. Trixie jumped up on Hazel's bed and snuggled in.

Across the hall, Neil was tangled in his covers and snoring lightly. Neither one of the kids were awake to have caused the noise. *There it is again! God, it sounds like a mouse. I hope it isn't. Gross. But it sounds like it's coming from the master bedroom.* Grace steeled herself to go in. The door to the master bedroom was closed but not locked. The sound was getting louder and to Grace's relief, she could tell it was a notification tone on a cell phone. She wondered if Julia or Matt had forgotten their phone, but they would have contacted her and given a number where she could reach them. She walked in the room, turned on the light and shut the door so she wouldn't wake up Neil and Hazel.

The room had a soft glow to it from the lighting that could be regulated from dim to bright with the switch. The California king-size bed had a Ted Baker Pistachio Border comforter and pillows with matching shams. There were a variety of throw pillows lined across the headboard that made the bed look cozy and inviting. The bed was made and everything was neat and tidy. It looked like it was ready for a catalog photo shoot. The matching nightstands had identical lamps but that is where the similarity ended. It was obvious who slept on which side of the bed. On the right nightstand was a stack of police journals and files neatly piled and some reading glasses lying on top. On the left nightstand were a couple of romance novels, some fingernail polish and face cream.

The chirping notification was getting louder but was sounding less often. When it sounded again, Grace could tell it wasn't coming from any furniture in the bedroom, but now sounded like it was coming from the master bathroom. *Why do you care what it is?* She thought. Now that she knew it wasn't a mouse she should have just let it go. *But now I have to know. Grant and Arden think I watch too many true crime documentaries but I feel that if a real mystery falls in my lap, I have to see where it takes me. Besides Matt or Julia could be without a phone and she might have to overnight it to one of them.*

However, when it chirped again, she didn't recognize the notification sound as belonging to either Julia or Matt. *But people switch those up all the time,* she thought.

As soon as she entered the master bath, the chirping stopped. *Of course,* she thought, *I'll just sit here until I hear it again.* The bathroom had the same color scheme as the master suite. There was a vanity with two sinks, a large medicine cabinet, a walk-in shower and a huge bathtub. When the chirp sounded again, Grace could tell it was coming from the medicine cabinet. *That's strange,* she thought, *who keeps a cell phone in the bathroom medicine cabinet?* When she opened the mirrored door, it looked like every other medicine cabinet in suburban America. On one side was shaving supplies, first-aid tape, bandages and ointment. On the other side, were outdated and expired prescription medicine bottles, lipstick, makeup, antacid, and aspirin. No electronic device or phone to be found. When it sounded again, Grace knew that it was somehow in the back of the medicine cabinet. *How can that be? Isn't it nailed directly to the wall?*

Grace shook her head and closed the medicine cabinet door. *Not my monkeys, not my circus,* she thought. But the medicine cabinet chirped again, but it was fainter this time. She turned and faced the mirrored door. She opened the door and began looking at the contents. Against her better judgment, she started unloading the cabinet as quietly as possible. She didn't want one of the kids to wake up, come looking for her and find her snooping through their parents' medicine cabinet. The last thing she took out was a bottle of Scope mouthwash that had clearly never been opened and was two years passed its expiration date. Behind it was a latch, so small that a person could not see it unless it was specifically being looked for. When Grace carefully tried to lift it, it wouldn't budge.

Grace was never one to give up that easily and the faint chirping sound egged her on. She opened the first drawer in the marble-topped vanity and grabbed a nail file. She used it to leverage the latch and was slowly able to unlock it. Once the latch was released the shelving in the cabinet swung open to reveal a storage space the size of a small wall safe. At first, Grace wasn't sure what she was seeing.

Taking Care of Grace

The chirp sounded again and then she saw it, a small burner flip phone. It showed a bunch of numbers on the caller ID with a 702 area code. Grace carefully flipped it closed and placed the phone back in the space. The next thing to catch her eye was the stacks and stacks of money in $500 packets. Besides the stacks of money she found prescription pads from a Dr. Granger in Columbus, Ohio, Dr. Jeffers in West Virginia, Dr. Singh in Cleveland and 4 other doctors from different hospitals and clinics in other states.

The other stacks of papers were insurance policies, medical files that matched the names on the prescription pads and prescription bottles all with Julia's name on them. Grace put everything back in the wall safe where she found it and carefully closed and latched the secret door. She put the items back into the medicine cabinet as best she could all the while trying to figure out why the secret storage area was there and what did all of those things mean? *I should have taken a picture of them,* she thought. *But that is ridiculous. I didn't know I would be finding a wall safe.* She slid the door across to close the medicine cabinet and quietly made her way downstairs to the den.

*****

Didn't most families have a wall safe? Arden had one in her bedroom. It makes sense that Julia's insurance papers were in there but there were some items that didn't make sense. Grace was trying to piece together the items she had just found. Maybe Grant and Arden were right. Maybe she did binge watch too many crime shows and she was seeing sinister plots where none existed.

She checked her phone for the time, 3:30am. She snuggled under that blanket on the couch next to snoozing dog Nancy and slept fitfully until 6:30am.

Chapter 26: Later That Same Day

Grace had about an hour and a half while Hazel and Neil were at soccer practice. She had left a note for Julia at the house as to where she and the kids were and that she would bring them back to the house at 3. Julia's plane was to get in at 2 so with any luck, all Grace would have to do is drop off the kids at home and not have to spend much time with Julia. While she loved the Brady kids and Matt was friendly and funny, there was something about Julia that made Grace a little uneasy. When she thought about it that was a bit of an exaggeration. Julia was always friendly and kind but Grace always felt there was something off about her. She seemed closed off at times, especially if her guard slipped a little bit. Maybe the edge was there because of Julia's childhood spent in the foster care system. And it couldn't be easy battling cancer. Grace was willing to take these facts into consideration.

After her discovery in the medicine cabinet, Grace hadn't been able to rest, not even the Calm app she had on her phone did the trick. When she finally gave up at around 6:30 am, she made herself some tea and read some more *Pride and Prejudice*. She gave another pass at her game theory paper, too. All the while trying to talk herself down from the wild theories she was forming based on her latest find and comparing it to all those true crime shows she had watched on TV. She remembered she needed to finish the inventory at the BrewHouse and now would be the time to do it.

*****

She was in the storeroom at the BrewHouse taking inventory as the thoughts regarding her discovery swirled again. *Why am I assuming a crime has been committed here?* She reasoned. *Julia is after all battling cancer. I probably stumbled upon their family safe. Everyone keeps money around the house, right? God knows they need it for Julia's travel and medical expenses. Insurance doesn't cover everything.* She had heard that plenty of times when refilling the coffee cups of the patrons at the BrewHouse. But what didn't make sense to her were the multiple prescription pads that were also in the safe. *Didn't doctors keep those under lock and key so that addicts couldn't write their own prescriptions? And none of those doctors were local. So how did Julia get a hold of the pads and why? As a nurse, was she authorized to write her own prescriptions? And if she could write prescriptions, wouldn't the pads have her name on them?* More information she would need to look up. Right now, she needed to keep her mind on her work so that she wouldn't have to count the to-go cups for the third time.

After an hour, Grace realized that the numbers weren't adding up and she almost requested an order for merchandise that they had plenty of on hand. *This is ridiculous,* she thought, *I am not going to be happy until I get another look in that safe.* She walked out of the storeroom and across the hall to Arden's office. The door was open but Arden wasn't there. Grace knew she was at a meeting at Melody's church to firm up the plans for the Brady fundraisers. Grace knew they were planning on surprising the Bradys with pancake breakfast and then presents them with a check to help with Julia's medical expenses. Today's meeting was to figure out how to get the Bradys to the breakfast without tipping them off and they were also going to firm up some of the details regarding volunteers and cleanup crew. Grace scribbled a note that she needed to run a quick errand and she would be back soon and left the note and the clipboard on Arden's office chair where she knew she would see it. Grace grabbed her backpack and lanyard with her keys and headed out the back entrance to her car.

*****

Grace got to the Brady house ten minutes later. The traffic was crazy with all of the new and returning students moving in this week. She thought about parking down the street but then realized that was silly. *I am here all the time. No one is going to think it's weird. If Julia or Matt gets home ridiculously early, I'll say I left my phone here and came back to get it.* With her excuse figured out, Grace slipped her phone in her front jeans pocket grabbed her keys and locked her car.

*****

Grace disabled the alarm and let herself in. Everything was just as she had left it this morning. She always made sure to clean up after herself and the kids so that when the Bradys returned home it was clean and welcoming. Grace slipped her lanyard around her neck and jogged up the stairs to the master bedroom and bath.

This time when she opened the medicine cabinet, she snapped a picture of the shelf so that she could put things back as closely as she had found them. Once in the cabinet she picked up the cellphone. It was a little flip phone that couldn't send or receive texts. The voicemail message light was blinking and just as Grace was pressing the button to retrieve them, the phone powered off because the battery was dead. Before it powered off, she was able to see that the messages were all from the same number with the 702 area code. Grace typed the number into the notes app on her phone. She then took pictures of the stacks of money.

When she had first noticed the money she hadn't read what was on the bands wrapped around the money. Now when she picked them up to photograph them, she could see what was printed on them. The bands were printed with the names of three casinos in Las Vegas. *Why would there be money from Las Vegas in the safe? She* snapped a picture of each of the stacks and did some quick addition in her head. There had to be at least a quarter of a million dollars here. Shaking her head to clear the shock and get back to snapping pictures, she took shots of the prescription pads and insurance papers. She placed everything back in the safe and then all the items back in the medicine cabinet the way they had appeared in the picture she had taken earlier. She grabbed her keys and phone and headed back to the BrewHouse to finish the inventory she had started.

Chapter 27: September 16

Early mornings suck, Grace thought as she poured the hot tea into her giant Yeti travel mug. She had enjoyed her weekend with the Brady kids but she was still feeling uneasy about what she had found in what could only be described as a wall safe. *But why? Why all of the prescription pads? Nurses couldn't write prescriptions could they? And if they could, wouldn't their own names be on it and not some Doctor? And what about all that money?* Grace's best guess was that there was a quarter of a million dollars there. *Didn't they trust banks? Wasn't it old people that lived through the Depression that kept money at home? Or drug dealers?* She couldn't imagine the Bradys being drug dealers. *So why would anyone keep that much money in their home? Granted it was in a safe but that was a lot of money for a wall safe. Plus, the wrappers indicated that the money was from a couple of casinos in Vegas. Wouldn't they have bank wrappers if they had cashed insurance checks?*

Arden was a freak when it came to money around the house. She made daily deposits to the bank for the BrewHouse and rarely had a lot of personal cash around. The only thing that makes sense were the prescription bottles. Grace and Arden as well as most of Camden Falls knew that Julia had battled cancer as a teenager, which resulted in total hysterectomy. When she had aged out of the foster system, she had put herself through nursing school and had vowed to adopt kids from the foster system when she married and settled down and was ready to start a family. *Maybe the prescription bottles were follow-up medicine from her cancer back in the day. I wish I had looked at the dates on the prescription bottles and medical files. They are probably from Julia's medical past.*

Grace tried to convince herself that there was a logical answer to this situation. Besides, she shouldn't have been snooping around anyway. After adding a little honey and 2% milk to her tea, she screwed on the lid and decided to get on with her day. She grabbed the tea and her book bag and headed to the door and then set the backpack down. *Wait a second, what about the burner phone?* Grace knew about burner phones. Grace had learned from the crime shows she watched that burner phones had their criminal uses. She liked both true crime and fiction on Netflix. Her favorites were *Making of a Murderer, Killer Women with Piers Morgan, Sherlock, Criminal Minds* and *How to Get Away with Murder. And whom do Julia and Matt know in Vegas?* She had entered the 702 area code in her phone app for notes and then had Googled it when she got home. *There were certainly a lot of calls from that Vegas area code.*

Grace gasped with a realization and relief, *we know Julia's cancer is back. That would explain a lot of what I found in the secret safe.* Grace sunk down on the bench near the mudroom that led to the garage. It was a lot for the 18-year-old to process.

What should I do? Is it really any of my business? What if Julia needs help? The kids seem to know vague information about it. Grace's mind was racing. She started to go through her list of friends and family trying to decide who would be the best one and most trustworthy to tell. Lindsay was out. Lindsay was her BFF but while Grace binge watched crime shows, Lindsay was all about the medical shows, *Gray's Anatomy, House, Chicago Med* and the classic *ER*. She would have the entire family needing to be quarantined. Arden, as cool as she could be, would probably focus on the fact that Grace had been snooping where she wasn't supposed to be. That is definitely not what Grace wanted her mom to focus on.

Aunt Mel was a consideration. *Wasn't there a law that said she couldn't tell anyone what people told her, or was that in the confessional? Wait, did Lutherans even have confessional?* Still, Melody seemed like a good choice. *Or what about Grant? We tell each other everything. Plus isn't his brother BFF to Matt. Maybe Grant already knows what's going on. But wouldn't he have told me? Ugh!*

Grace grabbed her backpack and tea and headed to the door again. She had decided to start with Melody and then check in with Grant. Having made up her mind, Grace felt a little more confident that she could tackle her Monday challenges.

Chapter 28: Later That Same Day

Melody was struggling with the sermon topic for Sunday. It was a Monday morning, the sun was steaming through the stained-glass window in her study at the church and the NPR classical radio station was playing softly in the background. Usually, by this time she had a pretty good idea of what she wanted to say. On Tuesday mornings, she and several of the other Lutheran ministers from the area met at the BrewHouse to offer perspectives on sermons and Bible studies as well as support in professional and personal matters.

This time the theme had already been decided. This coming Sunday the sermon needed to focus on money and giving to the church. The stewardship committee was expecting her to speak to the congregation about increasing their weekly giving. Melody had always felt blessed to serve this congregation. They had welcomed a female minister into their church when female ministers of any denomination were few and far between.

They had surrounded her and Arden during the 9/11 tragedies with support and caring. After the twins, Nicholas and Billy were born, the church members provided round-the-clock babysitting and errand-running services. The boys had more adoptive "aunts, uncles and grandparents" than they could count. The members had supported the boys every step of the way. In fact, the congregation tolerated the boys occasionally sitting on their mother's lap during the sermon and hiding under the giant Christmas trees during the annual Sunday School Christmas program.

She was grateful for their generosity of spirit and financial support. Whenever she or the church council went to the congregation asking for money or goods to support a community event or need it was given, no questions asked. She could feel God's presence at work in this church community. Nevertheless, she still got a little nervous asking the members to dig a little deeper into their pockets. And Melody was not meant for sales.

Growing up, selling Girl Scout cookies had been a disaster. Her parents had ended up buying 8 dozen boxes because she had been too shy to go around the neighborhood and knock on doors. That was the first and last year her parents allowed her to sell anything. When fundraisers at school came around, her parents just wrote a check rather than putting Melody and themselves through the torture.

Now she was faced with delivering the yearly sermon about the importance of giving to the church. She had plenty of biblical backing but in tough economic times, increased giving could be a tough sell. She had started to pray for guidance when there was a tentative knock at her study door. "Come in," she called, a little relieved that the interruption could lead to a full-blown distraction further postponing the inevitable.

The door opened and Grace walked in. "Hey, Aunt Mel, you busy?"

"Never for my favorite niece," Melody smiled, "Come, sit." Melody got up from her desk and came to sit on the couch with Grace.

"I'm your only niece, so there's not much competition."

"Ah, come on, even if I had loads of nieces, you would be my favorite one. So, what brings you to my neck of the woods?"

Grace paused. *Maybe this wasn't such a good idea.* Now that she was removed from the situation it seemed silly. And Melody seemed busy and worse yet, what if Grace told her and she didn't believe her?

Melody could see that Grace was struggling, "Everything okay, Sweet Pea?" Melody asked using the nickname that friends and family had used since her birth.

Grace wasn't sure how to begin so she tackled it like she would any other problem, set the parameters and ground rules. She took a deep breath and said, "If I tell you something, you have to keep it a secret, right? You can't tell anyone?"

Melody tried not to let her surprise show and didn't want to scare the girl off, "That's true speaking as your minister. The only times I can disclose information is if I have the permission of the people involved or if I feel they or someone else is in danger." She paused, "As your aunt, I gotta tell ya, kid, you're scaring me a little. What's up, you fail a quiz, forget to take out the garbage?" Melody was hoping that a little levity would relax her niece.

It did the trick, the tension slowly released it's hold on Grace, she smiled and said, "I'm sorry, it's just that this is pretty serious or at least I think it is and I could be all wrong…"

Melody took her hand and said, "Gracie, you are one of the least excitable kids I've ever met. If something is bothering you, you are right to talk it out with someone you trust. Speaking of which, have you mentioned this to your mom?"

Grace shook her head, "No. She's really busy with the semester starting and plus it involves people she sees on a regular basis."

Melody thought about what Grace said. *This kid told Arden everything*, "Okay, you set the ground rules earlier and I told you what my guidelines are. I need to ask two questions, are you in danger?"

"No," Grace said.

"Is someone you know in danger?"

Grace wasn't sure how to answer and then said, "Not in the way you think. No one is in physical danger. But I think people that I know and care about are being lied to."

Melody was relieved. "Okay, that is something we can deal with. Start at the beginning and we will see where it takes us."

Grace nodded. She told Melody about the impromptu weekend at the Bradys, how she found the hidden cabinet and what she found there. "I know I shouldn't have been snooping around, but I really thought there was a mouse or some other furry creature trapped in the house." Grace sighed, "That is the way this whole thing started."

Melody smiled and patted Grace's hand. "Wow, that is a lot to process. You didn't mention this to the Bradys when they got back?"

"No, I haven't seen them. The only contact we have had was through texts. Plus, I want them to trust me."

"I understand that but it sounds like you have stumbled upon something that they are not ready to make public yet."

"I understand that Julia is fighting cancer and they want to keep it a private family matter until they know what they are dealing with. But the prescription pads and bottles and the burner phone with the 702 area code, which by the way, is a Las Vegas area code."

"How do you know that," Melody asked. *This kid could have a future in the FBI.*

"I Googled it."

"I should have known. You watch all those crime shows, I don't know why I'm surprised that you would do your own investigation."

"Yes, well, and what Mom doesn't know won't hurt me. However, I still don't know what I should do."

"Well, I-" before Melody could complete her thought, Wilma Jean Powell burst into Melody's study.

"Pastor Mel," Wilma was breathless. Come quick, we have a situation with one of the quilters."

Mel jumped up and with a sidelong glance said to Grace, "We aren't finished." In a normal voice, she said, "Come on, Grace, maybe you can help us out."

Grace followed her aunt and the panicked Wilma Jean to the church basement where the quilters had set up their headquarters. They met every Thursday and sent their quilts all over the world through an international charity organization. They had tables with quilt tops laid out to be tied with yarn to the backing. They had three sewing machines where they finished the quilt tops and the backing. Two of the machines were up and running however, Gladys Brooks seemed to be attached to her machine in a very uncomfortable way. Melody, Wilma Jean and Grace rushed to her side.

Gladys was embarrassed. At 75 she had been quilting and sewing since she was a little girl, but her eyesight was beginning to fail and she refused to give up the hobbies she had enjoyed all her life. "I feel so silly, "she said on the verge of tears. "But I'm stuck and we don't know how to get me out of this and save the quilt top, too."

Melody was reassuring. "Gladys, we will get you out of this. Now let me see," Melody carefully looked at Gladys's sleeve and her position under the sewing machine foot. "Betty, could you grab one of the desk lights and hold it over this area?"

"Sure thing," Betty Smith was grateful to have something to do and to feel useful. She grabbed one of the desk lights that was clamped to one of the tying tables and brought it back to Melody. "Here you go, tell me where you want me to hold it."

"Right. Over. Here." Melody said carefully. She slowly moved the sewing machine foot up and like a surgeon and asked for "Scissors." Wilma Jean handed over the scissors with precision. By this time, the situation had drawn quite the crowd of the other quilters, the janitor and the church secretary. With a couple of snips, Gladys was set free. The relief of tension sent the tears flowing from Gladys's eyes. "Oh, Gladys it's all right." Melody gave the woman a reassuring hug.

"I'm sorry," Gladys said the tears becoming almost uncontrollable. "It's just that I don't see as well as I used to and my kids want me to move into assisted living and I-" Gladys couldn't continue. The other quilters exchanged sympathetic glances. Melody looked at Grace and addressed the rest of the group, putting a reassuring arm around Gladys's shoulders. "Gladys, let's go to the parsonage and have a cup of tea. I think we could both use it."

"Okay," she said between sobs, "or maybe something stronger."

Grace and Melody exchanged a look and both stifled the laughter about to bubble up. Grace took her cue.

"Listen, Aunt Mel, we'll talk later."

"Yes," Melody said firmly, "we will. And in the meantime you might want to run it by your mother."

Grace gave a wave and headed to the door leading out to the street while Melody directed Gladys to the parsonage next door to the church.

Chapter 29: September 15

"Grace, you are overreacting. What were you doing snooping around in the bathroom anyway? You obviously took the stuff you saw out of context. Have you been binge watching those true crime documentaries on Netflix again?" Grant Phillips teased and Grace shot him a warning look.

"Okay, if I'm overreacting, how do you explain these?" Grace handed Grant her phone and started scrolling through the pictures she had taken.

Grant was surprised, but thought it looked like the average family wall safe. "Come on, can't we just enjoy each other? It's the first week back and I've got pledges to torture." Grant was trying to cajole Grace out of her pensive mood and his charming, dimpled smile was having the desired effect.

They were standing in Grant's spacious, yet cluttered room at the Kappa Alpha Epsilon. They had met in a summer session calculus class and Grace had offered to tutor him when they compared quiz grades while walking out of class one day. Tutoring led to coffee, which led to more coffee, movies and dinner, which led to the two agreeing to be exclusive. One of the truly amazing aspects of their relationship was that Arden seemed to approve. She still set guidelines and curfews, but she seemed okay with Grant. Grace thought that part of the reason she was okay with it was that Grant's brother, Jack was a regular at the BrewHouse and the family attended Peace Lutheran Church.

This had been so exciting for Grace. Dating a college guy. The guys she went to high school with didn't have a clue. Grant was fun and caring and he never made her feel like a high school kid, until now.

Sensing that this was serious, Grant asked, "Who all have you talked to about this?"

Grace was inwardly relieved that Grant was starting to take this situation seriously, "Just you and Aunt Mel."

"Not Lindsay?"

"No," Grace sighed, "No, I love Linds but she doesn't know when to keep her mouth shut."

Grant agreed, "Good call, she is a great kid, but I think we need to be careful about how many people we tell. What did your Aunt Melody say?"

"At first, she was just listening and asking questions for clarification. Then the quilters interrupted us. One of the ladies had accidentally sewn her sleeve into the quilt."

"You're kidding," Grant said, trying not to laugh.

Grace was laughing a little too, "Poor thing, she was so upset. Aunt Mel and Betty, one of the other quilters, were able to get her sleeve out from under the sewing machine foot, but she was pretty traumatized. Aunt Mel took her over to the parsonage for some tea. I told her we would talk later."

"Good," Grant nodded. "The fewer that people that know, the better."

"So, you believe me?"

Grant hesitated, "I believe you saw something that seems a little sketchy, but it's the chief of police. Shouldn't they be the last family you should be considering as potential criminals?"

"I suppose you're right, but I have a bad feeling about it."

"I think I know how to distract you," he pulled her close, kissed her neck and whispered in her ear, "Come on, you know you wanna get me drunk and have your way with me." Grace grinned along with a shy giggle.

She pulled back and gazed coyly into Grant's eyes, "I guess my diabolical plan has been discovered." She gave him a lingering kiss. As she pulled away, she took on a serious tone, "Look, this isn't over, I know what I saw behind the medicine cabinet. We'll talk when you aren't so busy." She could see that dwelling on this right now wasn't going to help. Grant visibly relaxed and began kissing Grace's temple. Grace trying to lighten the mood said, "Don't be so hard on the little pledge boys. That skinny ginger assigned to Reed looked like he was going to pee his pants when you asked him to recite the Greek alphabet."

"I know, right? But we're stuck with him. He's a legacy. Little Moe's parents are movers and shakers in the financial community. The Pan-Hellenic Council and the college want us to make nice and keep them happy. They are big contributors all over campus." Grace nodded with a look of understanding. Some of the sorority sisters that she had met in CCP classes and around campus had mentioned their own issues with legacies as well as prominent contributors they needed to keep in a giving mood.

From outside, it was evident that the party was getting started with chaotic noise and throbbing music rising up from the backyard of the frat house to Grant's window. They could hear the DJ doing sound checks and the noise of equipment being moved around. He gathered Grace into his arms for a long, satisfying kiss. He reluctantly broke away and looked into Grace's large blue eyes.

"Your family is no slouch in the movers and shakers crowd," Grace commented. The Phillips family had been captains of the candy industry for a very long time. It still came as a shock that she was dating a college guy and one from a well-known family.

"The natives are getting restless down there and we don't want anymore unwanted attention from the council or the police," He nodded down at the party that, if possible, was getting louder by the minute. Grace's underage presence could only add complications to an already sketchy relationship with campus security and the local police department. Unfortunately, having an older brother, as a former cop and best friend of the police chief didn't cut any slack for the fraternity. Despite that, Grace was loath to break the connection as well.

She hesitated ever so slightly and said, "Will I see you after the party?"

Slipping an arm around her shoulders he leaned in and said, "You better. What will you tell Mama Arden? She keeps a pretty close eye on you.

Grace winced a little at Grant's reference to her mom. She understood her overprotectiveness but it didn't mean that it didn't get under her skin at times. Arden did her best and she really tried to let Grace be involved in a number of activities, but she could feel the undercurrent of fear that Arden tried to keep under wraps. Living life with the family dynamic she had, had its challenges. She decided to ignore the dig, "Wouldn't miss it. Our usual hangout?"

Grant winked and whispered gently, "I'll be there" kissing her he guided her to the bedroom door, sidestepping discarded t-shirts, empty Monster cans and dirty sweat socks. Grace gave him a quick wave and smiled as she headed down the stairs.

As she exited out the back door she was immediately enveloped into the crowd of bodies writhing and grinding to Lizzo's "Juice." Grace navigated the makeshift dance floor, gingerly avoiding the bouncing red Solo cups sloshing beer. The warring scents of roasted pig, beer, Nautica Blue and Marc Jacobs Daisy Eau So Fresh gave Grace an instant headache.

She worked her way to the edge of the partygoers. She had several hours to put in some study time before she hooked up with Grant. She just hoped that Arden would be working late tonight. It made sneaking out a lot easier.

Chapter 30: Later That Same Night

Grace checked her phone again. No message from Grant. She knew the party had gone on later than they had originally anticipated. He had texted her around midnight and said that the party didn't show any signs of letting up. He would text her in an hour. She had fallen asleep while reading her chemistry textbook and it wasn't until her phone started buzzing with an incoming text that she realized it was 3 am.

"Sorry, babe. Meet up 2 morrow?" Grant's text said.

Grace texted back, "Sure, Kiss." She dragged herself from the window seat in her room and plopped fully clothed on the top of her bed. Grace's bedroom looked like a million other teenagers' rooms across America. Her single bed had a trundle that she occasionally pulled out for sleepovers or when she had mountains of homework she wanted to spread out. By day, it looked like a little couch/daybed. She had a Vera Bradley comforter and pillow shams. Currently, the comforter was thrown back and two of the pillows were on the floor. Her water bottle was sitting precariously close to the edge of her nightstand that was covered with copies of *Teen Vogue, Elle* and

Prom. Grace figured it was never too early to start looking for a prom dress.

Her walls featured reprints of famous paintings such as Van Gogh's *Starry Night* and Renoir's *Ballet Dancers*. She also had posters of Panic! At the Disco and *Hamilton*. There were concert ticket stubs, pictures of family, friends, and places around New York City as well as schedules framed her huge mirror. While her room was usually neat and tidy, there was still the nail polish stain on the carpet near the end of her bed when she was hastily painting her nails Poison Green for a Halloween party and a fading tea stain where she stumbled into her room while studying for finals last year.

As she drifted off to sleep, the list of things she needed to do started scrolling through her mind and increasing exponentially as one item triggered another. She had the TimeTune app on her phone that kept her lists and obligations organized. Tomorrow or actually today was going to be especially busy. She had a before-school meeting with the student council she had to attend. This was her senior year and they were finalizing plans for homecoming. She didn't want to miss the opportunity to voice her opinion. She hoped to be voted onto the homecoming court, but being crowned queen seemed elusive. Besides Brandy Becker was a shoo-in as queen. She came from a long line of homecoming royalty dating back to her great grandmother. She wondered if Arden or Melody had ever been voted homecoming queen or even on the court? She would have to ask Arden in the morning.

After the meeting, she had the first of four periods of high school classes: AP English; Chemistry 2; Government and American Politics, Anatomy and Physiology and rounding out the morning Yearbook. She would be done by noon and that gave her a couple of hours to grab lunch, check in with her mom at the coffee shop and check on the Brady dogs. Julia and Matt were going out of town again this weekend. Once the kids were in bed it would be time to investigate the medicine cabinet again. She hoped to get Hazel talking about her parents to see if she would say anything that would help Grace figure out what was going on.

Aside from schoolwork, Grace was the epitome of the overachieving high school senior. Over the summer she had applied to a variety of colleges and was exploring her options. She and Arden had taken a couple of days last summer to visit some nearby colleges, but Arden had concluded that Camden Falls was the best choice for her. Grace was not so sure. She realized that part of Arden's decision lay in the fact that she didn't want Grace to stray too far from her home. Grace couldn't deny that Camden Falls University had an excellent Vet Tech program and she would be able to get her degree early and then start applying to Veterinary Medicine programs. Lately, however, she was wondering if she really wanted to pursue a veterinarian degree. Law enforcement and investigation was starting to interest her as well.

To help out Melody, Grace volunteered at the local soup kitchen and on Thanksgiving every year, Arden and Grace volunteered at Peace Lutheran's Thanks and Giving Dinner, feeding the homeless and delivering meals to shut-ins. She was a member of the girls' tennis team, women's chorus and had been inducted into the National Honor Society her junior year.

Besides working at the coffee shop, she also dog/house sat for four families in the area. Two were college professors who used her when they went on vacation, which usually coincided with her school vacations. One family consisted of an orthopedic surgeon and his wife who scheduled three-week trips to exotic locals for conventions. Their five Labradoodles ranging from youngest to oldest kept Grace on her toes.

However, her last client employed her steadily to let the dogs out on her lunch hour and also feed and walk them occasionally when their schedules overlapped. The Brady's were a busy family with a very irregular schedule. They had a standing arrangement with Grace to feed and check on Trixie and Nancy every day between noon and one. She also helped out when one or both Bradys were detained at work. She would walk Hazel and Neil home from school, fix them a snack and help them get started on their homework. The Brady's paid her handsomely, gave her a huge Christmas bonus and invited her and Arden to their annual Halloween and Christmas parties.

Later after the noontime check on the dogs, she would head over to campus for her College Credit Plus classes of World Religions and Abnormal Psychology. She usually spent an hour or two on weeknights and more time on the weekends working at the coffee shop and hanging out with Grant. Grace loved her life. She hated having idle time. Her relaxation included running, to stay in shape for tennis and playing with the dogs she sat for, reading and the occasional Netflix binge with Grant.

She still had a hard time believing Grant was her boyfriend. Even though he hadn't put any pressure on her, Grace felt she was ready to take the next step with Grant. They had been talking about it more and Grace was ready. The sorority girls talked about more than legacies and study tables during the small group discussions in class. Almost all of them who had steady boyfriends were sexually active. And to be honest, when Grace and Grant had met up at their secret hideout, things were progressing to the next level. Both had backed off and agreed that it was a little early. But Grace knew that Grant wouldn't wait forever. And honestly, Grace didn't want to either. She was falling in love with him. He was kind, funny, smart, ambitious and drop-dead hot.

So she had become proactive, she had gone to the university health center and met with the gynecologist on staff. She had ordered the required exams for Grace and had issued her a prescription for birth control pills. She had been taking them for a couple of weeks now with no adverse side effects.

She knew she should have talked it over with her Arden, but it just felt too new and fragile. Besides Grace was 18 and could make these life decisions for herself now. At first, she hadn't been sure how far this was going to go with Grant. But, whom was she kidding? She had already made up her mind when she sought out the pills. Rolling over on her side and positioning the pillow into a more comfortable place the drowsiness was winning the battle and as Grace drifted off to sleep her thoughts were filled with Grant.

Chapter 31: September 17

Arden and Grace had rescheduled their dinner for the following night. The Golden Palace had been a favorite place for Arden and Grace since moving to Camden Falls. While popular with the college crowd, they rarely ate at the restaurant. Their carryout and delivery business made up the majority of their profit. Grace and Arden would do carry-out occasionally but tonight Arden felt as if the atmosphere of the restaurant, as well as the memories they had shared there, would have a calming effect on the lingering tension in their relationship.

Arden arrived first and Suzy, the waitress who had served them for years, took Arden to their favorite booth. The red leather crackled as Arden slid into the seat. Without asking Suzy brought Arden a pot of tea, a cup and the menu. Arden gave her a grateful smile and said thank you.

The restaurant had not changed in all the years they had been coming here to eat. The red velvet wallpaper with golden dragons and pagodas looked as fresh as it had the day they had first walked in. The lights were kept low and the Chinese Imperial music played softly in the background.

Arden took a sip of tea and let it and the calming music release the tension that she didn't realize she had been holding in. She checked her phone again to see what time it was and to see if there had been a text from Grace. To be fair, Grace wasn't late yet but Arden hoped she would get there soon. The quicker they could clear up the tension, the quicker the two of them could get back to normal.

While she waited, she decided to check her emails. Most were either order confirmations or shipping details for the shop. A couple were from tech companies seeing if she was interested in opening an online store. Arden didn't know if she was quite ready for that or if it was even a good fit for the BrewHouse. She liked to think that coming to the BrewHouse wasn't just for legal stimulants but also for the experience. It was a place to meet up with old friends and new ones. She had several regular study groups who debated and quizzed each other on everything from Russian politics to calculus equations. Subgroups of the Camden Falls Chamber of Commerce came in and while sampling the pastries and coffee, determined the next steps for the community.

Aside from the campus and special groups traffic, a couple of book clubs and a knitting club came in and took advantage of the cozy, welcoming atmosphere. One aspect of technology she had been considering was developing an app that would keep track of a rewards system and order ahead online. Travis, one of the IT guys for the campus, along with one of Jack's students said they would be glad to work with her on it. The only payment would be free coffee for life. Arden had laughed and told them she would consider it.

She went back to the main screen of her phone and checked the time again. She let out a sigh, looked up and saw Grace entering the restaurant. Greeting and smiling at the staff who had known her since she was a toddler putting Lo Mein noodles on her head, to the beautiful, grown woman she had become made Arden realize just how fast time has gone by. These thoughts brought tears to Arden's eyes. *Ben and Jess would be so proud. I just hope we can get back to where we belong.*

Grace made her way to the table. She placed her backpack against the foot of the booth and hung her yellow rain slicker on the hook next to the booth. Arden always thought it made her look like the Morton Salt Girl.

"Hey," Grace said as she slid into the booth. "Have you ordered yet?" Grace, too, was trying to keep the mood light ignoring the tension in the air between her and the only mother she had ever known.

Taking Care of Grace

"No," Arden smiled brightly, "I was waiting for you."

Before they had a chance to say more, Suzy returned with a pot of tea and a menu for Grace. Both Arden and Grace smiled at Suzy as she left and then both began studying their menus as if there would be a final exam later. This was merely to put off the impending conversation. Neither one of them ever deviated from their regular order.

Suzy returned to take their orders, Chicken and Broccoli with steamed rice for Arden and Happy Family for Grace. Once the menus were removed and teapots refilled there was nothing to distract them from the issues before them.

Arden looked up to see Grace looking at her. "Look-" she began.

As Grace said, "I-" and then "You first."

"Okay," said Arden, smoothing out the invisible wrinkles on the paper placemat before her. She took a deep breath and said, "Look, I know you are a senior and think you have the world all figured out."

Grace started to interrupt but Arden put a hand up to stop her. "Please let me say this. I remember 18. I thought the same thing. I knew exactly what I wanted to do. I couldn't wait to get out of Bucyrus, get out of Ohio and show the world that I was going places. And then life happens. You have to start being an adult. I know I've said it before, but I'm going to say it again. I don't want you to look back 10, 20 years from now and think 'I really missed out on some fun in high school.'"

Grace rolled her eyes,

Arden was taken aback, "What's with the eye-rolling? What's gotten into you? The snarky teenager is out of character for you."

Grace let out a sigh that could only come from a world-weary eighteen-year-old.

"Mom," Grace paused trying to soften what she was about to say, knowing that no matter how she said it, it was going to hurt. "I know you mean well, and usually you listen to what I have to say, but this time you seem focused only on what you want for me. What about what I want?"

Arden folded her hands because she didn't know what else to do. She said quietly, "Okay, I'm listening. No judgment. Tell me what you want."

Grace looked at Arden ensuring that she was listening and started, "I know you think I'm not spending enough time at the high school and too much time on campus and with Grant. You are afraid I am missing out on quintessential high school opportunities." Grace paused, looking for a reaction from Arden.

Arden nodded and said, "True."

"However," Grace continued. "I spend over half of my day at the high school. I go in early for student council meetings and I'm one of the top photographers for the yearbook. I go to every pep rally, football game and musical for pictures. I'm on the tennis team and I'm a TA for Mr. Lockhart."

Arden couldn't help but concede this point but said, "I still don't understand why you spend so much time on campus since the majority of your classes are at the high school and some college classes are online. You'll have plenty of time next year to hang out on campus."

Yikes, thought Grace, *One thing at a time.* Grace clarified, "The reason that several of my friends and I spend so much time on campus is because we can get a lot more studying done that way."

Now it was Arden's turn to be sarcastic and she hated hearing herself but plunged ahead anyway. "Really? What are you studying? The effects of Frisbee on the shirtless male population?"

Grace fired back, "That's just one of my studies!" Grace shook her head and whispered, "You are never going to listen to me."

Arden apologized, "I'm sorry. That was a cheap shot. I'm frustrated and scared and trying to understand why you and your friends find it easier to study on campus."

Grace paused before answering, ensuring Arden's question was sincere. "Because at King Library on campus, they have several quiet rooms manned by what I assume are former prison guards who shush you if you breathe too loudly."

Arden was surprised by this answer and asked, "What's wrong with the high school library?"

Grace explained, "They have turned it into a classroom/media center. Students and teachers are constantly going in and out. Lots of conversation. It's not very quiet. Just when I get in the study mode, someone interrupts and the next thing I know I haven't gotten anything done. At the King Library, I can hole up in a study carrel and no one bothers me."

Again, Arden couldn't argue and to be fair, Grace's grades had been high and steady. Arden was pretty sure that scholarships were in Grace's future. Grace had given her a justified reason for using the campus library, but the Grant situation needed to be addressed. Taking a deep breath, Arden said, "I'm concerned about how much time you are spending with Grant."

"Why is this an issue now? We have been seeing each other since the beginning of summer."

"I know that, but he's 21."

"No, he's not. Not until February. Besides, I thought you liked Grant." Grace was trying to keep calm, but her tension was simmering to the surface again.

"I do, but I think he is too old for you. He's going to want to do more things, dangerous things that his frat brothers put him up to. He'll be able to buy alcohol legally from what Roxie told me the other morning, available alcohol for the Kappa Alpha Epsilons has not been a problem."

Grace was livid, "Unbelievable, you take the word of a gossipy old professor over mine?"

"Roxie is neither old, or gossipy and she has been a wonderful role model for you. The point is, the Kappas have an awful reputation and Grant is 21."

"Ugh," Grace was beyond frustrated. "What are we really talking about here? What are you really afraid of, Mom?"

Arden hated this, they had always been able to talk and they rarely fought. Not like this. Arden felt like she was racing down a roller coaster track with no stop in sight. She chose to not answer Grace's question directly, "I'm not going to forbid you to see him, but I want to be more in the loop. I want him at our house more and not meeting him God knows where." She paused to let that sink in and then plowed on, "And this is non-negotiable, no going to the frat house."

"What? You have got to be kidding me!"

"I assure you I'm not. I went to college, too. A lot has changed but the concept of the frat house has not."

"You can't control me! I'm 18!"

"Keep your voice down," Arden hissed. "As long as you live under my roof, you will follow my rules," Arden was shocked. *Where did that come from? When did I start channeling my dad?*

"There is no talking to you." Grace started to gather her things.

Arden didn't want the conversation to end this way. "Wait, hear me out."

Grace considered it. She too felt as if the conversation had taken on a life of its own and she wanted them to get to some sort of solid ground. She sat back down.

"I like Grant. Don't get me wrong. And I realize you are 18, but I don't want you to think that I'm taking these facts for granted. I also want the absolute best for you. I don't want you to get stuck in a relationship or situation where you can't pursue what you want to pursue. I made the mistake of dating the same guy all through college and then ended up marrying him because I thought that was what was supposed to happen. It was awful. Getting a divorce was almost as painful as losing your dad and mom. I don't want you making the same mistakes that I did."

"Who said anything about marriage? I have plans, Mom, that may or may not include Grant."

Arden was a little relieved. "I'm glad to hear it. I still want to see Grant at our house more."

Grace relaxed a little too. "I can live with that."

"But I still maintain, the frat house is off."

"Why? That doesn't make any sense. The frat has been improving its rep and I'm never there when a party is going on."

"I would hope not. Your presence during a party could get them brought up before the PanHellenic board. Besides, why do you want to hang out there? If memory serves, frat houses are beyond disgusting."

Grace could feel her anger rising. "We are never anywhere but Grant's room and then it's never for very long."

"Alone in his room at the frat house. That makes me feel so much better." Arden was beginning to feel the tension again.

"I'm done. I can't get you to see this my way." Grace started gathering her stuff and got up and put on her slicker.

"Wait, where are you going? We haven't eaten yet."

"Oh, I don't know. Maybe I'll see if Grant can score us some booze while we hang out at the frat house."

"Grace! Grace!" Arden tried to get her attention without raising her voice but Grace was too focused on getting out of the restaurant as quickly as possible.

Suzy's look of concern as she brought their meals to the table and saw Grace headed out the door brought tears to Arden's eyes.

"Um, could I have these to go, please? Thank you."

Suzy took the meals back to the kitchen to place them in carryout containers. She met Arden at the cash register where Arden paid and tipped Suzy handsomely. As she took the tip, Suzy laid her hand over Arden's. "It'll be okay. The teenager comes out in all of them once in a while. You two will figure it out."

Arden smiled and squeezed her hand. "Thanks, Suzy. I hope we weather this storm soon."

Arden gathered up her order, coat, purse, and umbrella and headed through the driving rain to her car.

Chapter 32: CFPD- September 18

Jason Stage had worked at the police station almost as long as Matt. He, Matt and Jack had all gone to school together and Jason had followed them to the police academy. Jason didn't have any aspirations of becoming police chief or even making detective. He had enjoyed being a beat cop from the very beginning. He had his regular neighborhoods that he kept a check on and had more than once saved a kid from going to juvy.

Tonight, however, he was working the tip line. Donavan had called off sick and they were running short-handed. Jason didn't mind working the tip line and once in a while, a good lead came through. Most of the time, however, it was drunk college students pulling a fraternity prank or the regulars calling in complaining about their neighbors.

It had been a slow evening tip wise, so he decided to check the email inbox to see if anything interesting turned up there. He was scrolling through and saw an email with the subject line Trey Brady. It was from the Las Vegas PD. Jason, as well as everyone on the force knew that Matt kept an eye out for anything regarding the whereabouts of his brother. It was also common knowledge that Trey had a very different relationship with law enforcement than his brother did. Jason scanned the text of the email and saw that Trey had turned up in Vegas and was caught on a security camera at one of the high-end casinos. Since he wasn't causing any problems, the PD let it slide. They sent a video of what they caught. It was clearly a courtesy to Matt.

Jason scrolled down to the attached video and clicked on it. Sure enough, there was Trey looking like a high-end poker player hitting on a petite redhead at the bar. *Some things never change,* thought Jason, *those Brady guys always had luck with the ladies*. Jason couldn't hear what was being said and it really didn't matter. It was obvious from the body language that the couple was into each other. It wasn't until the redhead turned around and faced the camera that the cup of bad station coffee Jason was holding slipped out of his hand and spilled all over the floor. *Unbelievable!*

*****

Sheila removed her reading glasses and rubbed her eyes. Paperwork was one part of the job she hated. With governmental changes and new regulations coming from the higher-ups almost daily, the paper trail was endless.

She checked her phone for the time and realized she had been sitting in front of the computer for two hours. She got up to stretch. *It is time for me to head home. I hope Clyde remembered to get the casserole out of the freezer*. Sheila smiled, *I am so lucky to have the family I do. I would be lost without them.*

As Sheila stood up and grabbed her jacket, Jason came careening toward her. Sheila held up a hand and said, "Oh, no, Jason, I am done for the day. No new cases tonight." She looked up and realized that something was seriously bothering the normally calm cop. "What is it, Jason?"

"Sheila, I think you need to come see this immediately!"

*****

"Wow, I don't believe this. Where did you get this footage?"

"I was checking emails and you know how the Chief keeps tabs on Trey. Las Vegas sent us this out of courtesy to Matt." Jason paused and then said, "Look, it doesn't surprise me to see Trey on that video. He couldn't stay out of trouble even if he wanted to but the woman he is with doesn't make any sense."

"Agreed," Sheila said. She had seen a lot of things while being a cop and very few things surprised her anymore. But the human condition was anything but predictable. "But we can't jump to conclusions. This could be a very innocent situation."

"With Trey involved? I doubt it. And what's with the hair?"

Sheila dismissed the comment, "Women and men change their hair color all the time. We need more information." She had a million different scenarios playing through her head. Very few of them had a good outcome.

Jason drew her out of her thoughts, "What should we do with this?"

Sheila looked Jason in the eye and said, "The chief will have to know. This might be a situation that he is aware of and we are blowing it out of proportion. Let me do a little investigating on my own before we tell the chief."

Jason nodded, relieved that confronting the chief would not be immediate. "Sounds good. I will let you know if anything else comes through."

Sheila gave a faint smile and nodded, "Thanks, Jason. I think our best course of action is not to mention this to anyone in the department right now."

Jason agreed, "Understood." He walked back to the counter as Sheila struggled with this new information.

Chapter 33: September 17

What a great weekend and I made some fabulous contacts, Julia thought to herself. She had been able to talk Matt into meeting with his law enforcement buddies while she "went to the specialists." Julia's idea of specialists was the blackjack tables at the nearby reservation casino. Julia knew that if she told Matt that she had to meet with the doctor on her own to review her medical records, he would be willing to stop by the local city police department and pick their brains about new law enforcement tactics and she knew they would have him occupied for hours. She knew he cared about her "illness", sometimes almost too much. But she was aware that he would get antsy listening to her medical litany again, so she hadn't even bothered to line up one of her contacts to play the doctor.

Before leaving on this trip Matt had insisted on going with her to give moral support. That always made things more complicated. First, she had gone to the local library, to run off her medical records and the "diagnosis by the oncologist" to show Matt and her "doctors back home." The only non-fiction in this story was Matt. There were no specialists in this town or any other of the places she took Matt to. But there were plenty of casinos and floating poker games to be found.

And there was Trey. They had been hooking up at the casinos and poker games whenever possible. It hadn't always been easy. It wasn't until Matt showed her a photo album that his mom had sent for Hazel to use in a family tree school project that she realized why Trey had looked so familiar to her. This was the wayward brother Matt occasionally talked about.

Trey had a hard time keeping himself out of jail. But after this weekend, his boozy aggression had worked on her last nerve. He was getting careless and drawing unwanted attention to them. It was time to cut him loose. She had called in an anonymous tip regarding Trey violating parole. He would be arrested tomorrow and be none the wiser that she was the one who turned him in.

Besides, she had scored a high roller. Antonio Cervantes was her ticket out. He happened to be at the last two floating high stakes poker games she had played in. They had exchanged some pleasantries but the first time, Trey had gotten in the way. Antonio was an up and coming high roller that was inserting himself seamlessly into this world. Word on the street was that he had hit it rich and bankrupted himself a number of times, but now seemed to have gotten his act together. He owned casinos all over the U.S. and Canada and was starting to acquire casinos worldwide.

Julia had been daydreaming about Antonio. She could see herself jet setting all over the world on private planes and yachts, sipping champagne and eating gourmet meals. As she looked in the mirror in the master bath she thought, *You've come a long way from foster care.*

She was tired of life as a cop's wife. She was constantly putting up a front. If she were completely honest, being with Matt in the beginning was fun. Then he got serious and at that point she did want to go straight. No more hustling, no more con jobs. She had been one of the best of the grifters. She had conned two families out of their life savings. That had gotten her through two hedonistic months in Vegas. But once the money was gone, so were the men, friends, hotel suites and fairytale life. But it had gotten old and she wanted stability. So she put herself through nursing school and went legit. The only truths about her past that Matt knew was that she had been in foster care and that she had put herself through nursing school. The cancer, her cons, the rest of it had all been a lie.

She thought she had everything figured out until Matt wanted to have kids. She couldn't tell Matt the real reason she couldn't have kids, so she made up the lie about the cancer to explain the hysterectomy and in a flash of insight suggested they adopt foster kids. She thought it was a long shot at best. Who would let a cop and a nurse adopt kids? The crazy hours, the imminent danger made them seem like a long shot. She figured they were safe. But Matt wanted to please her so he pulled some strings and before she knew it they were an instant family.

Taking Care of Grace

Julia was starting to get restless again. She had put down really solid roots this time, but she had gotten herself out of worse spots. Matt had called to check in and delivered the news that Trey was back in jail for violating his parole. Julia had made the appropriate sympathetic noises and inwardly breathed a sigh of relief. There was no indication of her involvement. And bonus, Matt had to work late. Once the kids were in bed, she could play the online slots.

Now while the kids were at school, she was going to transfer her winnings from the liner of her suitcases and put it in her secret cubby. She went into the master bath to open up the medicine cabinet and unlatch the cubby. As soon as she opened the medicine cabinet she knew someone had been in it. She always took a picture of the contents before leaving to make sure that no had messed with it. She didn't need her snapshot to tell her that everything was out of place or slightly out of place. *Great! All these years and no one has ever bothered my space. Now someone has been snooping around*. And in going through the medicine cabinet, the intruder had moved the bottle of Scope. *Okay, calm down. It doesn't mean anything. Check the latch.*

Sure enough, the latch had been moved. She could tell because she always latched it completely and it was currently lifted a little above the tiny bar that stuck out.. *Shit! Someone has found the cubby and had looked in it.* It was at that point that the burner phone chirped behind the phony shelving. Ice went through her veins as she realized that she had forgotten to silence it after talking to Antonio. Julia lifted a shaky hand to the latch and opened the cubby. Yep, someone had been in this cabinet for sure. The phone had been moved, the money, while still in neat piles was no longer in the same place she had put it. The prescription pads were out of order as well as her faked medical records. She was going to have to be sly to figure out who was behind it.

She thought about Neil and Hazel. They had been told on many occasions that they were not to be in mommy and daddy's room without permission. For the most part, they listened. Besides, Hazel would feel too guilty for breaking the rules and would have texted her admitting the crime. Matt was not under suspicion. For one thing, he had left for the trip before she did and hadn't been back to the house since they had arrived in Camden Falls. Even though he obviously used the master bath, he rarely got into the medicine cabinet. Most of the items in the cabinet were things that Julia used. He had had the Uber driver drop him at the station and then take Julia home. Besides if it had been Matt he would have gone into cop mode and questioned her.

It was a pretty safe bet that no one broke in with Grace here all weekend and the kids in and out. Plus there was the state of the art security system. She had a sneaking suspicion that Grace had been in the bathroom and let curiosity get the best of her.

Julia closed the cabinet and slowly turned to leave. She would question the kids and then casually ask Grace. Once she had her answers, action would be taken.

Chapter 34 - September 17

Arden had been trying to track down Grace since noon and it was now nine o'clock at night. The panic was creeping in. She knew that Grace had a crazy schedule and with it being the beginning of the school year, neither one of them had settled into a routine yet. She kept going over the same information and kept coming up with the same results. Grace wasn't here and she wasn't answering calls or texts.

Arden had checked her phone for reminders, her planner for notes and the calendar they had on the refrigerator so that they didn't have situations like the nightmare she was living now. She had called a couple of Grace's friends but none of them had seen her since classes ended for the day. When her cell phone rang she jumped practically dropping it. She hit the accept button without looking at the caller ID and said, "Grace?"

"No, it's Melody. You still haven't heard from Grace?"

"No," Arden said, her voice starting to get shaky. "I don't know what to do."

"Okay, I know you have contacted everyone you know and that she knows. You've tried calling and texting her?"

"Yes, and still no response. I texted Roxie, too to see if Grace had shown up at her office. She hasn't seen her since earlier this week at the BrewHouse. This isn't like Grace. We are in constant contact with one another. Both of us check in with one another especially if there is a change in plans."

"I hate to ask this, honey, but have you contacted the police?"

"Not yet, but I'm starting to think I don't have a choice."

"I have to agree." Melody continued, "listen, you call the police and I will send out a text to my congregation that we need help finding Grace."

"Thank you. I'll make the call and let you know what is decided."

*****

"Okay folks, we are going to spread out and search for Grace. Have on your walking shoes. Most places that we will be going entail a lot of walking. An officer will be assigned to each group of searchers. We will keep in touch through cell phones. Peace Lutheran Church is the headquarters. The BrewHouse, here, will be our checkpoint. Thank you for your help," Officer Evan Green nodded to the crowd and went to lead his group.

Melody was standing next to Arden. She put an arm around her and said, "How you doin', Artie?" She hadn't called Arden that in a very long time.

Arden shook her head trying to keep the tears from starting. "I don't know."

"Listen," Melody said, "We have most of the town out looking for Grace. We'll find her and everything will be okay."

"I sure hope so. I-"

"Arden! Is there any news?" Grant came towards her, tears in his eyes.

"Oh, Grant, no news yet, "Arden said, giving him a hug.

"I just don't know where she could be," Grant said shaking his head.

Jack worked his way through the crowd and stood next to Grant. "Hello, we are here to help. Grant and I, along with a few guys from the frat house are here to join the search."

"Thank you so much," Arden said," I feel I should be out there looking, too."

Melody and Jack exchanged a look. Jack gave a slight nod and took Arden by the arm and said, "Could we talk over here just a minute? Grant, get your fraternity brothers together and check with Officer Green as to where he wants us to search."

Grant nodded and headed toward the group of young men standing near the baked goods counter.

Jack turned to Arden and said to her quietly, "Listen, I understand your first instinct is to go out and lead the search. I think it would be better for you to stay here. Grace could show up any minute and you are going to be the first person she'll want to see."

Arden nodded, "You have seen many of these cases. What are the odds that Grace is okay and not-" Arden didn't trust her voice to complete her thought.

"Every case is different-"

"Jack, don't sugarcoat this for me. I would much rather know what I'm facing than be wandering through this limbo."

Jack paused, "Honestly, I don't know enough about this situation to give you odds about anything. Tell you what, let me check with some of my contacts at the station and maybe I can give you a more educated guess."

Arden took Jack's hand, "Thank you. I'm sorry I put you on the spot."

"You didn't. You are a mom worried sick about her kid. It's an impossible situation."

"I would appreciate anything you could find out for me."

"I'll be back soon and let you know what I find out." Jack touched her arm and strode out the door calling Matt on his cell as he headed to the police station.

*****

"Hey, Jack, come on in. Have a seat. You want some coffee?" Matt asked casually.

"No thanks. I just stopped by to see what you know about the search for Grace."

"Crazy, huh? I don't have a lot of intel yet. The search parties have been out for about two hours. I will be going to the BrewHouse to check on things here shortly."

Jack was a little taken aback. *Why wasn't he over there already? After all, Grace was their house sitter, baby sitter and pet sitter. Shouldn't he be more concerned?* He asked carefully, "Everything okay? How is Julia's new treatment going?"

"Ah, so far so good. She doesn't seem to be having too many side effects."

"Good. That's good." Jack saw this as his cue to leave. "I guess I'll see you at the BrewHouse. Let me know if there is any way I can help. I know you were pretty upset the other day."

"I was and I appreciate you listening to me. I went home, Julia and I talked and we are working it out."

"Good. I hope you are reconsidering liquidating your retirement accounts."

"We aren't going to go down that road. We are checking out other sources, loans, that kind of thing."

"Glad to hear it." Jack said and thought to himself, e*specially since we have these fundraisers planned*. Aloud, he said to Matt, "I'll see you at the BrewHouse."

Matt came around the desk and gave Jack a hug. "Thank you so much, my friend. I don't know what my family and I would do without you. Now, I will see you soon, I am going to check a couple of my sources here at the station regarding Grace and then I'll be out to search."

"Say hi to Julia and the kids for me."

"Will do."

Jack waved and started making his way back to the BrewHouse. He felt a little bit better about Matt's reaction. No doubt he has a lot on his mind about Julia's illness and Grace's disappearance. As he walked, he started thinking about his meeting with Matt. At first, it had seemed that something was off. He didn't expect Matt to be in full-blown panic mode. That was never a good approach in law enforcement, or anything else for that matter. But this was different. Maybe he was overreacting. He pulled out his phone and sent a quick text to Grant.

Jack: Where r u?

Grant: Heading towards the main gate of campus.

Jack: See u there.

He headed to the campus main gate. He knew that Grant and his friends were with Officer Sheila Hastings. If anyone could give him some insight into this situation it was her.

*****

Jack saw the group he was looking for heading towards the main gate of the college. He caught up to them and said, "Hi, Sheila, how are things going?"

"Hey, Jack, good to see you. I wish I had better news, but we have nothing yet."

"That's what I was afraid of." Jack looked around to make sure they were out of earshot. "Can we talk a minute?"

"Sure, Jack. I need to talk to you as well. Let me get this group started and I'll walk back to the BrewHouse with you."

"No problem."

Sheila made her way back to the group that Roxie was leading. She gave them a list of the areas they needed to search and her cell number for them to check in with her every half hour or sooner if they found anything. It didn't matter how immaterial it might seem to the volunteers. She made her way back to Jack and they started walking toward the BrewHouse.

Jack and Sheila had become reacquainted when Jack moved back to Camden Falls. She had picked his brain on more than one occasion when she was stuck on a case. He had done the same with her when a felon they were looking for was headed towards Ohio or had connections there. She, Jack, Matt and eventually Angela Rossi had all gone through the police academy together. While Jack had gone on to work in Chicago, Sheila and Matt had stayed in Camden Falls working their way up the chain of command. They had built up both a professional and personal relationship over the years.

Jack had a great deal of respect for Sheila. She was able to keep a family together in spite of the high-pressure career she had chosen. Clyde, her husband, had been a couple of years ahead of them in school. She and Clyde met after high school. Shortly after they met, they got married and started a family. They had the same type of marriage he and Edie had had. At least, that was what he had observed from the outside looking in.

Sheila hesitated and then asked the question that had been on both her mind and Jack's, "Do you think everything is okay with Matt and Julia? I know you are good friends with them, but I've been wondering if the experimental trial she's in is helping."

Jack shook his head, "I don't know. I know that before the treatment they had hit a rough patch. I just talked to Matt at the station about how Julia is doing and it's part of the reason I came looking for you. He says that Julia has had very few side effects and they are hoping that the upcoming tests will show either an improvement or at least a stabilization of her condition." Jack was still confused by Matt's behavior, "I've gotta tell you, his reaction to Grace's disappearance is off. I can only chalk it up to worrying about Julia's health concerns and Grace's whereabouts."

Sheila nodded with a look of relief, "I'm glad to hear you say that. I have been thinking the same thing. You know him and Julia better than I do, but I figured he would be more worried and active in the search."

"Me, too. That's what's bugging me."

"Tell you what," Sheila said, "We are working out a timeline of Grace's whereabouts leading up to the disappearance. In an unrelated area, I also have some surveillance tape that might give us insight into Matt's recent behavior. I want your opinion. It's at the station. Maybe you'd like to come take a look? Fresh eyes and all that?"

"Sure, anything to help. I just don't want to step on any toes."

"You know you are welcome at the station." Sheila continued with updates about the investigation, where some of the holes in the timeline were and besides the search what other evidence they were looking at. "But there is one other thing I need to tell you." Sheila hesitated.

"Out with it, Hastings," Jack said, knowing that whatever Sheila was going to say he was not going to like. He hoped that he could lighten the mood, however, her words hit him like a punch in the gut, "We have to bring Grant in for questioning."

"What?! Why?!" Jack knew this would be coming but he still wasn't prepared for it.

"Come on, Jack. You know why. It's standard procedure."

Jack paused and realized this had to be treated like any other situation. The difference here was that he was personally involved. "Yeah, you're right, but it doesn't make it any easier. Especially when it is someone in your family."

Sheila looked around to make sure there wasn't anyone within earshot, "Look, I'm not supposed to tell anyone this, but I trust you. Grant is not a serious suspect. He's on our radar for two reasons. Number one, he's the boyfriend. The public, the head honchos at the station and the press would be all over us if we didn't question him."

Jack nodded. He knew Sheila was right.

"And second, the fraternity he is involved in does not have the greatest reputation."

Jack started to speak but Sheila held up her hand to stop him so that she could finish.

"However, we are glad that Grant is working his way up to the office of president of the fraternity. So far he has been a great influence on them and the guys seem to respect him. They listen to him which gives us hope that the frat is turning itself around. Their GPAs have improved and the reports of hazing have decreased considerably."

Jack looked relieved, "Who knew Little Stinky would turn into such a role model?"

Sheila laughed, "Little Stinky? I bet you are the only one who gets away with calling him that."

Jack nodded and smiled, "Pretty much. Look, I'd like to be in there when you question him."

Sheila shook her head, "You know you can't do that. I shouldn't have told you as much as I have." She could see the disappointment and frustration on his face. "I tell you what, I will text you when we are getting ready to bring him in. That way you can be there to pick him up afterwards. That's really all I can do."

Jack nodded. "Thank you, Sheila. I realize the huge risk you are taking."

Sheila puts a hand on Jack's arm. "I will keep you posted as best I can."

Jack thanked her and headed to the coffee shop to relay the information he had found out to Arden.

Chapter 35- September 17

Grant had never been so scared in his life. He had gotten in trouble before. Being the baby of the family, they had shrugged off his antics as being precocious and adorable. But those had been things like playing tricks on his older siblings and almost blowing up the small pool house when he found leftover firecrackers from their Fourth of July cookout and party.

He had never been in trouble with the law. He had come close a couple of times but no one knew about it. At least not in his family. Once, during high school, he and his buddies went out to Old Man Green's farm and had gone "cow tipping." Old Man Green, who was not an old man but he was the oldest Green left, had been lying in wait with his shotgun and a cell phone primed to dial 911. One shotgun blast in the air and a loud "I'm callin' the police!" sent the boys flying like shrapnel to their cars parked one road over and they were out of there by the time the cops arrived.

The other time was just last year. He and some of his fraternity brothers were in one of the bars uptown waiting to hear one of their brothers play in a band. Brandon, the current president of the fraternity had bought a pitcher of beer and Grant and the other three guys had been sharing it. As they were finishing up, Brandon and Gill still had beer in their glasses, but Grant's beer was gone so the waitress took the empty pitcher and Grant's glass and Brandon ordered another. While she was gone, a guy who looked like an extra from *Duck Dynasty* approached their table. *Here we go,* thought Grant, *a good ole boy hating on the fraternity.* Grant putting on his charming, winning smile as the bearded man pulled out a DEA agent ID and said, "Let me see your ID's." Brandon, Grant and the other guys handed them over. The agent looked them over, handed them back, thanked them and moved on.

"Whoa, that was a close one," Gill whispered.

"Yeah," Brandon said, "Good thing that waitress had taken away your glass or we would have been arrested for buying alcohol for a minor. The frat and this bar would have been in big trouble."

Grant was still shaking a little but kept his cool. He didn't want to put a damper on the party, so he switched to Pepsi for the rest of the night while his frat brothers continued to drink beer.

And now, here he sat in a police station and was possibly going to be charged with his girlfriend's disappearance. How did he get into this mess? He loved Grace. More than he let himself or anyone else know. He had been freaking out since Arden had called him asking if he knew where Grace was.

It wasn't like her to stay out of the communication loop, especially with Arden and Lindsay. The two of them might as well be surgically attached. Grant was a little jealous of how close their relationship was. Grant had never really felt that close to anyone. He loved his parents and they were incredibly good to him and he did feel like he could tell them anything and they would still love him. They might yell and scream if he really screwed up, but at the end of the day, they would be there to support him.

His siblings were so much older than he was but he felt closest to Jack. Even when Jack lived in Chicago, Jack made it a point of calling every week, just to talk to him. His sister had taken him on a couple of digs, but at the time he was too young to appreciate it. Cory had been cool and got his fraternity into a hockey game for drastically reduced ticket prices and they got to meet the team afterward. He was wishing that one of them, any one of them were with him right now.

They must jack up the air conditioning in here. It's freezing, Grant thought. He was trying to keep from shaking, his hoodie and jeans seemed to be seeping the cold in instead of keeping him warm. He couldn't be sure if it was the icy room or his nerves that were making him shake. It was probably a combination of both. He thought back to the pictures Grace had shown him on her phone. *Could they have anything to do with her disappearance?* It was unlikely. It was a common wall safe at the house of the chief of police. Families had those in their homes all across America.

He wondered if they were watching him through the two-way mirror to see if his body language gave anything away. He had to stop watching those crime shows with Grace. That thought made the tears flood his eyes and he tried hard not to let them overflow. He wanted so badly to find her. He felt he was wasting his time sitting in this police station when he could be out looking for her. They didn't know about the out-of-the-way places he and Grace would meet up.

He put his head in his hands as Officers Tristen Bennett and Carl Coleman entered the interrogation room. Grant looked up.

"Grant Phillips?" Bennett asked.

"Yes," Grant said, barely above a whisper.

Carl pulled his phone out of his coat pocket, "Mind if we record this conversation?"

"No," Grant said, "Are you going to read me my rights?"

"You're not under arrest, Grant. We are bringing in all of the people who are close to Grace and may be able to give us insight into where to look for her."

Grant nodded his head trying to keep from falling apart.

Carl began the questioning, "So Grant, how did you and Grace meet? She is a high school student after all and you are, what, a sophomore in college?"

Grant cleared his throat, "We met about four months ago in a calculus class at the university."

"Was this a summer class?"

"Yes, Grace is in a CCP program and was trying to get her math credit out of the way."

"What is CCP?"

"College Credit Plus. Kids can take college classes while they are in high school. The classes are free as long as you pass. I did it. By the time I graduated, I was able to register as a sophomore in college."

"So you met in the class. Were you partners for a project or something?"

"No," Grant shook his head and started rubbing his hands together. "Actually, Grace is a math wiz and I'm not. I failed my first quiz and the instructor suggested I get a tutor. I happened to see over her shoulder that she got an A. So I asked her if she would be willing to tutor me."

"So she was your calculus tutor. When did you two start dating?"

"I guess it was towards the end of June. We had been talking about how we both liked old movies and there was a revival of *Rear Window* at the State Theater so we went and then we started seeing each other."

"Hmm," Carl said as he took notes about what Grant was telling him. He usually played bad cop to Tristen's good cop but it just wasn't working for him. He and most of the other officers knew that Grant wasn't a serious suspect, but the protocol had to be followed and to be honest, stranger things had happened since he had been working in law enforcement.

Looking up at Grant, Carl said more than asked, "Everything been going okay between you and Grace. Any fights or disagreements?"

"No," Grant answered quickly, trying to make eye contact and failing. He did not want to tell them about what Grace had confided in him about the police chief and his wife before the party.

"Grant, I'm not making this up! I went looking for a mouse and instead, found a burner phone, tons of cash, prescription pads and files."

"Grace, sweetie, I believe you think that's what you saw and it sounds sketchy, but haven't you been binge-watching those crime documentaries on Netflix again?"

"Grant? Did you hear the question?"

Grant looked up, feeling scared that he had been thinking about the past and not paying attention to the present. He stammered, "Uh, sorry, What was the question?" but he still didn't hear. His mind went back to the last time he had seen Grace.

"Grant! Listen to me! This is serious! What do they need with that stuff? I know she's a nurse, but isn't it against the law to write your own prescriptions especially if you are not a doctor?"

"Probably not, but he is my brother's best friend. They have known each other practically since birth. And besides that, he is the chief of police! You know they have to be squeaky clean."

"The chief of police should be but that doesn't mean his wife has to be," Grace was trying to hold her ground in the argument. And then she brought up, "What about the wigs in her closet?"

"Grace, did you go snooping through their closets too?"

"After I found that stuff, I wondered what else she or they could be hiding. Turns out I think it's all on her. I snooped through her closet and found several wigs of various colors and lengths. And more duffle bags filled with cash. She also had some pretty slinky outfits stuffed down in one."

"Grace! You are unbelievable! What is Saint Arden going to say? Why didn't you stop instead of snooping more?"

"I don't know. It felt like I was in too deep and couldn't find a way out."

"Grace, you are going to be in so much trouble. You know they are going to find out and probably fire you for this."

"I don't care, something is up."

"What? What could possibly be up? So, you found this stuff, what do you think it means?"

Grace took a deep breath, "I think Julia is lying about her cancer."

Grant looked at her shocked and speechless.

"I don't mean that she doesn't have it at all, I just think maybe it is not as bad as they are letting on."

"You think Matt is involved, too?"

"He lives in the house with her doesn't he? He would have to know."

Grant started to pace back and forth, his mind was spinning. "I don't know about that. But if what you are saying is true, where is all the money coming from? What could she possibly be up to?"

Grace looked puzzled, "That's what I can't figure out. The only thing I keep asking myself is why does she have to go out of state all the time for these check-ups and trials? I mean, we have The James right here in Ohio. Aren't they supposed to be cutting edge? And why does she have all that money in wrappers from Vegas casinos?"

Grant didn't have an answer for that one. "So what do you think she is doing?"

Grace shook her head, "I don't know. Gambling?"

Grant came towards her, "That seems a little out there Grace. Look, no more snooping. You have been lucky twice not to get caught. You might not be so lucky next time."

"I promise I won't snoop anymore, but if she is not as sick as she says she is, then she is committing fraud and stealing from the citizens of Camden Falls."

"I can tell this isn't over for you. What have you got up your sleeve?" *Grant paused and then said,* "Wait, you aren't going to tell Lindsay are you?"

"No, but I think someone needs to know. I can't tell Arden, at least not yet. I think I might test the waters with Aunt Melody. Besides she has to keep whatever I tell her a secret."

"Good call," *and I'll try to see if Jack has any feeling about this. I won't come right out and ask him, but he and Arden have talked about doing some fundraising for the Bradys. I think if Jack had any idea, he wouldn't go through with it and he certainly wouldn't have involved the entire community."*

"Grant? Did you hear the question?" Tristen asked kindly. *What was up with this kid? He is keeping something from us.*

Grant looked up, feeling scared that he had been thinking about the past and not paying attention. "No sorry. What was the question?"

"Is there something you're not telling us?" Tristen asked.

"No, why?"

"Because you kinda zoned out on us twice. We thought maybe you were thinking about something you might have remembered that could help us."

"No, nothing like that."

Taking Care of Grace

"Then what were you thinking about?"

"The last time Grace and I were together."

"Good, that was what we wanted to ask you about. Can you give us a timeline of the last time you talked to Grace?"

"Sure," Grant cleared his throat again. "Uhm, I was at the frat house getting ready for the party. We had finally gotten through Hell Week and we had invited the new pledges to the party along with a couple of sororities."

"What do you mean, getting ready?"

"We were having a hog roast and a DJ was coming, so Tyler and Ethan had been working on the hog, making sure the coals were hot enough and that it was turning on the spit. I had been out to talk to the DJ and had shown him where to set up."

"Okay, so how does Grace come into play here?"

"After I finished with the DJ, I went up to my room to grab my keys to lock up so that no one would come into our room while the party was going on."

"Smart thinking. And then...?"

"I was getting ready to leave and Grace showed up."

"Had you invited her to the party?"

"No, she's only eighteen. We are trying to clean up our rep. No underage guest as the party. We hired a couple of bouncers to check IDs. We didn't want to get in trouble again, we finally have the Pan-Hellenic Council on our side."

"So why did she show up?"

Careful Grant, this could get you into trouble. "We hadn't seen each other in a couple of days. Just texts and stuff. I had been busy with the pledges and Hell Week."

"So, why did she stop by?" Carl asked.

"Like I said we hadn't seen each other in a couple of days and we wanted to, you know, talk, in person."

"Ah-huh, talk huh, don't you mean hook up? Isn't that what you kids call it? Did you sleep with her?"

"No! We just talked! I swear!" Grant shouted, on the verge of tears.

"Okay, you talked. What did you talk about?"

"We talked about our schedules. We talked about the fact that she had a couple of house sitting gigs coming up for the Bradys and I was telling her about a couple of pledges that had been giving us fits but we had to keep them because they are legacies."

"Did you argue? A couple of witnesses said they heard raised voices."

Think fast, Grant thought to himself. "We raised our voices because the music was starting to get loud out in the backyard and we couldn't hear each other very well."

"So you guys talked. For how long?" Tristen asked this time.

"Uh, about a half-hour."

"And did you make plans? Did you set up a time to meet after the party?"

Might as well tell the truth. "Yes."

Tristen could tell that the kid wanted to protect himself and Grace, but there would be plenty of time for that later. "Look, Grant, whatever you tell us can get us that much closer to finding her. That's what you want, isn't it?"

Grant looked from one cop to the other, let out a big sigh and said, "We have a place we like to meet near campus. Especially when it's warm like it has been."

"Where is it?"

"The Edison Park near the auditorium."

Tristen nodded to Carl, got out of his chair and headed out. "I'll let you know what I find out."

Carl turned back to Grant, "You did good, kid. This is the first real lead we've had. Is that the only place you guys would meet?"

Grant hesitated and then said, "She wouldn't be there."

"Why don't you let me be the judge of that."

Grant let out a sigh. "Sometimes I would sneak her up the backstairs at the frat house. Up to my room."

"Backstairs case?"

"Yes, it's an old servant staircase that leads from the upstairs down to the kitchen. The house was originally a private residence, then remodeled into apartments and finally we bought it and made it into our fraternity house."

Now it was Carl's turn to sigh, "You're right. We have searched the frat house from top to bottom. Where else?"

"Sometimes, when Arden was working late, she would sneak me into her room."

"Right, again. If she were in her room we wouldn't be having this conversation. Is that it?"

"No," Grant said, barely above a whisper.

"Jeez, kid, getting information out of you is like pulling teeth. Tell me everywhere you two hook up."

"We haven't been hooking up. We've been talking about it but Grace isn't ready."

"Okay, save the love story for the fraternity. Where else have the two of you been meeting?"

"At the Bradys," Grant hung his head.

"The Bradys? You mean the chief of police?"

"Yeah, Grace has been house/pet and babysitting for them for several years."

"Would she have any reason to be there now?"

"No, she just finished up a weekend there."

"Okay, one last question. Grace was last seen around noon. Can you verify your whereabouts between 11 am and 3 pm yesterday?"

"Yes, uh. I had class until noon. Business Law with Professor Jameson. I had a question about the upcoming exam so I followed her to her office and we met until about, I don't know, twelve-thirty."

Carl took notes while Grant talked. "Where did you go next?"

"After meeting with Jameson, I went to the student union to the food court and picked up a couple of burritos."

"Did you eat there or go somewhere else?"

"I ate them on the way back to the frat house. I needed to take over for Gill. He was manning the pledges' study tables. I was there until four o'clock and then a few of us hung out in the rec room playing pool."

"Okay, we'll check it out. In the meantime, here is my card if you remember anything."

"Are we done? Am I free to go?"

"Yes, but keep us in the loop."

"I will." Grant took the card and on rather shaky legs headed out of the station.

Chapter 36: Later That Afternoon

After the questioning at the police station, Grant had gone back to the frat house. He needed a shower and coffee to get the feel of the police station off of his skin. He wanted to go back to the BrewHouse and see how the search was going. He knew that Grace hadn't been found, otherwise, someone would have notified him.

When he got back to his room, Jack was waiting for him.

"Jack! Am I glad to see you! Any news?"

"Afraid not. How ya holdin' up? Bennett and Coleman weren't too hard on you were they?"

"You knew I got called to the station? Why didn't you come with me?"

"You know better than that, kid. Besides, you have been cleared."

Grant grew so pale, Jack thought the kid was going to pass out. "I was a suspect?"

"Relax, it's protocol. In missing persons' cases, the first suspects are the people closest to the victim, the parents and a significant other, if there is one in the picture."

Grant sighed and sank into the recliner near his desk, "I guess that makes sense. How has the search been going? I take it Grace wasn't at our secret meeting spot."

"No and I hate to tell you, it's not a secret any longer."

"Yeah, I know."

"Why have you two been sneaking around? Mom and Dad love Grace and I thought Arden was supporting this relationship. Whenever I'm at the BrewHouse and you two come up in conversation, she has nothing but positive things to say about you."

"I don't know. It just seemed fun. You're right, everyone supports us, but Arden keeps a pretty tight leash on Grace and sometimes she likes to sneak out and meet when we both know Arden would freak."

"Well, of course, she would. You realize that Arden has good reason to keep a close eye on Grace."

"I do and I know Grace does, too. But sometimes she wants to shake things up and rebel a little."

"I just hope that her rebellion hasn't gotten her into trouble."

"When Grace comes back, if she gets back-"

"She will get back and then I think she will be grounded until you're ready for the nursing home."

"Way to make me feel better. Actually, if it meant Grace walking through that door right now, I would be willing to take a grounded-for-life sentence."

"Grant, listen, we have most of the police force as well as friends and family are looking for Grace. We will find her. You can't give up hope. Unless-"

Grant let what Jack had just said to him sink in and then when the realization hit, he practically jumped out of the recliner, "What do you mean, unless? What are you implying?"

Jack sighed and rubbed his neck, "Look, you have already admitted to sneaking around. The next leap to make is that something happened and-"

"No, stop right there. Nothing happened. And now that I think about it, how did you know we had been sneaking around? Wait, did you listen in on my interrogation?"

"No," Jack said quietly, "I tried, but I knew that Sheila couldn't do that without losing her job, but she did fill me in. She watched your interrogation."

"Oh, great. What else did she tell you?"

"That you have been cleared, your story checks out and-"

"And, what?"

"And they think you know more than you are telling them. They think you might be trying to protect someone."

Grant's silence was sending up red flags to Jack. *Shit, what has this kid gotten himself into? I hope this wasn't some harebrained fraternity stunt gone wrong.* "Okay, out with it. Who are you protecting? Did Grace take off for some reason? Is it a bone-headed frat prank gone wrong?" Jack was starting to lose patience. "Grant! Who are you protecting? Answer me now!"

Grant got up slowly from the recliner and walked toward Jack and said quietly, "You."

Chapter 37- September 19

The rain had started up again and this was going to slow down the search. If he was honest with himself, Jack was starting to get a bad feeling about Grace. She had been missing going on three days. The longer she went missing the less likely they would find her alive. He hated cases like this one. They rarely ended happily.

As he entered the police station he realized one thing, that all police stations looked and smelled the same. The bustle, the cramped work quarters and the delightful aroma of stale coffee, disinfectant and sweat. It didn't matter if it was a small Ohio town or a big city. All police stations were the same. The first person he saw was Carl Coleman. "Jack Phillips! Doin' a little slummin'?"

"Nah, feels good to be back in the old house. How's Katie, she still putting up with you?"

"Yep. Going on twenty-five years. I am the luckiest guy in the world."

"That you are, my friend, that you are."

"Hey listen, is Grant okay? We had to be a little tough on him but he is really a good kid. Since he's close to the victim, we had to bring him in for questioning."

Jack appreciated what Carl was telling him. He knew they had to follow protocol. "I appreciate that. You know, he's pretty tough but

Grace's disappearance has really thrown him. I think he really cares about her."

Carl nodded his head in agreement. "I think you're right. We've watched that kid grow up around here. And you may not know but he was quite the ladies man in junior high and high school. Grace seems to have tamed him a little bit."

Jack agreed. "I think so too. Any updates?"

"No. We finally got Arden to go home and get some rest."

"How did that work out?"

"Melody took her home and offered to stay with her. Arden told her no. She took a half-hour nap, took a shower and was back to the BrewHouse within two hours."

Jack shook his head in amazement. "I'm surprised you got her out of there for two hours. How is she holding up?"

"She's one of the toughest people I've ever met. But you can imagine the extra baggage she carries regarding Grace. I don't know what she will do if this ends badly."

"Then we can't let it." Jack looked around the station, "Have you seen Hastings? I had a couple of questions for her."

"Yeah, she said you might be dropping by. Come on, I'll take you to her."

"Thanks." And the two walked back to the conference room where Sheila was working on the timeline.

*****

Sheila didn't hear Jack come into the conference room because she was so absorbed in the papers before her.

Jack gently said, "Wow, that's a lot of data."

Sheila jumped being jolted out of her isolation.

Jack laughed a little, "I'm so sorry. I didn't mean to startle you."

Sheila laughed it off as well, "It's okay, Phillips, but you know what they say about paybacks."

"Well, at least you still have your sense of humor."

"I have to or tears of exhaustion and frustration will take over."

Jack nodded, "Understood. What's the latest?"

"Not good, I'm afraid. I want you to take a look at this timeline I've been putting together on the whiteboard. I'll talk you through it and maybe it will shake something loose for me, too."

"Sounds good. Let's do it."

"Okay, here goes."

9:00am- Grace leaves her house at 1993 Willow Lane and proceeds to Camden Falls High School.

9:20- 11:45-Grace signs in at the main office in the high school and goes to her first class and fulfills the rest of her schedule.

Sheila pauses momentarily and says, "Here is one area that is pretty sketchy. She leaves the high school and there is an hour and a half that is unaccounted for. According to Arden, she didn't go home for lunch. We have checked with Lindsay, Grant and some of her other friends and no one had heard from her or seen her during that time. To be fair, on any other day, they may not hear from her during this time. We have to factor in travel time and sometimes she would go to the library on campus or the student union or the BrewHouse between the time she left school and her class on campus at three which is- let me see, here it is, Abnormal Psychology with Tom Pritchard."

"That makes sense. Have you checked with Pritchard?"

"Yes, unfortunately, it's a pretty big class and he doesn't take attendance. He recognized Grace from the picture we showed him. He said she tends to sit at the back of the class and attends regularly."

"How does he know that if he doesn't take attendance?"

"That's what Evan asked and he said that Grace is an excellent student. Sometimes she volunteers information and at other times when he calls on her she knows the answer. But the day in question, they had divided into groups to work so he wasn't sure if she was there or not."

"He didn't group them himself?"

Sheila shook her head, "He said, 'No, they are adults, they can group themselves. I leave it up to them.'"

Jack blew out a sigh, "Okay. How many students are in his class?"

"There are two sections of Abnormal Psych. Each section has around 50 students. We've got a couple of rookies tracking down the students to see if any of them remember seeing Grace or working with her that day in class."

"Good. Who knows, we might get lucky. So when does Grace show up on the timeline next?"

Sheila looked at her notes and then at the whiteboard, "The next time Grace shows up is walking across campus. More like running. She needed to drop off some papers at the administration offices and she ran into her best friend, Lindsay McManus. They took shelter from the rain in the Commons Archway. Lindsay said they talked about making plans to go shopping for Homecoming dresses. Grace had promised her that she would text her later on to finalize plans for the shopping trip. Grace never did. Lindsay texted several times, the last one being a little angry and even called but got no response from Grace."

"What's the time frame for the texts?"

"Let me see," Sheila said consulting more of her notes, "here's the transcript of the texts. They are time and date stamped:

Lindsay- (7:02 pm; 9/17) Hey, have you figured out when you want to go?

(7:15; 9/17) Hello? Anybody there? Text me.

(7:30; 9/17) Getting ready to leave 4 swim prac. I will be MIA. Text me soon. Worried :(

(10:02; 9/17) I give up. If you didn't want to go in the first place you should have told me.

"And that was the last text?" Jack asked.

"Yes."

"Have you questioned Lindsay?"

"Yes," Sheila gave an eye roll. "I thank God everyday I had boys instead of girls."

Jack laughed, "Were you able to get any useful information out of her?"

Sheila shook her head, "Not really. She was a sobbing mess for most of it. Felt guilty that she had sent the last mean text. Her parents were a trip, too. Mom made sure to tell us that she was extremely busy and didn't have time for this. Dad kept looking at his phone and asking repeatedly if they needed to get a lawyer. Stepmom was surprisingly normal. She confirmed what Lindsay told us and said she tried to reason with Lindsay as to why Grace wasn't answering her, but Lindsay had her mind made up by then. With her parents being so self-absorbed, I'm surprised Lindsay is as normal as she is. The only useful information we got from her was what I told you about their meeting on the Commons. So at least we know things were progressing normally through Grace's day until 2:52 pm."

"Why such an odd time?"

"That is the time stamp on the video footage from the ATM machine on State Street. In the background you can clearly see Grace getting into her car."

Jack stared pensively at the timeline and the papers spread out on the conference table. "Have there been any updates on the missing students from the other universities?"

Sheila nodded, "Yes, as a matter of fact, but no help for this case. I've been in contact with Angie Rossi with the CPD. She was working the case until the Feds took over the show. Turns out the guy they have in custody has quite a setup." Sheila moved her swivel chair to access the laptop on the conference table. "Here is the latest info we have on him. The man they have in custody is 38-year-old Kirk Mead and he has a Rap Sheet that speaks volumes. He has been in and out of jail since he was 14. His latest crime spree is abducting young men and women from various universities and feeding them into a sex trafficking situation. He is just the tip of the iceberg. Four of the five missing persons had contact with him. His cover is a food truck called "The Paddy Wagon." He travels from campus to campus and scopes out potential victims. He chats them up finding out about schedules and habits, comes back after dark and abducts them for his bosses."

Jack nodded, "Sorry, it turned out to be a dead-end for you but maybe he can cut a deal to help nail the higher-ups." He paused, "Angie Rossi. That's a name I haven't heard in a while. How is she doing?"

Sheila smiled to herself, glad that Jack still remembered Angie, "She's great. She has worked her way up through the ranks. The FBI has tried to recruit her on a couple of occasions."

"Hmm. Good for her. I remember she was always at the top of her game." Jack lost himself in thought for a moment and then said, "Sorry, what else do you know about this guy?"

Sheila paused then continued, "After checking his whereabouts and the timeline we have formulated for Grace's disappearance, he is not our guy. He hasn't even been to this campus yet. He also isn't linked to the Green case at Ohio State. Turns out his death was due to alcohol poisoning. No foul play involved. Mead is singing like a canary. My sources tell me they have given him a pretty sweet plea deal in order to take down his bosses. He has been pimping for a sex trafficking network that is wanted in four states." Before Sheila could continue or Jack could ask any more questions, they were interrupted.

"Hey, what's going on in here?" Matt Brady asked from the doorway. "Jack, I thought you were out searching? Has Grace been found?"

"No," Matt said, knowing that his presence at the police station looking through police files without the permission of the chief wouldn't usually be a problem, it could garner some reprimand for Sheila since his younger brother had been one of the suspects. He was hoping the friend card would help ease any possible tension. Matt ran a tight ship and liked to be in the loop.

"Officer Hasting. A word," Matt said calmly but both Jack and Sheila knew that Matt was unhappy with both of them.

Jack tried to intervene, "Hey, Matt, this is my fault. I put Sheila on the spot. It won't happen again. Thanks, Sheila and sorry I got you into this."

Sheila smiled, "No worries, Jack." Sheila knew this could happen but she felt strongly that Jack would have insights that would help them break the case and find Grace.

*****

Matt closed the door to his office after he and Sheila walked in.

"Have a seat, Officer Hastings." Matt said formally as he moved to sit behind his own desk. He began, "We've worked together for a long time and I thought we had built a professional relationship of mutual respect."

Sheila began, "We have. I know you are upset that I had Jack come in to look at the evidence, but he has been a huge help in the past."

"Agreed. However, he hasn't been personally invested in the outcome before. If word gets out about this, IA will be crawling up our backsides."

"What are you talking about? Personally invested? You mean Grant? He was never a serious suspect."

"You know that and I know that but the public sees what it wants to. Young girl goes missing and the first suspects considered are the parents and significant others. If we give anyone special treatment, especially someone who has family connections to law enforcement, we all come under the microscope."

Sheila had to relent. "I suppose you are right. I didn't think about it from that angle. All I had in mind was that we had a missing girl from a prominent business owner in Camden Falls and very few leads. Jack has been extremely helpful in the past."

"I can't argue with that but your actions could put this department in jeopardy."

"Understood. It won't happen again."

"See that it doesn't. This is your first and last warning. If any other information makes it into Jack Phillips hands, I'll be forced to take disciplinary action."

"Understood."

"Now, I need you and Green back out on the streets searching."

"Yes, sir," As Sheila left Matt's office, she felt cut down to size as well as a little confused.

*****

Something is up with the chief. I have seen a change in him since the last trip Julia took out of town seeking new treatment. And what was up with that? Why did she and Matt travel separately? I realize someone has to stay with the kids and grandparents aren't always available for that. Maybe her condition is worse than any of us thought?

And another thing, in the past he has never cared when we brought Jack in on a case. In fact, he welcomed it. There was the Grant factor that I hadn't considered and it did seem like it was the only reason that made sense. In my mind it is a pretty lame excuse for a couple of reasons. Number one, Jack has been welcomed around the station since he came back from Chicago. Jack had been at loose ends after losing his wife. But pretty soon, when he wasn't teaching, he offered to consult. It wasn't like I brought him in for the first time on this case.

Number two, I brought him in on the case after Grant had been cleared. This case had to move fast. Once Grant had been cleared, I didn't see any reason why I couldn't bring him in to consult.

Sheila had been considering all of these conflicting feelings as she walked back to the conference room. She gathered up the papers and put them in the file. She stared at the timeline on the whiteboard. She still wanted Jack's take on the video footage from Vegas before they presented it to the chief. She would have to find a way to get it to him. The clock was ticking on both of these situations. No time to waste.

Chapter 38 - September 20

I hate this part, Carl Coleman thought. The only bright spot in this whole scenario is that Grace was still alive when they got her to the hospital, however, there hadn't been any updates. As he and his partner Tristan Bennett approached the BrewHouse he could see Arden through the window. She was smiling at something one of the college student regulars had said. He and the others sitting at the table had been part of an earlier group searching for Grace. When the rain started to pour, Melody had sent them back to the BrewHouse to dry off and eat something before they went back out.

Carl hated having to be apart of one of those life-altering moments. Especially one this stressful when life before and life after the event took on a whole new look. He hesitated a moment before opening the door, the bell giving a friendly jingle.

Arden was still talking to the group and topping off their coffees when Carl and Tristan approached her. He took off his hat and said softly, "Arden, can we see you for a moment?"

Arden sensing their mood but fearing the worst, trying to postpone the inevitable said, "Sure, Officers, what can I get you?"

Tristan did not want to do this in front of an audience, "Arden, is there somewhere we can talk?"

Terror and panic started to enter Arden's eyes, "Ah, sure, ah, let's go to my office." She almost dropped the coffee pot when she put it on the counter and absently called, "Tabby, I'm going in the back."

"Ok," Tabby called concentrating very hard in filling the sugar canisters. She as well as the other workers were praying for Grace's safe return.

Arden led the way back to her office trying not to jump to the worst possible conclusion. It seemed as if the hallway got longer and longer as she walked back to the office. She hoped the roaring in her ears would die down enough to hear what the officers had to tell her.

She opened the door to her office, offered the officers the chairs in front of her desk while she went around to her chair and sank down trying not to shake. Arden summoned the courage to end the silence, "You've found Grace haven't you?"

"Yes," Carl confirmed.

"Is she-" Arden couldn't go on. The horrible situation of 9/11 came rushing back and took her breath away. Tristan got up and came around the desk kneeling next to her.

"She is alive. But we need you to come with us to the hospital right away."

"Oh my God," Arden wailed in fear and relief. "What happened? Where was she?"

"I'll fill you in on the way to the hospital. Carl, please radio in and tell them we have Arden and we are on the way to the hospital. Please radio the other officers heading up search teams and let them know the situation and they can call off the search. Also, see if you can get an update from the hospital." He gave Carl a pointed look so that he could talk to Arden alone. He put an arm around Arden, pulling her up from her desk chair.

"Come on, Arden. Let's go. Grace will want to see you as soon as she wakes up."

"Wakes up?"

"I'll fill you in on the way. "

Arden grabbed her purse and allowed Tristan to lead her out the door.

*****

Lenore was working the desk when Tristan and Arden came through the emergency room doors. Carl had gone to park the cruiser and check in with the precinct.

Lenore came around to Arden. "Tristan, thank you for getting Arden here so quickly. The doctor wants to talk to you. I paged her when I saw the two of you coming in the door. Let's go into this conference room while we wait. Can I get you two anything, water? Coffee?"

Arden shook her head, afraid to speak. Tristan said, "No, thanks, Lenore. Appreciate it."

Lenore nodded, "She'll be here soon." Lenore left and closed the door.

Arden began, "I don't understand how she ended up in the tunnel. It must have been some kind of freak accident."

Tristan asked carefully, "When was the last time you saw Grace?"

Arden thought back and said, "Yesterday morning, before work. She said she wanted to get to school early, she was meeting some friends to study for a chemistry test that was later that day. We were both trying to call a truce from our argument at the Golden Palace the night before. We had agreed to get salads for supper that night. We were trying to be a little more health-conscious about our food habits. I tried to text her that afternoon to see if she just wanted to meet at Applebee's rather than eat at home. When she didn't text back, I called and it went to voicemail. When she didn't come home, I started calling all of her friends. Then I called the police."

Tristan nodded. "Okay, what did her friends say?"

Arden started giving Tristan the rundown of what she found out from Grace's friends. "Lindsay had seen her at the study group at school and all through the morning as was their normal routine. I think they have chemistry and yearbook together and then they go their separate ways, but they see each other in the halls. I think their lockers are close to each other, but I don't think Grace uses hers too much. She had also seen her on campus and they had made tentative plans to go shopping for Homecoming dresses. A couple of other girls that I know said Grace was present throughout the day and maintained her normal schedule. They had seen her at school and in the university classes but after that, they didn't hear from her."

Just as Tristan was preparing to ask about Grant and if Arden had spoken to him, Dr. Millicent McGregor walked in and closed the door. Millicent had been an ER trauma doctor for thirteen years. She had been at Camden Falls Memorial for ten of those years. She had been a regular customer at the BrewHouse and she considered Arden and Grace friends. It was hard enough to deliver serious medical news to strangers, but when you knew the parties personally, it was even more difficult.

"Hi, Arden, Tristan."

"Hi, Millicent," Arden said it was barely a whisper.

"Arden, is there anyone you would like us to call?"

"Melody and Roxie," she said without hesitation.

"Already done," Tristan said. "They are both on the way."

Arden visibly relaxed. Tristan said, "I'll let you two talk." He got up to leave.

Arden put a hand on his arm, "Thank you, for everything,"

Tristan nodded, "I'll send Melody in as soon as she gets here. Sheila will be here later to check on you." Tristan left, closing the door behind him.

Millicent put the file on the table and sat down next to Arden. "I want you to know that your daughter is quite a fighter."

Arden smiled, "She comes from a long line of fighters."

"We are doing everything we can. Things are serious, but we have a lot of positives on our side."

Arden shook her head. "Don't sugarcoat it, this limbo is driving me crazy. Good or bad, I need to know what we are facing."

"Okay," Millicent said, taking a deep breath. "It appears Grace took a serious tumble into the tunnel. She has a broken leg and three broken ribs. She has a concussion and some internal bleeding that we were finally able to get under control."

Arden nodded, "That sounds pretty bad, is she awake? Has she been awake? Can she tell us what happened?"

"No, she hasn't been conscious since they brought her in. In fact, we have her in a medically induced coma so that her body has a chance to heal before we try to wake her up. One of the complications she is facing is that one of the broken ribs punctured her right lung causing it to collapse."

Arden sobbed.

Millicent took Arden's hands. "We have it under control. Her left leg was a clean break. We set it and it won't require surgery."

"That's a relief."

"I agree. Now we just have to monitor her progress and be sure that we have stopped the internal bleeding." Millicent continued to outline the treatment they would be giving Grace.

Arden nodded. "How soon can I see her?"

"She's in ICU right now. They are getting her settled in. Give us about an hour. Do you have your cell phone on you?"

Arden nodded. She got it out of her purse.

Millicent took it. "Here, I am putting my cell number in your contacts. I will text you when you can come in and see her. Why don't you go get a cup of coffee or something? I promise as soon as she is settled, I will personally text you."

Arden smiled and nodded. "Thank you so much, Millicent. I know she's in good hands. I think I'll go down to the chapel." She got up gathering her things.

Millicent grabbed the file and patted Arden's arm, "We'll talk soon."

"Thank you."

As the women exited the conference room, Lenore came up to them, "Arden, Melody is on her way. She was in Columbus at a meeting at Trinity Seminary. She's about 15 minutes away."

"Thanks, Lenore. I'll be in the chapel."

"I'll send her right to you when she gets here."

"Thank you." Arden walked to the elevators. When one of them arrived, she got on it and went to the first floor to the chapel.

*****

Arden entered the hospital chapel and was relieved to find it empty. The dim lighting had a calming effect. There were six rows of chairs with a center aisle that led up to an altar. There was a candle, cross and an open Bible on the altar and a stained glass window depicting the Nativity backlit behind it.

Arden walked up to the second row and sank down into one of the chairs. *Where to begin,* she thought. *I feel like a complete failure. You entrusted me with Grace and now she's hurt, seriously hurt.*

Arden looked at the stained glass window and then the candle and began to pray.

"God, I know I don't pray as often as I should. I know I could do better. I know that making deals is not Your style. It's not mine either. I love that little girl up there. I love her more than I've ever loved anyone in my life. In many ways, she is my life. When she lost her parents, I know I was hesitant about taking her on. But I wanted to make Ben proud. And now, she is in danger, real danger. God, please spare this child. She is just starting her life. Please, bring her back to me. I love her and I know I should be asking for Your will to be done. But I just can't do that. Please, God, bring her back to me."

Arden had her head resting in her hands when she heard the door to the chapel open. Melody came up the aisle and slid in next to Arden and hugged her.

"Arden, honey, what's going on? I got a call from Carl Coleman with the police department saying that Grace has been found and I need to come back to Camden Falls right away."

Arden began to fill in the blanks for Melody. Once she was up to speed Arden asked, "Where were you? Lenore said something about Columbus?"

Melanie nodded, "I had to meet with the Bishop at the Seminary. I would have rescheduled but he was only going to be there for a short period of time. I couldn't pass it up."

"That's right. In all the excitement, I forgot you were doing that."

"Enough about me, what about Grace, what is her condition?"

"Critical but stable. She's in the ICU but they are hoping to move her to the step-down unit within the next couple of days. It depends on when they bring her out of the medically induced coma."

"I assume you've been down here praying. Mind if I offer my own?"

"Please," Arden said, "I'm afraid my prayers are-"

"Don't even think that what you have to say has to meet some standards. Did you speak from the heart?"

Arden nodded.

"Then that's all it takes. Come on pray with me." Melody took Arden's hands in her own and the two women bowed their heads and

Melody said, "Dear Lord, please keep Grace and her mother Arden in your loving care. Grace has fought to live through this so far. If it be Your will give her the strength to continue to heal. Keep her mother Arden in Your loving care. In Your name we pray. Amen"

Arden gripped Melody's hands, "Thank you." At that point, Arden's phone buzzed with a text. "Oh, that could be Millicent telling me that I can go in and see Grace." She pulled out her phone and was right; it was the text she had been waiting for. "Come on, we can see Grace."

"Lead the way," Melody said as the women left the chapel.

Chapter 39-September 17

Now all she had to do was send the text. Julia had cleaned out the two hiding spots. She had stuffed the clothes she didn't want and some of the shoes in nondescript black trash bags. Three of those were stuffed in the trunk of her car. She was going to drop them in random dumpsters on her way into her last shift at the hospital. A suitcase and carry-on were in the backseat. She had it all figured out. Take care of Grace; work her last shift at the hospital and two days from now she would be another nameless face on the Vegas Strip. Antonio would be in town by then for the big game coming up and he had promised her that after this big win, they would fly to parts unknown and try their luck at casinos around the world.

Julia shook her head trying to rid herself of the fact that things had gotten too messy. She had started to feel cocky and had forgotten to double-check that the burner phone was off. None of this would have come to such a crisis if Grace hadn't gone snooping around.

Besides, this suburban life had run its course for her. She was tired of it. Tired of the wife and mother routine. She would have been able to make a clean break and planned a little more if Grace had kept her nose out of her business. That kid was too smart for her own good. Julia wasn't sure how much she knew and who all she may have told. She wasn't your typical 18-year-old. Her charming personality and good looks opened doors for her that remained shut for the rest of the general population. Plus losing her parents to the 9/11 attacks gave her opportunities through collective public sympathy. Julia hated girls like that. They always got whatever they wanted. Well, now she decided it was her turn to get what she wanted.

With the money she had amassed from her winnings plus the money from her medical insurance, she could afford to fly away and disappear to anywhere in the world she wanted. And Matt would be fine. The town would take pity on him and the kids and they would be the new cause for Arden and her band of merry followers to crusade for.

She had grown tired of Matt. He threw himself into his work. Sometimes she felt like he cared more about the citizens of Camden Falls than he did about her. The kids didn't suffer, that was for sure. He moved heaven and earth to be at every one of their events. Every time he made a romantic overture, she told him she was too tired from working or she didn't feel so well after one of her treatments. They hadn't slept together in months and she had been able to convince him that she slept better alone. She didn't want to wake him up with her restlessness or if she felt ill in the night. He had been sleeping in the guest room and using the guest bathroom for a couple of months now. At least she knew he wasn't poking around her nest egg behind the medicine cabinet.

The kids were starting to develop their own lives and hadn't picked up on the distance between her and Matt. If anything, they focused on her "illness." Neil seemed a little oblivious to it, but Hazel was the one to watch. She has been hanging around Grace too long. That was another reason they needed Grace out of their lives, she was messing with her kids' minds.

Julia shook her head again. Maybe because she was so close to her goal she was starting to feel paranoid. No time to dwell on that train of thought. The first order of business was to take care of Grace. Then she could get on with the life she knew she deserved.

*****

Grace checked the next to the last item off of her To-Do List. That was always a satisfying feeling for the highly structured teenager. She had been a list maker practically since the day she could write. When she had asked Arden for a planner for her tenth birthday, Arden had given her a puzzled look but went in search of a planner appropriate for a child. Through her connections and some online searches, she had found a Franklin Covey Agenda for Elementary students that was positive, fun and colorful. Grace had taken to it like a fish to water. She had kept some sort of planner from that day forward. Her TimeTune app was the lifeline she needed to keep all of her commitments straight. If she were more creative, she would try one of those Dot Planners that everyone was crazy about.

Her last stop was going to be the library on campus. She needed to drop off a couple of books she had borrowed for AP English and do some reading for her Abnormal Psych class. Professor Pritchard had put a couple of books on reserve and if overachievers wanted some extra credit, they could head to the library and write a response to the case histories he had marked for them. Grace could not pass up an extra credit opportunity. Her grades didn't need it, but she liked the challenge. Besides, she was not looking forward to dinner with Arden. Normally, it wasn't a big deal. Especially since they had fought the night before. She loved spending time with her. She was the only mother she had ever really known. But, lately, because it was near the 9/11 anniversary, Arden was in prison guard mode. She got this way every fall and with good reason. Plus, keeping the discoveries at the Brady house a secret was beginning to take its toll. Maybe if she said something to Arden about it, it would take the focus off of Grace and her plans for senior year. She knew that if they discussed her plans after graduation, Arden was not going to like the fact that Grace wanted to consider an out of state college.

*****

Why is my butt vibrating? What is that annoying buzzing noise? Grace slowing awoke to realize that she had dozed off in her favorite chair in the library. That annoying vibrating and buzzing sound was from her cell phone notifying her of an incoming text message. She focused on the screen and realized she didn't recognize the number. *Wonder if it is one of those annoying telemarketers or college reps wanting to interview her? Or that car dealership that keeps calling her KiKi and telling her that they have a few options in new pickups they would like for her to test drive.* She typed in her code and read the message: Hey, GG- phone dead again. Meet me at ED @ 9. Luv ya- G.

Of course, his phone was dead again. He was constantly letting the battery get too low. She wondered how they ever got messages to each other in a timely manner with his phone on silent or dead.

Grace: Whose phone did you snag this time? Craig's?

There was a pause and she could see the pulsing dots indicating he was replying.

Grant: No, one of the pledges. We on? (Heart emoji)

Grace laughed and typed: We on. See you later. (Double heart emoji)

She was going to need a little Grant time after dinner with Arden.

Chapter 40- September 17

She watched from behind the bushes at the side of the Education Building. The ground was soggy from all the rain and it smelled musty and gamey. *Where was that kid? She texted her an hour ago.* She hated waiting like this. Better to get it over with. Her bags were packed, letters written to the kids and one to Matt. Mere formalities at this point. All she cared about was tying up this loose end and getting out of town and into the arms of Antonio. They were going to be jetting to locations unknown as soon as his tournament in Vegas was over.

She saw headlights coming up the street and Grace's little compact car parallel parking on the side of the street. *Good,* she thought, *I won't have to move the car. It can sit there for a couple of days without calling undue attention to it. Grace's campus car tag hanging from the rearview mirror will keep the parking patrol at bay.* She watched as Grace sat in her driver's seat, turning off the ignition, grabbing her cell phone and backpack as she exited the car. She locked it, looked both ways and crossed the street towards the education building and dance studio.

Wasn't it lucky that Grace accidentally left her cell at our house after her last stay and I am the one that happened to find it? What teenager chooses their graduation year as a four-digit code to lock her phone? Before she had returned it to her, she had searched through her contacts and noticed that at times, Grant used someone else's cell to contact Grace. *Perfect,* Julia thought, *I know just how to get her alone.* She watched Grace as she carefully made it to the walkway between the two buildings.

*****

Grace paced back and forth checking her phone every few minutes. *Where is he? This rain will only hold off for a little while.* Tired of looking at her phone and not getting any texts, she unzipped the front pocket on her backpack and secured it in case it started to rain again.

Grace found this area of campus a little creepy. She never liked it when Grant wanted to meet here, but it was near one of his frat brothers off-campus houses and they often met up there for some alone time. The frat brother went home every weekend to see his girlfriend that he went to high school with and he had given Grant a key. She heard a noise, relieved that Grant had finally arrived. She turned in the direction of the noise, only to come face to face with Julia Brady. Startled, Grace said, "Oh, hey, hi, Julia. I thought you were someone else."

Julia smiled, "Grace, what are you doing out in this weather? Won't Arden be worried about you?"

Grace stammered, thinking frantically for a plausible reason as to why she was standing outside on this soggy evening, "Arden knows I'm here waiting for a friend from Abnormal Psych class."

Julia paused, looking closely at the teen. She cocked her head and said, "Really. A friend from Abnormal Psych? Isn't there someplace a little safer you could have met? The BrewHouse, perhaps?"

Did Julia know something? Was she aware that Grant and I are sneaking around? Did she look at my cell phone before returning it? Thinking fast, she said, "Makenna is meeting me here for my notes and-"

"And there is no Makenna and if there is she isn't meeting you here. Isn't G supposed to be here soon?"

A chill ran through Grace, *Oh, God, that text wasn't from Grant it was from Julia. She's on to me.* Trying to buy some time, Grace said, "I'm pretty sure Makenna told me to meet her here. Let me check my phone," Grace twisted to grab her backpack front pocket and saw Julia withdraw her hand from her pocket. She was holding a small revolver pointed at Grace. "Cut the games and leave the phone alone. You and I have some talking to do."

Still trying to buy some time, Grace said in a shaky voice, "Julia, what are you doing? What do we need to talk about?"

"I think you have been nosing around where you don't belong." Julia could see that Grace was trying to figure out a way to call for help. Julia nudged the gun closer, "Don't even think about screaming for help. Besides, you try to tell them the story that the wife of the chief of police tried to kill you and they would never believe it." She paused, "Now, I know you've found my secrets and I have a feeling you have told your frat-boy boyfriend." Julia could see by the expression crossing Grace's face made pale by the streetlight that she was on the right track. She continued, "Now Grace, you really disappoint me. I thought you were someone we could trust. We let you into our home, let you take care of our children and pets and how do you show your gratitude? By snooping through our house, finding things that are none of your business."

Grace swallowed hard and lied in barely a whisper, "I didn't tell anyone and I won't. Your secrets are safe with me. Besides, I really don't know what I was looking at. I was just trying to find a bandage for Hazel because she cut her hand while we were playing outdoors."

Julia chuckled and her steel-blue emotionless eyes settled on a steady gaze on Grace. "Cut the bullshit, Grace. You know exactly what you found. My guess is that you have pictures of it on your phone right now and you can't wait to turn me in. So I can't trust you any more Grace. And I'm not going to let you stand in the way of my new life."

Grace fought the tears that were threatening to spill, "I won't stand in your way. I'll erase the pictures and forget we even had this conversation."

"So I was right, you do have pictures. That is a shame, Grace. You had such a bright future ahead of you. Hand over the phone." Grace twisted the backpack around, getting a pretty solid grip on it swinging it toward Julia, trying to knock the gun out of her hand. Julia sensed what Grace was attempting to do and deflected the backpack with her other hand. Julia grabbed Grace by the arm and shoved her toward the heating grate. "I don't want anyone to interrupt our conversation. Lift the grate and start down."

Grace started to panic, "You don't want to do this Julia! Think about Matt, Hazel and Neil! Think about yourself and your medical situation!"

Julia laughed, "There is no medical situation. I'm as healthy as you are, but in your case, that is about to change. Now, start down the ladder."

Grace, stunned by this latest admission, grabbed the grate to slide it off the opening into the heating tunnel. Because of the recent rain it was slippery and hard to keep a hold of.

"Come on, I have a plane to catch. Stop stalling." Julia kept the gun trained on Grace as Grace took a shaky step on the metal ladder that led down to the heating tunnel. Grace frantically tried to think of a way to reason with Julia but by now it seemed pointless. Once Grace made it to the third rung down, Julia was tired of waiting for this kid to get down in the tunnel. She decided to lend a hand. When Grace looked up to try to reason with her once again, Julia's foot shot out hitting Grace squarely in the forehead, sending the teen backward into the tunnel. Her arms pin wheeled struggling for balance while a strangled cry escaped her lips. Grace hit the cement floor with a sickening thud. Her body twisted at an odd angle and blood was starting to pool underneath her.

****

Julia climbed slowly up the ladder, cautiously peering to see if anyone was around. There wasn't. She carefully negotiated the last few slippery rungs and lifted herself out of the grate. She had followed Grace down to ensure the girl was dead. It had grown darker and the clouds were playing hide and seek with the moon. She straightened up and gave one last look down the shadowy tunnel. Luckily the generators had kicked on just as the commotion started. If there were any workmen in the tunnel or anyone else near the area, the scuffle and Grace's scream was muffled by the ambient noise. Julia felt an inkling of guilt about taking care of Grace in this manner, but she had been the only obstacle standing in her way. Julia took a deep cleansing breath. She carefully replaced the grate and looked around to ensure there were no witnesses. *Now it's time to get back to the house and finish packing. My new life awaits!* She casually strolled to her car and freedom.

Chapter 41: Present September 21

Sheila had finally gotten some sleep. Grace had been found. She had been awakened from her medically induced coma. Sheila felt they had turned a positive corner in the case.

It was 7:45 am and Clyde had let her sleep, turning off her 6 am alarm. The smell of fresh-baked blueberry muffins had awakened her. She had taken a shower and padded downstairs to find the muffins. *I do love that man of mine. He might not be able to boil water, but his blueberry muffins rival anything on the Food Network.* He had left her a note under the plate of muffins. Along with wishing her a good day and telling her how proud he was of her, the note said: Angie texted me. Didn't want to wake you since you were probably getting some much needed sleep. She will be in town today and will stop by with coffee. Said she would be here around 8. I'll be home around 5 to get dinner started. Love you Beautiful.

Oh, Lord, and I look like a scarecrow. Just then her phone pinged an incoming text message. It was from Tristan. Hey, Sheila, you awake? Call me.

Sheila hit the call button on the message. As soon as Tristan answered, she said, "What's up Tristan, any updates on Grace?"

"Yes," he said, "She is out of the coma and resting comfortably. She isn't up to visitors yet. The Doc is all mama bear about her patient. We are hoping to get in and question Grace later today. Also, the internal bleeding wasn't as extensive as they initially thought. Believe it or not, the angle in which she fell and the backpack breaking the fall may have saved her life."

Sheila breathed a sigh of relief, "That is good news. Anything else to report?"

"A lot. The IT guys cracked the code on Grace's phone. They were able to retrieve some of the last text messages Grace received. They were from a burner phone by someone identifying themselves as Grant Phillips."

"What do you mean 'identifying as Grant'?"

Tristan went on to say that they had brought Grant in and questioned him. While on occasion he has borrowed someone else's phone to text Grace, this was not one of those times. In fact, the time stamp on the messages is for 7:49 pm, the day of the disappearance. At that time, Grant was leading a meeting at the frat house. There are 20 witnesses that can testify that at no time between 7:30 and 8pm did he leave the room or have a cellphone in his hand. Also, this was a burner phone, paid for with cash. In the past, he has used a friend's phone and the number had shown up in Grace's contacts. This message indicates using a pledges phone, therefore it wouldn't be in her contacts. However, the pledge has his own phone and the numbers do not match." He paused and before Sheila could ask he said, "We did get some interesting leads from some pictures we were able to retrieve."

"Good. Can you email them to me? I'm going to work from home for a little while and then head over to the hospital to check on Grace."

"Already done. I will be interested to know what you think."

"No hints?"

"Nope. I want to hear from you."

Sheila sighed, "Okay. I'll let you know. Keep me updated on anything else you find."

"Will do." Sheila disconnected from the call just as her doorbell rang. She checked the time. *That will be Angie,* she thought as she went to open the door,

*****

"Are those blueberry muffins I smell?" Angie called out as she walked through the living room and into Sheila's sunny kitchen. Angie felt this was her second favorite kitchen in the world. In first place was her mother's kitchen in Columbus. Maria Rossi, always had a sauce or some other Italian treat simmering on the stove while her kitschy collections made the space warm and whimsical. The Hastings' kitchen surrounded its inhabitants with effortless comfort like a cozy blanket. There was always a bowl of fresh fruit and the ceramic red cardinal cookie jar was always full of homemade chocolate chip cookies. Both of these items resided peacefully on the white marble island that was the center of the kitchen. The rest of the kitchen color scheme included white countertops and cupboards with accents of red and black.

Angie looked around the kitchen letting the hominess surround her. The black side-by-side refrigerator still sported the giant dry erase calendar on the side. It isn't nearly as full of commitments as it was when the boys were still living at home.

'Hey, girl! Is that BrewHouse coffee I smell?"

Angie turned toward Sheila and smiled, "They are the only game in town."

"Funny you should say that…"

Angie looked puzzled, "Care to fill-in-the-blanks?"

Before Sheila had a chance to answer, there was a knock at the back door. Sheila held up a hand and said, "Hold that thought. I have called the other criminal expert to lend us a hand."

Realization dawned on Angie. *That could only be one person.*

*****

When Jack got there, the last person he thought he would be seeing was Angie Rossi. *Wow,* he thought, *she is still as beautiful as she was at the police academy.* "Hey, Angie, good to see you. It's been a while." Jack walked toward her clasping her hand because a hug felt too awkward.

"Good to see you, too. Sheila told me you were back in Camden Falls. I was sorry to hear about your wife"

"Thank you," Jack said. "It's good to be back. I hear you are taking down the bad guys in C-bus."

Angie laughed, "I'm doing my best. I keep trying to get Sheila to come work at a big city precinct, but she's not having it."

"I'll leave that crazy town to you. We have enough to take care of right here in little ole Camden Falls."

Ever the diplomat, Jack said, "Both situations have their pros and cons. After Chicago, I like being back in my kinder and gentler hometown."

"And we're glad your back" Sheila said and touched his arm. "Angie brought coffee and Clyde's famous blueberry muffins are in the kitchen. I'll warm them up while you two start looking through these files."

"We're on it," Jack said smiling.

Sheila smiled as she walked to the kitchen to get the muffins. *This is working out better than I could have hoped,* she thought.

Chapter 42: Same Day: Morning

The emergency ward, as well as ICU, had been more tension-filled than usual with the discovery of Grace. It seemed as if the nurses and doctors, as well as the community at large, had been holding their collective breath hoping and praying that the young girl would pull through.

Outside of Grace's family and friends, no one was more grateful than Lenore. She had been praying since the first alert about Grace's disappearance had been dispatched. Now from everything she was hearing about the young girl and her doctor, Millicent, the girl was going to recover. Texts had been flying among the staff especially to those off duty, keeping them up-to-date on Grace's condition.

Taking Care of Grace

As Lenore finished recording the vitals of several patients in Emergency that were still waiting for rooms as they were being admitted, she realized that Julia Brady had not replied to her text. She knew that Matt would notify her as well, but she felt if Julia wanted any medical updates, Lenore could fill in the blanks for her. Come to think of it, Julia had seemed a little off when she left the hospital earlier. *Granted,* Lenore thought, *that poor child has enough to think about with this new treatment waiting for her. Worrying about Grace has probably added to her stress.*

Lenore completed the last report and then left the nurses station to go to the staff locker room to pick up her lunch bag and purse from her locker. As she walked down the hall, she checked her phone again. Her brother had texted asking if she wanted to join him and his wife for Sunday dinner after church. No other messages or missed calls. *I'll try again later,* Lenore thought. *I'm sure Matt has told her by now anyway.*

*****

Hey, Baby, Good News! Grace has been found. Barely alive but Millicent is in charge. I'll text when I know more. Let me know you got this. Love you.

It had been four hours since Matt had sent that first text. Every half hour since then he had sent another, but nothing came through from Julia. *Where could she be? Her flight to Minnesota doesn't leave until 10 tonight. Is she ill? Is she experiencing side effects and trying to hide it from me?*

Matt had lied to Jack that day at the police station. Things were not better between him and Julia. If anything they were worse. They were like the proverbial ships that pass in the night. Matt wondered if she had been taking odd shifts at the hospital just to avoid him. They hadn't slept in the same room in months. She had said it was because she didn't want to wake him unnecessarily when she was feeling ill or restless. Matt didn't buy it. There was something else going on.

In his mind, there were too many things not adding up. He knew the experimental treatments could wreak havoc with her system and maybe cloud her judgment. But she wasn't even putting on an act in front of the kids anymore. She was short with them and withdrawn. It seemed so out of character.

Cancer was an insidious disease, and it was tearing his family apart.

Chapter 43: Same Day: Afternoon

Julia was checking around the house to make sure she had gotten everything she wanted to take with her and bagged up the stuff she was going to throw in random dumpster on her way out of town. She had stuffed the cash into her carry-on bag strategically wrapping a sweatshirt and some well-placed toiletry items around the packets so as to throw off the airport security guards and the x-ray machine.

During her cleaning and packing frenzy she had pushed back the occasional pangs of guilt she felt. Matt would be okay. Deep down he was a good and decent man. A much better man than she ever deserved. There was some part of her albeit small that wishes she could have continued on the straight and narrow path that Matt offered her but the call of the cards and the jet setting lifestyle was stronger.

She had written letters to Hazel and Neil, but really, what was the point. Grace had been more of a mother to them than she ever was. She was sure they would miss Grace more than they would ever miss her. And now that she had taken care of the Grace issue, she could begin life anew. No strings to pull her back or loose ends that would reveal her deception.

The last bag had been loaded into the car. Her carry-on bag was on the front seat and her cross-body purse was resting on her hip. She had put her phone on silent while she cleaned up what was soon to be her former life. She took it out of her purse only to discover it had been blowing up with texts from virtually everyone in Camden Falls.

Julia's mouth went dry with a silent scream of shock and rage. Matt said this was good news! Grace was alive? Good news for whom? Is this some cruel joke the universe was playing on her? Julia quickly scrolled through the litany of texts from Matt that morphed into texts from Lenore and the other nurses that she worked with. All of the messages were the same, Grace was alive. Wasn't that wonderful. Julia leaned against her car fearing that her anger and shock would weaken her. *What should I do now? She is too much of a threat to my new life. She knows too much.*

Julia checked her watch. She still had several hours before she had to be at the airport. She took a deep breath and texted a reply back to Matt. She told him she had turned her phone off so that she could take a nap. It was great news. Any word on Grace's condition? *Please God, let her still be in a coma.*

Matt texted back: Thank God you're okay. Grace is holding her own. They think she will be awake pretty soon so that she can tell us what happened.

Good, She texted back. I'm so relieved. I will stop in and see her before my shift tomorrow. She had already finalized her resignation with the hospital weeks ago, but as long as Matt thought life for them was heading towards normalcy, she could buy herself a little time. She proceeded to answer the other texts as she formulated her next plan of action.

Grace's condition? *Please God, let her still be in a coma.*

Matt texted back: Thank God you're okay. Grace is holding her own. They think she will be awake pretty soon so that she can tell us what happened.

Good, She texted back. I'm so relieved. I will stop in and see her before my shift tomorrow. She had already finalized her resignation with the hospital weeks ago, but as long as Matt thought life for them was heading towards normalcy, she could buy herself a little time. She proceeded to answer the other texts as she formulated her next plan of action.

Chapter 44: Same Day: Evening

"This case has taken a turn that I never saw coming," Sheila said with a sigh.

"I'm not sure these two situations are related." Jack said. "It's obvious that Julia is pulling some kind of con from the pictures we found on Grace's camera. But how does that connect her to Grace's attack."

"I might have the answer to that," Angie said as she walked back into the den of Sheila's home that had become their makeshift war room. She still couldn't believe that she was in the same room as Jack Phillips. He still took her breath away. After he and the rest of her friends had graduated from the police academy she didn't think she would ever see him again, let alone help solve a case with him. "I just got off the phone with Carl. He and Tristan have been tracking down the doctors named on the prescription pads. As we all suspected they are fake. They are checking into the insurance claims to see if those are fake as well. Jack, they also contacted Grant and to see if he was aware of any of this."

"Was he?" Jack asked nervously.

"I'm afraid so." Angie went on to tell him about the conversation at the frat house before the party during pledge week. "He also said that Melody was aware as well. He also confirmed that the photos were taken in the Brady home. Before they try to get a search warrant they want to know how you want to handle this, Sheila."

Sheila turned over the alternatives in her mind. None of them seemed painless. She was still unclear as to how much Matt was aware of the situation. Was he covering for Julia or would he end up being collateral damage?

"Why didn't either of them tell me or you, Sheila, for that matter." Jack said, trying to keep his frustration at bay.

"Grant told Carl and Tristan that he had encouraged Grace to talk to Melody or better yet Arden about what she had found. He said she had been able to talk to Melody but they had been interrupted before she was able to give her any real advice. Grace went missing before she had a chance to talk to Arden. As for Grant coming to you, Jack, he was afraid. He knows how close the Bradys have been to the family and he didn't want to jeopardize that until he was absolutely sure."

Jack shook his head in fear and anger and said, "Great. All the while letting this fraud continue, and look at where keeping secrets got him."

"Listen, I understand your frustration" said Sheila, "but we have an even bigger issue at stake." She paused, "Do either of you think Matt is aware of what his wife has been up to?"

"No," Jack said firmly, "No way. Matt is no saint but he wouldn't be a party to a con that would cost him his job and damage his reputation. Besides, we aren't even sure how Julia amassed all that money."

Sheila stood up, went to her desk by the living room picture window and brought her laptop over to the couch where Jack was sitting. "There is something I've been meaning to show you."

*****

Jack shook his head in disbelief. "Has Matt seen this yet?"

Sheila shook her head. "No, I wanted you to see it and get your take."

Angie asked, "Do we know who the guy is she's talking to? He sure looks familiar."

"He should," Sheila said, "That is Matt's younger brother Trey."

"And he didn't recognize his own brother's wife?"

"It's not that far-fetched. Trey has been on and off the family grid for years. He was doing time for aggravated assault when Matt and Julia married," Jack offered, "Come to think of it, I don't think Julia and Trey ever met in person before this Vegas situation."

Angie nodded. She looked at Sheila and then Jack and then said, "I think there is only one way to handle this. You and Jack need to confront Matt and see what he knows. It won't be easy for you two, but Matt should get a chance to explain himself."

Sheila held up her hand, "I agree, but we also have to do this by the book. If Matt has any idea or is covering for Julia in any way, we have to consider that possibility."

Chapter 45: A Couple of Hours Later

Jack had called Matt to meet him at the police station. He had been upfront and said that he and Sheila had some information they wanted to get his take on. At first, Matt had been reluctant. He had been trying to track down Julia, but she wasn't answering her phone. Jack promised to help him after they met. Sheila and Jack had arrived at the station ahead of Matt and decided that the most neutral place to meet was in the conference room.

Jack felt sick to his stomach. After all, Matt had been through, dealing with a spouse who he thought was gravely ill, the possible breakup of his marriage and a brother who just couldn't stay out of trouble. Jack didn't know how he was going to deliver the news to Matt and not totally derail their friendship. They had been through so much together. He wasn't sure how they were going to weather the current situation without imploding.

Sheila was lost in thought as she sat waiting as well. She and Matt had never been close and on a few occasions had disagreed professionally on various cases. But if Matt was innocent, she did not want him to become collateral damage and lose his job and community respect.

Both she and Jack were startled when the door to the conference room opened and Matt walked in, checking his phone for contact from Julia. When Matt looked up and saw their faces, he knew immediately that something was wrong.

"What's going on? Do you two know where Julia is? Is there bad news regarding Grace?"

Both Sheila and Jack were at a loss as to where to begin. Sheila hesitated, then asked, "Matt, have a seat." After he sat down across from Sheila and Jack, she continued, "When was the last time you talked to Julia?"

Matt replied, "Late yesterday afternoon. She had a shift at the hospital and I was out looking for Grace with the rest of the community. Has something happened? Is she hurt?" Panic was starting to creep into his voice.

Jack tried this time. "Not that we know of, but something has come to light and we are not sure if you are aware of it." Jack took a deep breath and asked, "When was the last time Julia went out of town for a consultation and where did she go?"

Matt brought up the calendar on his phone. "Let's see. It was late last week and she got back on Sunday. It looks like this was a follow-up appointment with a treatment trial in West Virginia."

Sheila consulted the file in front of her. "Would that be a Dr. Jeffers in West Virginia?"

Matt looked back at his phone, "Yes, that's the one. Julia has consulted with her several times regarding some new treatment trials."

Sheila looked at Matt trying to gauge his reaction. *Was he really that oblivious to his wife's situation?* Then she said, "I'm afraid the only consulting Julia and this Dr. Jeffers has been doing is at the casino."

Matt's face grew pale. "I knew it. She's been having an affair."

Jack and Sheila looked at one another, then Jack said, "That is a possibility, however, I think there is more going on than an affair." Sheila passed the file to Matt and closely watched his face and body language. It was becoming obvious that Matt had no idea about the double life his wife had been leading.

Matt slowly paged through the file, "How did you get a hold of Julia's medical records? It looks like someone has been digging through our private files and took pictures of what they found."

Sheila asked, "Matt do you know where Julia keeps all of these records?"

"Yeah, we have a filing cabinet in the home office." He continued to look at the 8 x 11 photos in the file and stopped at the prescription pads. "These do not look familiar to me." Then he saw the photos of the cash and burner phone. "What is this? Where did this come from?"

Jack said, "You haven't seen them before, Matt? Not anywhere in the house?"

Matt shook his head, "No, I have seen written prescriptions but I never really paid a lot of attention as to who wrote them."

"Did you ever pick up medication for Julia? Was there ever a problem doing so?"

Matt nodded, looking more and more confused, "Yes, I have picked up a prescription or two, but that has been rare. Usually, Julia uses the pharmacy at the hospital."

Sheila said, "Matt, we did some checking. Julia hasn't been getting any prescriptions filled or going through any treatment."

"Wait, what are you saying and where did you get these pictures?"

Jack leaned in, "Matt, what do you know about the wall safe in the master bath?"

"What wall safe? What are you talking about?"

It was Sheila's turn to lean forward, "So you claim to be unaware of the wall safe behind the medicine cabinet in the master bath."

"That is not a claim. That is the truth," It was obvious that fear, disbelief and anger were starting to mix inside Matt. He continued, "Now it's time for the two of you to tell me exactly what the hell is going on?"

Jack and Sheila took turns explaining how Grace was the one who heard the burner phone chirp and went to investigate. The pictures they had shown him had come from Grace's cellphone. Through their investigation of her disappearance, they had discovered that she had told Grant and Melody and was unsure of what she had uncovered and what to do with the information. When they recovered her phone after finding her in the heating tunnel, the detectives and IT guys started tracking down the doctors, money and insurance claims. Jack finished up by saying, "Buddy, it looks like Julia doesn't have cancer and never has. She has a list of priors involving fraud and prostitution that date back to her leaving foster care. By the time she met you she had changed her name and started a new life. From what we can piece together, she was trying to leave her old life behind and be a law-abiding citizen." He paused, "The insurance claims, medical records, doctors are all a part of the fraud. She has been billing the insurance company for hundreds of thousands of dollars and making trips to Vegas and other casino hotspots gambling it away. All of the trips she has made out of town have been to casinos, not hospitals."

After listening to what they had told him, Matt sank back in his chair, his tall, solid build almost shrinking before their very eyes. When he spoke, it was barely above a whisper, "Are you sure?" And then it dawned on him, "Do you think she had something to do with Grace's disappearance?"

Jack nodded, "And we also think she is the anonymous caller that notified authorities that Trey had violated his parole."

"What?! That's impossible! They've never even met!" Matt was ready to jump to his feet.

It was Sheila's turn to talk, "Matt, a few days ago, we received an email from the Las Vegas Police Department. This is footage from the Island Bar and Casino. They knew you were keeping tabs on Trey and as a courtesy, sent this to us. I don't think they realized who the woman was in the footage." Sheila turned her laptop toward Matt and hit play. Matt watched in stunned silence as his brother picked up his barely-dressed wife in the bar. *Is it possible that I don't know my wife at all?*

Once the video was finished, Sheila closed the laptop and said, "Matt we have reason to believe that Julia could have had something to do with Grace's disappearance. In checking the texts, we found messages from a number not found in Grace's contacts. Someone posing as Grant lured her to the walkway between the education building and the dance studio on campus." She paused, "As you know, burner phones are nearly impossible to trace, but we were able to track the serial number on the phone to a Wal-Mart, two towns over. Store footage shows a woman Julia's size with red hair purchasing the phone. The woman in the Wal-Mart footage is the same one in the Vegas video. So that's why it is imperative to find Julia. She can shed light on this whole situation."

"I can't believe this is happening. All of this going on under my nose and I never picked up on any of it."

Jack said, "Look, Matt, I feel for you, but we really need to find Julia. Time is of the essence."

Matt worked to pull himself together and started to think more like a cop than a wronged husband. He looked at his phone, "I texted her to let her know that Grace had been found and taken to the hospital. I sent several other texts letting her know my movements, but no response."

Sheila and Jack shared a look, Jack said, "What about the hospital? Has she been in contact with anyone there?"

Matt flipped through his contacts and pressed Lenore's number. "It's ringing," he said.

The three patiently waited and after the fifth ring, Lenore answered, "Hi, Matt. Calling to check on Grace?"

Matt said, "Yes, is it okay to put you on speaker? I'm here at the station with Sheila and Jack."

"Of course. The news of Grace continues to be positive."

"That's good news, Lenore," Sheila said.

"Yes," Jack said, "Is Arden still there?"

"Yes," said Lenore, "We got her to go home and take a shower and get a bite to eat, but she refuses to leave that darling girl's side."

Trying to not set off any warning bells, Matt said, "Hey, Lenore, I've been trying to get a hold of Julia. Doesn't she have a shift today?"

There was a pause and then Lenore said puzzled, "No, Matt. Yesterday was her last day. She turned in her resignation two weeks ago. We sure are going to miss her around here, but the new treatment she is going to be receiving in Nevada will hopefully stop the cancer in its tracks. You and the kids will miss her. I hope you can take some trips to see her while she's out there. "

Stunned looks went around the conference room table. Matt quickly recovered, "That's right. We have both had crazy schedules, I'm not sure if I'm coming or going."

Lenore laughed, "I understand. But to answer your question, I haven't seen or heard from Julia. As a matter of fact, I texted her hours ago to update her on Grace and she never answered back."

Matt said, "Thanks, Lenore, I appreciate the help. If you happen to see Julia, tell her I'm looking for her."

"Will do. I'll probably see you at the hospital later to talk to Grace?"

"That you will. Talk to you soon." Matt ended the call.

Immediately Sheila said, "Did you know about any of the information Lenore just told us about Nevada and Julia resigning from her job?"

Jack said gently, "I think this is the first time Matt is hearing about it. I'm so sorry, Matt."

Matt appeared to be moving even deeper into cop mode. "Thanks, but there is no time to waste. I have a feeling that if Julia is behind this she was not happy to find out that Grace is still alive. Sheila, you need to start working on a search warrant for my house. Jack, come with me to IT. I'm going to see if they can trace Julia through her car's GPS. I want Coleman and Bennett stationed outside of Grace's room. No one gets in without an ID."

Sheila said, "All of what you just said is already in place. In fact, Green and a couple of other cops are at your house right now. Coleman and Bennett are at the hospital. All they have told staff and Arden is that they are worried that whoever attacked Grace might come back to finish the job. They are also to let us know if Julia shows up. As for the GPS, we already got the readout and it shows that she was in the area where we found Grace."

Matt thought for a moment, "That's not enough to bring her in for Grace's attack."

Jack said, "You're right. There are no security cameras between those buildings but we were able to find footage of both Grace and Julia walking towards the area, and then later only Julia walking back."

Matt let out a sigh, "Okay, time to pick her up and end this once and for all.

Chapter 46: September 22

The ICU was probably one of the most quiet and intimidating places in the hospital. The rhythmic beeping of monitors and the soft murmurs of nurses and doctors conferencing about the patients interrupted the quiet, dimly lit area. The shadows seemed lengthened and the gentle beeps provided reassurance to family and staff alike.

The tranquility was broken only in crisis. A patient in distress brought a flurry of activity breaking the silence and perhaps a few hearts.

As she entered the unit, her eyes adjusted to the dim lighting and she trained them on the monitoring hub where a variety of monitors and equipment was keeping the staff aware of the slightest change in a patient's condition. To her relief, she could see that the head nurse, Trudy, was noticeably absent. On break, no doubt. Trudy had the uncanny ability to keep an eye on patients, update files and doctors, all while maintaining a proficiently run unit.

Alexis was new to the staff. She was young and still learning the ropes. She was in Cubical One, checking IVs, smoothing sheets and recording vitals on the computer next to Harry McDonald's bed. His stroke had incapacitated him and the doctors, family and friends weren't expecting him to recover. If he did, the 72-year-old would have to give up his independent living. Alexis looked at her former elementary teacher with love and concern. She decided to pray for a miracle.

The only other nurse in attendance was Jolene. She was the oldest nurse in the unit and had been at the hospital the longest. She was set to retire in three months and it couldn't come fast enough for her. She hated all these computers. Where was the human touch? A squeeze on the arm and a reassuring word were more healing than reading a computer readout. She longed for the good old days of white, starched uniforms, handwritten charts and more of a personal connection with the patients.

She breathed a sigh of relief when she realized Jolene had her back to her as she entered and made her way to Grace's cubical near the entrance. She had overheard in the hallway that Arden had left for a couple of hours to check into things at the coffee house and get a shower and clean clothes. A guard had been placed outside the ICU to protect Grace. She almost laughed at how easy it was to come in here. She had on red scrubs that she stole from the phlebotomy department. She had on a red scrub cap that covered her blonde hair and a mask over her face. People had a fear of the red scrubs almost as much as they feared the doctors in white coats. She flashed her ID that she stole from the same department and the cop barely looked at her. In fact, she thought he turned a little green at the sight of the red scrubs. *Fear of needles, no doubt.*

She silently made her way into Grace's cubical. She could take care of Grace, hide behind the curtain as the commotion started and sneak out unnoticed while everyone was trying to save the beloved teenager.

She couldn't help but pause to look at Grace's still, sleeping frame. Deep down she had liked Grace on some level. Grace had had the adolescent life that she had dreamed about. She also was a little jealous of how Grace seemed to be a better mother figure to Hazel and Neil that she had ever been.

She was angry with herself that the fall didn't end this whole situation. She was taking a risk, but that's what it was all about. Isn't that what she lived for? What got her blood pumping? Everything was a gamble, a risk. The cards, the dice and life. She lived for it. Craved it. She had come too far to let anything stand in her way. No matter how much she liked Grace, she was an obstacle to her happiness.

She set down the phlebotomist kit on the nightstand. There was barely enough room with the huge bouquet of flowers and two stuffed animals bearing get well wishes taking up most of the space on the nightstand. She pulled the rubber gloves out of her right pocket and drew the empty syringe out of her left pocket. She took the protective tip of the shaft of the needle and drew back the plunger filling the barrel with air that instead of giving life, would be taking it away. She moved closer to the sleeping girl and grasped the port and slowly inserted the needle.

"You won't feel a thing," she whispered to Grace. Before she had a chance to continue, Julia was grabbed from behind, dropping the lethal syringe to the floor. Detective Evan Green had Julia slammed against the wall and her hands in handcuffs in record time. Cops had materialized around the cubicle and five guns were trained on her.

Sheila Hastings moved towards Julia as Evan turned Julia around to face her. "Julia Brady you are under arrest for assault, two counts of attempted murder of Grace Winters and ten counts of fraud." She Mirandized Julia and she and Evan along with the other officers led her out of the ICU. Trudy was back as well as Alexis and Jolene. Each were checking Grace's vitals. Sheila bagged the syringe and phlebotomy kit. Evan had escorted Julia to the undercover police car. As Sheila and Carl walked to the other cruiser, Sheila shook her head and said, "I never would have believed that Julia was capable of this."

*****

"Is she gone?" Arden entered the ICU glad to see that Grace was awake and smiling and Jack was waiting for her as well.

"Yes," Jack said, "I know this was hard. Trusting us to use Grace as bait was a risk, but I guarantee, we had everything covered and the sting went off according to plan."

Arden visibly relaxed and turned her attention to Grace, "Oh, Sweet Pea, I am so happy you are awake. I have been scared to death." She embraced the girl carefully keeping the tubes attached to Grace intact.

"Well, I'll let you two talk. Grace, I am so glad everything worked out for you. I know Grant will be by later to see you." Jack leaned down and kissed Grace on the forehead. He started to leave.

"Jack," Arden said, "could I speak to you a moment?"

"Sure, let's step out here," They left the ICU and stood in the hallway.

"I don't know how to thank you. Your presence and help during this whole ordeal means more to me than I can say,"

"Arden, I am so glad she is okay. It is going to take a while for Matt to move on from this, but I know he feels partly responsible because he had no idea about Julia's crimes."

Arden shook her head, "I don't blame him at all. We were all fooled. I'm so sorry he is going through this. And the kids.." she trailed off.

Jack agreed, "Matt and the kids are going to have a lot to overcome. It will take time, but they will all move on."

Arden smiled, "I hope so. And thanks again. Grace and I owe you so much."

Jack smiled, "You two owe me nothing. If you need anything, don't hesitate to call."

"Thanks, Jack. Stop by the BrewHouse anytime. Free coffee and sweet treats for life."

"How can I pass that up," He laughed. He drew Arden into his arms and hugged her. "Take care." he whispered and then he was gone.

Epilogue

At first, Matt didn't believe that the woman he married could have pulled off such a devious plan. In order to support her gambling habit, Julia had faked the entire cancer story in order to collect money to support the life she wanted to become accustomed too. At first, she tried to deny everything, then as the pieces of evidence revealed themselves, she could no longer deny her crimes. She pled guilty and was sentenced to 20 years at the Ohio Reformatory for Women in Marysville, Ohio.

***

Matt cooperated fully and it was determined that he was completely unaware of his wife's duplicity. The Camden Falls Police Department had wanted him to stay on but for Matt, this town held too many painful memories. Hazel and Neil were still reeling from the breakup of the family. Matt decided to sell the house and move to Colorado. He had always enjoyed the area when he had traveled there for law enforcement conferences. A former cop had opened up a sporting goods store specializing in ski equipment. He had offered Matt a job as head of security for all of the stores in his franchise. Matt decided to finally take him up on it. It was a good change of scene for him and the kids. From the research he did, there were a couple of good schools in the area and they could all learn to ski.

***

Grace made a full recovery and was voted Homecoming Queen. Due to her injuries, the school postponed the game and the dance for a week in order to have the newly crowned queen attend, with bedazzled crutches and a beaming Grant on her arm.

*****

October was in the air and brought with it the crisp air, wood burning stove smoke and crunching leaves beneath his feet. Classes were well underway and a new normal had been established.

Jack was in his home office standing near the window scrolling through his contacts. He looked up to see a doe and her fawn getting a drink from the pond outside his window.

I don't know why I'm making such a big deal of this. It's just dinner. If it's a bust, the relationship will stay the same and everyone will move on.

That wasn't exactly true. Taking a friend or an acquaintance to the next level presents a risk.

I haven't felt this nervous since I asked Edie out the first time. Stop being ridiculous and just do it.

Jack scrolled through his contacts and found the number he was looking for. He punched the number waiting for her to answer.

"Hello."

"Hi, It's Jack."

"I know, I saw your name on caller ID. I was hoping you would call."

Jean A. Smith